PRAISE FOR
LOVE & VIRTUE

'An absolute cracker, *Love & Virtue* lobs right into the current moment with a clarifying light. I hope EVERYONE reads this book.'—Helen Garner, author of *The First Stone* and *The Spare Room*

'Reid is a young author to watch.'—*Marie Claire*

'*Love & Virtue* is a formidable debut novel. The writing is punchy and clever, with characters so deeply drawn that they feel like friends and enemies from a former life.'—*Guardian Australia*

'wonderfully readable prose, offering a nuanced and often very funny portrait of privilege and betrayal that probes complex questions about consent, trust and what it means to be a truly "good" person'—*The West Australian*

'Reid writes with ferocity and intelligence, and this novel demands attention and commands respect.'—*Sunday Times Magazine*

'*Love & Virtue* is an accomplished novel—by turns funny and furious, and full of the plangent longing and confusion of early adulthood.'—*The Saturday Paper*

'The prose crackles fiercely, luring readers in with phrases to mull over and taste before devouring the next delicious sentence.'—*ArtsHub*

PRAISE FOR
SEEING OTHER PEOPLE

'Diana Reid, you are in a total league of your own.'—Zara McDonald, *Shameless* Podcast

'The prose sparkles on the page, as effervescent and drinkable as a glass of prosecco on a warm summer's evening.'—*The Australian*

'Reid hasn't lost her skewering wit.'—*The Sydney Morning Herald*

'Reid's witty and insightful social observation is something to relish.' —*The Bookshelf*, ABC Radio National

'There is a genuine warmth as well as capacious intelligence and sly humour to Reid's writing, and a dynamic energy to the novel that's always compelling.'—*Guardian Australia*

'This charming, insightful and clever follow-up to *Love & Virtue* is an immensely readable novel that explores the bonds of family, friendship and principle.'—*Books+Publishing*

'I love Diana Reid's writing and *Seeing Other People* hit the mark once again.'—*Women's Agenda*

SIGNS OF DAMAGE

Also by Diana Reid

Love & Virtue
Seeing Other People

SIGNS OF DAMAGE

DIANA REID

ultimo press

Lines from 'Gerontion' on page 167 from *Collection Poems 1909–1962* by
T.S. Eliot used with permission from Faber and Faber Ltd.

Published in 2025 by Ultimo Press,
an imprint of Hardie Grant Publishing

Ultimo Press
Gadigal Country
7, 45 Jones Street
Ultimo, NSW 2007
ultimopress.com.au

    ultimopress

All rights reserved. No part of this publication may be reproduced, stored in a retrieval system or transmitted in any form by any means, electronic, mechanical, photocopying, recording or otherwise, without the prior written permission of the publishers and copyright holders.

The moral rights of the author have been asserted.

Copyright © Diana Reid 2025

 A catalogue record for this book is available from the National Library of Australia

Signs of Damage
ISBN 978 1 76115 109 5 (paperback)

Cover design George Saad
Cover images Broken glass by Sergey Feel/Shutterstock; White Lily by Lucas Ottone/Stocksy
Author photo Courtesy of Daniel Boud
Text design Simon Paterson, Bookhouse
Typesetting Bookhouse, Sydney | 12/1.5 pt Baskerville MT Pro
Copyeditor Ali Lavau
Proofreader Rebecca Hamilton

10 9 8 7 6 5 4 3 2 1

Printed in China by RR Donnelley.

 The paper this book is printed on is from FSC® certified forests and other sources. FSC® promotes environmentally responsible, socially beneficial and economically viable management of the world's forests.

Ultimo Press acknowledges the Traditional Owners of the Country on which we work, the Gadigal People of the Eora Nation and the Wurundjeri People of the Kulin Nation, and recognises their continuing connection to the land, waters and culture. We pay our respects to their Elders past and present.

For Tom Davidson McLeod

'Unexpressed emotions will never die. They are buried alive and will come forth later in uglier ways.'

—Source unknown

CONTENTS

Prologue 1

MONDAY

1 2024 11
2 2008 24
3 2024 36
4 2008 52
5 2024 65
6 2008 76

TUESDAY

7 2024 93
8 2008 106

WEDNESDAY

9 2024 123
10 2008 136

THURSDAY

11 2024 149
12 2008 161

FRIDAY

13 2024 175
14 2008 186
15 2024 203
16 2008 214
17 2024 229
18 2008 244

SATURDAY

19 2024 263

Epilogue 277
Author's note 289
Acknowledgements 290

PROLOGUE

THE CORONER IS difficult to take seriously. I think it's mostly his eyebrows, which are very thick and tilt upwards, giving him an expression of constant, wounded shock. And it's his manner: his kindness is irrepressible and dispels any sense of formality. A few minutes ago, I was talking to a police officer in a private room at the station. The coroner charged in without knocking, introduced himself by his first name, and before I could ask him to repeat it, took my right hand in both of his. He gave it a prolonged shake. 'Sorry,' he said, his head shaking too. 'Terrible. Terrible.' The effect of all this was to make our meeting seem less like an interrogation and more like a catch up between old friends.

Now, sifting through the papers on the table between us, he pauses to wipe his forehead, then looks at me—those eyebrows reaching up and inwards, forming a peak.

'Hot,' I say and suddenly we're both laughing in an obliging, self-deprecating way, as if that's what's unusual about this situation: that it's hot in Tuscany in July. Not that he is a coroner and I am at the police station and, therefore, someone has just died.

We are here because, a few hours ago, poolside loungers at one of this town's many boutique hotels had their leisure violently disrupted. A body falling from a rooftop balcony. The descent was too startling to decipher. For most it was a mere flash across their periphery, more random than sinister, as they bent their eyes to a book or blinked against the sun. It might have been a bug or a bird, were it not for the sound—the unmistakable, punctuating thud of skull on stone—which made sense of what they'd seen.

I am here, the first of two people whom the coroner needs to speak to, because I was up on the balcony from which the body fell.

He finds his piece of paper. With almost theatrical officiousness, he clicks a ballpoint pen. 'Tell me, please, what happened?'

He's regarding me without suspicion. But circumstance imposes it. We both know why I'm in his office so soon after the event. What he's really asking, the morally relevant question, is: *Did that body fall, or did somebody—you, or the person up there with you—push it?*

There is a prolonged silence. After several seconds, I realise that I am expected to break it.

Until now, I have been watching the scene as if I am not a participant in it.

To my Australian eye, this bland, yellow-plastered building looks quaintly historical. The foreign police uniforms have all the gravitas of costumes. On the way into this room, I passed several white helmets sitting inanely atop messy desks. They looked like meringues. Even in here, where there are no windows and no adornments, barely any furniture, just a table and four chairs, a red chip packet winks at me from a bin in the corner. Noticing it, I think: *we don't have that brand at home.*

I am aware, even as I collect these details, that I am in shock.

Earlier today, when it happened, I howled. It took me a long time to realise that the sound was coming from me. I think people were trying to comfort me: I remember hands at my shoulders. I remember batting them away.

But since my arrival at the station—no, since I was ushered into the back of the police car—I have been comparatively calm. I have responded easily, instinctively, to authority: answering questions as they are asked, standing and sitting where instructed. I can do all this at a great distance, marking the many small absurdities, never thinking: I am here, this is me.

The coroner clicks his pen again. Twice: once to sheath it, once to re-release the nib.

'Please. What happened?'

I swallow. My mouth is dry. I start with the truth, which is nonetheless misleading for its apparent simplicity.

'I had a seizure.'

I WAS DIAGNOSED with epilepsy a little over two years ago now. Over that time, my seizures have varied in length and frequency, but they usually follow a similar pattern: there are certain beats that I always hit.

For many seizure-sufferers, the onset of an attack is heralded by a sign so bizarre, it's almost mystical. Even doctors use the decidedly non-medical, almost rapturous term: *aura*. The patient might hear a voice or see coloured lights or feel a sudden and intense burst of joy, their mind flooded with a dazzling light. There are reports of one epileptic, who knew he was about to fall whenever he heard the rousing strains of Beethoven's Fifth. He must have been prolific: every doctor I've ever spoken to on the topic claims to have treated him.

My own aura is comparatively prosaic. I smell burning.

My first seizure occurred while I was making a cup of tea in the office kitchenette. I wondered, before I hit the tiles, whether somebody had burned their toast.

At the hospital, the registrar on duty asked me greedily whether anything 'strange' had happened before I fell. Did I smell anything? Like burning? When I confirmed that yes, actually, someone had burned their toast, he smiled with childlike triumph. As if he were a student and I was the teacher, who had just confirmed that, yes, he got the answer right.

He was so excited he could only whisper. 'But there wasn't any toast, was there?'

With this question, my malady seemed much more insidious. It wasn't a physical ailment—a matter of brain tumours or cancers. It was in my *mind*. *I* was the problem. I had lost touch with reality: imagining toast that wasn't there, fainting in the office kitchenette.

'I don't understand,' I said. And then I burst into tears.

That was when the registrar explained to me that my aura was normal—diagnostically useful, even. Now I was the student and he was congratulating *me*. Well done, you had the perfect seizure.

After two years of intermittent attacks, my initial assumption any time I smell burning is that I'm having an aura. When I'm cooking, for example, the slightest whiff of charring is enough to raise my heart rate. Even when I can see the smoke coming off a frying pan—even when I can locate the source of that smell with my actual human eyes—there's always a moment, pre-logic, in which I panic.

After the smell comes the dread: the numbing fatalism, in which fear is an opioid and I accept that the worst is coming and there's nothing I can do to prevent it. It's a sensation of retreat, as if I am a drone zooming out from my own life, adopting an ever wider, more remote perspective.

It's at this point that I know I'm on the verge of blacking out.

Then there are the moments after I return to consciousness. The disorientation of an abrupt, unflattering angle. If I'm outside, I'll have a jarring glimpse of the sky: a bald and mocking blue. Or I'll see other people's shoes: the dirty rubber sole of a sneaker, fake tan caked at an ankle.

Most often, the first sensation that returns to me is not sight but touch. Strangers' hands on my neck, my legs, under my armpits—all those hands, touching me.

Then, once I've sat up, shaken myself off and checked that I didn't break anything in the fall, there will follow what I think of as the final phase. It's the most protracted: it continues into the following days and weeks. This is when I attempt to deduce what, exactly, transpired while I was unconscious.

SO WHAT HAPPENED on that balcony—who hit who, whether intentionally or not, whether there was a push or a fall, how the whole scene played out—I don't know. In a sense, I wasn't there.

I was sitting in the morning sun, baking among the bricks and the roof tiles with my oldest friend, and my best friend, when I started to have an aura. By the time I regained consciousness, one of them had gone over the edge.

The interview with the coroner doesn't last long. The coroner lets me go after just twenty minutes. I am able to pull up medical records on my phone to show I suffer from epilepsy. Only weeks ago, these documents caused me real grief: some international airlines are reluctant to take passengers who are at high risk of a seizure. Now, they are essential proof of my innocence. Whatever happened on that balcony, it wasn't the result of any deliberate action by me—not when I was unconscious at the time.

On parting, the coroner holds my hands again: both of mine encased in his. Subject to his next interview, he says, he is happy to write up what happened as an accident.

At the front doors, three large steps lead down to the street. I have just reached the bottom when I have a sudden need to sit. I place my hands on the hot stone to steady myself. Worried that I'm going to faint, I put my head between my knees. My hair falls on either side of my head. The sun finds its ruthless way to the nape of my neck.

I sit there for several minutes as light-headedness morphs into nausea. I retch onto the cobblestones.

Like someone who has done the wrong thing and immediately thinks about how they might get away with it—what lies they could tell to make it go away—I find that I am in the wrong life. I wonder what I could possibly say, how I can understand the events of this morning, what story will make it all go away.

I may have satisfied the local coroner, but my own doubts are punishing.

Although I did not intend to push anyone, it is possible that, while they were attempting to move me from the edge or to protect my head, my limbs lashed out, knocking my would-be saviour off balance. That would still, for the purposes of the coroner's form, constitute an accident. But it would be an accident—a fatal accident—that I personally had caused. My first recourse is guilt: was there something I could have done—medical advice I might have taken—to prevent today's attack?

I think back to my last seizure, which was only a week ago. Quickly, I become overwhelmed and need to retch again. It seems impossible that so much could have happened in one week.

It started on Monday with a funeral in Sydney. Now it's Saturday afternoon. My head is still in my hands, but I know that if I looked up, I would see market stalls in the square. In less than a week, I have travelled halfway across the world and have been forced to confront a second, more shocking death. A new country, a fresh tragedy.

Eventually, I resolve to stand up and go back to the hotel, back to my top-floor room and to the balcony that adjoins it—carved into the roof like a wound. Even before I have crossed the square, I stop by a stall selling fish and lean my hand against a tentpole for support.

I realise that this is a futile exercise, that tragedy is random and its senselessness is precisely its cruelty. Still, it's only natural to look for an explanation. We turn to the past and try to identify a turning point, an originating trauma, a moment after which the tragedy became neither random nor senseless, but inevitable.

So I proceed, panting more with each step up the gentle, cobbled incline. As I go, I scour this week just passed, and all the history it contained, looking for a sign.

MONDAY

CHAPTER 1

2024

IT WAS BRUCE Kelly's wish to be cremated, his ashes scattered in Sydney Harbour. Like all his final wishes, it was written in a neat hand and altered recreationally in the final months of his life—whenever he had fought with one of his relatives, or whenever he *hadn't* fought with them and was growing bored by peace. At the time of his death, he had also stipulated a private burial (family only) and a more public funeral service. The latter was to be hosted at his home.

A clear winter's day. Guests arrived at the Kelly residence with raw cheeks and shawls askew. While the men removed their coats, their wives pretended to admire the white lilies that adorned the hallway so they might better see through to the mirror that hung behind. Peeping between petals, they flattened their hair.

The wind was aptly dramatic: it bent heads until they bowed as if in grief and slammed doors portentously. But from the comfort of the Kellys' family home, the weather seemed to mock them. In the kitchen the sunlight was relentlessly benevolent. It ravished the marble surfaces until they cried out and shone; it set the champagne flutes twinkling, yet, somehow, stopped short of getting in anyone's eye. And in the living room just beyond, where the heater was on and the windows were double-glazed, the wind was impossible to feel. They could only see it: in the lawn, which looked freshly polished, and in the leaves, which danced in the trees.

As she surveyed her set-up, Bruce Kelly's widow, Vanessa, wished she hadn't thrown herself into the preparations with quite so much vigour. Every surface had been cleared: Bruce's pill tray thrown away, the masses of condolence bouquets out of sight in an upstairs bedroom. The furniture, too, had been rearranged. The motorised armchair, which usually sat in morbid proximity to the TV, was inconspicuous in the corner, its back against the wall. The shadow of it still stained the floorboards, beneath a row of rented fold-out chairs.

Vanessa feared she had, without intending to, set the scene for a party. *A Celebration of Life*, the invitations read. But that didn't mean it actually ought to be fun.

She was right: solemnity would elude them all day. At first, the mood was festive—almost frivolous—and then, when drama eventuated, it was not in a sombre, reflective vein. It came instead with flashing lights and sirens.

IT WAS INEVITABLE, given Bruce Kelly's age, that his funeral would feel like a reunion. If he had been young enough to still be working full-time or old enough to be fully retired, then his mourners may have been familiar with each other, either from an office or from a regular funeral circuit. Instead, dying at the inconvenient age of seventy-seven, he managed to assemble under one roof a great many people who had not seen each other in several years.

For his peers, Bruce's death was a blow. It knocked their lives into perspective. For the first time, they had to admit to themselves that they had arrived at *late* middle age. Perhaps even had arrived there some time ago. The water was rising. And so they opted for overt displays of vivacity: booming greetings, pumping handshakes, telling each other that they 'hadn't aged a day' (although, privately, they thought the changes were alarming).

Even the younger generation was caught up in a flurry of reconnection. Bruce's two daughters, Skye and Anika, were surrounded by friends they hadn't seen in years: people they'd grown up with who had since scattered across the world. People who'd returned today because they could remember, as only old friends can, who Bruce Kelly's daughters were before they'd had a chance at self-invention—when they were, first and foremost, the children of their parents.

In the back corner of the room, trapped within a punishing shaft of light, two women of about thirty were conducting one such conversation. One, Cass, was a friend of the family. The other was Skye Kelly, Bruce's eldest daughter. With a white father and a Chinese mother, Skye had inherited none of her late father's looks but much of his personality.

'The whole thing's fucked,' she was saying now.

Cass gripped her tighter. 'And with your wedding and everything. What terrible timing.'

'Well, there's never a good time for your dad to die.'

'Of course not.' Cass felt chastened. She had approached Skye bearing a sombre: *I'm sorry for your loss.* But then Skye had hugged her with such warmth and squealed at such a pitch that Cass had immediately adopted a tone better suited to gossip than to condolences.

It didn't help that Skye was looking incongruously glamorous. Skye Kelly was not only very attractive, she was so meticulously groomed her beauty seemed to insist on its own importance. Her black hair had the 'natural' waves that were only achievable by first straightening then curling. Her nails were painted a deep plum colour that extended to her toes, which were crammed into violently strappy heels. Cass, on the other hand, was wearing mascara—but only out of respect. And her black knitted dress was so inoffensively dull she might have been going to a job interview.

To her credit, Skye was more interesting than people who command attention before they've opened their mouths tend to be. Now, she continued her riff on the inconvenience of her father's death, scheduling-wise.

'No, but this has been particularly bad. Like, a few months ago and I could've thrown myself into wedding planning as a distraction. A few weeks later and Dad would've walked me down the aisle. But dying *right* before my wedding?'

Cass nodded. 'It's hard.'

'It's just rude! It's too late to cancel anything. So here I am. Burying my father on Monday, getting married on Saturday.'

'You poor thing.'

'To be fair, when we first told Dad we were going to have a destination wedding, the phrase "over my dead body" was thrown around.'

'Oh my god. I guess he wasn't bluffing.'

'Ha! Yeah. Anyway . . .' Her mouth twisted as if she were about to say something, but broke, instead, into a watery smile. 'It's good to see you.'

In the tears that threatened, Cass saw that they were approaching a precipice. And she saw that it was only the pretence of normalcy—little jokes, chitchat—that might drag Skye back.

'Well, I can't wait for Saturday,' she said. 'It's going to be so special.'

Skye grabbed her arm, resuming her earlier enthusiasm. 'Yes! I know, it'll be good.'

'And it's so nice of you to include Sam.'

'Of course. You can't drag people all the way to Tuscany without letting them bring their partners.'

'I would've come solo.'

'You know,' Skye said, 'I told Anika the other day: there's a spare plane ticket and everything, if you want to bring a special someone.'

At the mention of Skye's younger sister, they both switched from their inane banter to an equally familiar conversational mode: concern for Anika.

Cass scanned the crowd but couldn't spot her. 'What did she say?'

'She wasn't amused.'

Cass bowed her head closer to Skye's—orange hair next to black. 'Poor Anika.'

'Yeah, poor thing.'

Their pity was not generic. Yes, like Skye, Anika had just lost her father. But when they said 'poor Anika' they expressed the same thought. Not: *Poor, grieving daughter*, but: *Poor, fragile Anika, who struggles to cope at the best of times.*

Cass hadn't seen Anika in years. But she still felt protective towards her. In fact, this protectiveness was the foundation of Cass and Skye's friendship.

In school, Cass had been in the same year as Anika. Skye was always the cool, intimidating older sister; the embodiment of womanhood too remote even to aspire to—glamorous, like a celebrity, precisely because she was unrelatable. Then, when they were young women themselves and Cass and Anika started partying, Skye became a co-conspirator, buying them alcohol and sending them event links and street addresses. While Cass and every other girl they knew made bad choices and accidentally hurt themselves in all the usual ways—vomiting and blacking out and telling tall stories the following day—Anika was giving quiet expression to a lifetime of self-loathing. Gradually, it became apparent that her behaviour was not normal, that the situations she found herself in were not so much reckless as self-destructive. It was around this time that Cass became more closely allied to Skye than to her younger sister. She would call Skye to ask her to pick them up, or to tell her the fucked-up things Anika had said while drunk and speculate about whether or not she meant them. Then, when it turned out that she did mean at least some of them, they counselled each other about how best to stage an intervention.

That was years ago—over a decade now. Cass left Sydney straight after her three-year degree, travelled, lived overseas. Around that time, Skye graduated medical school and took a year off before starting as a junior doctor. She stayed in Cass's flat when she visited London. Sometimes curled up on the communal couch, sometimes stretched out on Cass's bed, they talked about Anika late into the night. Eventually, they talked about their own lives instead. So theirs became a friendship that didn't need Anika at all—that turned to her and sighed about her every now and then. A safe place where they could both complain about Skye's unstable little sister without seeming callous. If they saw Anika's flaws, the depressing predictability of her patterns, it was only because they loved her. Loving her, in that sense, granted them a licence to judge.

Meanwhile, on social media, Anika always appeared self-assured. She had wandered through academia at the leisurely pace of the privately funded. Five years for an undergraduate, another four for a master's, who knew how long for the PhD. On the side, she worked in bookshops and clothes shops and occasionally wrote online articles, which she shared in carefully roundabout ways. Like: *Look at this sunset, oh and I did a thing.*

Anika always photographed well. She was unhealthily thin, of course. But in that clavicled, lip-filled corner of the internet reserved for the genetically blessed—the children of hot people or rich people—she didn't stand out. She was just on the sickly side of normal. Cass liked to linger on her photos: zooming in or holding her finger on the screen to study an Instagram Story. Every time she saw her, she wondered how Anika *really* was; whether she occasionally said those same fucked-up things and who listened when she did.

Understanding where Cass's thoughts had turned, Skye clarified, 'Anika's been amazing, actually. Like, completely stoic.'

'Really?'

'I know. Grief does strange things to people. Anika's all serene. I, on the other hand, have turned into a crazy baby.'

'Oh, Skye.'

'It's fine, I'm kind of enjoying it. I'm being so insane.' Skye raised a plum-coloured nail and with it—without even using the pad of her human finger—she dried the corner of her right eye. 'Anyway, tell me about Sam.'

'Oh, I don't know. He's fine; he's a person.'

'I'm so excited to see him at the wedding. It's been . . . what? Fifteen years?'

'Sixteen, yeah.'

Sixteen years ago, when Cass was thirteen, she had been invited on the Kelly family holiday. Bruce and Vanessa had rented a house in the south of France for the European summer. Cass didn't have a passport. No one in her family had ever been to Europe. It was a strange, upsetting extravagance even to be invited. But the Kellys had insisted. They were anxious that Anika bring a friend with her, given her mental health at the time. They would pay for it all, even the flights. Cass begged her father to let her go. He thought thirteen was too young for international travel. She reminded him that she was 'almost fourteen'. He said he didn't want to be in the Kellys' debt. Cass countered that she was performing a service, not accepting charity: the Victorian novels she liked to read were full of paid 'companions'. Because her father adored her, and because he always did, he relented.

The whole holiday was, to Cass's mind, impossibly chic and cultured. A rich writer stayed in the place next to them (or *chateau*, as everyone called it). At the Kellys' villa, they were joined by family friends: Bruce's oldest friend, Harry, and a young man called Sam. Even *family friends* was a thrilling concept; Cass's own parents just had friends. The Kellys, by contrast, were a single, irreducible entity, such that to befriend one was to befriend all. Like royalty, or the mafia.

But it was Sam, nineteen at the time, who most captivated Cass. After returning to Australia, she periodically looked him up on Facebook and used him as a standard against which to measure all other men.

When, a year ago, Cass found Sam on a dating app and not only matched with him but proceeded to date and fall in love with him, Skye had declared it all 'too good to be true'. Given that she had never actually seen the two of them together (Sam was always 'at work' when she and Cass hung out), she also liked to joke that it wasn't, in fact, true.

'Is he here?' Skye asked now.

'No, I'm sorry.'

'Of course not.'

Cass smiled. She knew where this was going. 'He sends his condolences.'

'I bet he does.'

'He couldn't get out of work, I'm sorry.'

'Except he doesn't have a job, because he doesn't exist.'

Before they could indulge their personal joke any longer, a hush from the other end of the room confirmed that it was time to take their seats.

Looking over her shoulder, Cass saw that the fold-out chairs were almost all taken. Both women arranged their faces and, with a hand squeeze, parted. Skye went to the front row to sit between her mother and her sister. Cass sat demurely at the back.

WHEN EVERYONE WAS finally seated, the tone became, for the first time all day, something akin to mournful. The assembled crowd enacted the rituals of respect: exchanging unhappy smiles, checking that their phones were on silent (they were).

Bruce's widow, Vanessa, stood to explain the program for the afternoon. Anika would speak first, she said, then those gathered would be invited to share their favourite stories about the deceased.

Those who knew Bruce's family well were surprised by this announcement. First, because it appeared Vanessa did not intend to say anything about her late husband. Second, because it was Anika, not Skye, who was going to speak.

People always compared the Kelly sisters. Perhaps it was a natural impulse towards neatness, but Anika's deficiencies were exaggerated to heighten the contrast. A pair of opposites: one fair, bright, glittering. The other shy and cringing. And although both were clever, one was witty, the other tortured.

And those who didn't know the Kelly girls—who knew Bruce from work, or barely knew him at all, who had not sat at their family table, charmed by Skye, unnerved by Anika—got the gist as soon as Anika stood and made her way to the front of the room.

There was an audible gasp. Anika Kelly had the kind of emaciated body that reveals the human skeleton in intricate, upsetting detail. Beneath a navy silk blouse, her collarbones were so prominent they foreshadowed a latticework rib cage and jutting hipbones. Her hands trembled when she took the microphone, and she had what looked like an abundance of elbows, protruding as they did in three different places.

In the static near-silence the microphone created, the crowd held its breath—each person gripped by that primal fascination that anticipates disaster. The feeling that arises when someone takes to a microphone and makes it obvious, in the panicked pause before they begin, that they're afraid of what they might do with it.

After a long wait, Anika cleared her throat.

Were her voice louder, it might have trembled, but it lacked the commitment even to waver. She spoke quickly, sprinting to the end of each sentence. Several people leaned forward to better catch the phrases that knocked each other over then doubled back and apologised for the inconvenience. Her hands, too, flapped, as if to wipe away the words, which, however well-chosen, were tenuously strung together.

It was not difficult, in this atmosphere of rapt attention, to hear a thud, and the scrape of a chair from the back row. But nobody turned to look.

More rustling at the back, followed by the unmistakably expensive sound of something breaking.

The assembled heads rotated. Although not all eyes were yet fixed on the exact cause of the disturbance, most were looking in the right direction when somebody let out a scream.

They found her then, some standing up to get a better look. Several jaws dropped.

If it had been an old person wriggling on the floor, they might not have been so surprised. That would be dramatic, yes, but in a predictable way. Heart troubles—even choking on a canapé—these were twists they could anticipate.

Instead, they found a red-headed woman, her black knitted dress bunched up around her knees. She couldn't have been much older than thirty.

The scene, for all its strangeness, had an eerie familiarity. Few had witnessed it before, but almost everyone present had absorbed the sight from the general cultural imagination.

The woman was having a fit.

Open, unseeing eyes. Lips moving as if chanting, limbs twitching against the floor.

Skye was the first to reach her, arriving at Cass's side just as twitching turned to thrashing.

It was obvious from her position that Cass had fallen backwards off her chair. Miraculously, there was no blood, despite the sharp fragments of porcelain that covered the floor. But she was lying only a few centimetres away from the uncompromising corner of the marble kitchen island.

Skye eased herself into a cross-legged position and began to inch across the floor until she could pick up Cass's head and place it in her lap. With those purple-tipped fingers, Skye placed her hands at Cass's temples, and held her in place.

A middle-aged man arrived at her side a moment later. He stood with his legs apart on either side of Cass.

'Stop, don't touch her.' Skye spoke in an authoritative tone that she usually reserved for work. Nevertheless, the man began to crouch.

'Stop,' she repeated. Then, when he was almost straddling Cass: 'I'm a doctor.'

He stopped, mid-squat.

'Don't touch her.'

He deliberated, which only prolonged his awkward pose, and gave the onlookers more time to notice that he was poised above the thrashing woman the way one might squat over a toilet seat.

An errant giggle from the crowd was all it took to make the man retreat.

'Nobody touch her,' Skye repeated. 'I've got it under control; I'm a doctor. It will pass in a few minutes. Everybody step back.'

She was right: Cass's seizure lasted for about four minutes. During that time, as Skye's competence became increasingly apparent, the panic in the room subsided. In its place, a grim fascination took hold. Cass seemed to be performing an age-old dance of aberrance; writhing as if possessed by demons, as if gripped by hysteria, as if her veins were alight with electricity. Although it wasn't true, by the end of the day several onlookers would earnestly recall that she had been foaming at the mouth.

As strange as this brief scene was, it was stranger still for the three Kelly women—the only people in the crowd, who knew Cass well.

Seizures, like strokes of lightning, do not discriminate by character. Even so, there are always people, who seem like they *would* be struck by lightning; who *would* lose something precious; who *would* board the ill-fated flight. Because there are always those whom life bends to accommodate, and those whom it attacks. Cassandra Playfair was so unambiguously in the former camp that Vanessa, Skye, and Anika all thought, as they witnessed her seizure: 'She doesn't seem the type.'

Cass was usually a vessel for other people's pain, rather than the sufferer of her own. She was the sort of person who might meet someone at a party and within minutes find out the most distressing thing that had ever happened to them. Not because she was an over-sharer. On the contrary, her very restraint encouraged the opposite response in others, like she was always strong enough for one more burden.

And yet here she was, stripped of her characteristic composure, the focal point of her own drama. The Kellys, who had known Cass since she was a child, had only seen her like this once before. Sixteen years ago, in a foreign house, older and grander and otherworldly, they had witnessed a similar scene. It came back to them now: vaguer than memory, more evocative, too. Three spines tingled with deja vu.

It was as if the present and the past were linked: a spider's web, wherein a shock to one strand could make the whole structure shake.

CHAPTER 2

2008

THE VILLA IN the south of France had a storybook quality. It was impossible to imagine a less-than-perfect day—let alone a crisis—occurring there, amid such graceful dereliction.

Guests turning off the main road were greeted first by glimpses: a pert square structure, an orange facade, six windows, white shutters spreading their wings on either side. As they drew near, they would see in front of the house the stone steps, curved and soft at the edges, that led up from the pool to the arched front door. The laundry, the crack-tiled terrace, the wrought-iron furniture—all of these were only visible from the back, through the house or down the gravel drive that encircled it.

And lurking just behind, as if placed there by a painter to emphasise the villa's quaintness, was a much larger property. Its walls were an exposed grey stone, webbed with ivy. Not only was it situated higher up the hill, it boasted three storeys to the villa's humble two, with a wide balcony on the second floor. The whole effect was of a child and its parent: one innocent, the other knowing.

A little over a week ago, Bruce Kelly had been spending his days watching the stock market, making grim predictions with his colleagues. Despite what all the financial journalists seemed to think, it was obvious the disaster hadn't been contained; they were yet to hit rock bottom. Now, after six nights here, he continued to wonder about the world outside, but his curiosity was mild and benign. Tranquillity had etherised his mind.

Today, the villa, as Bruce Kelly thought of it (publicly, he called it 'an old farmhouse'), had never looked less foreboding. It was almost eight in the morning. Somewhere nearby, past the cypress trees and the olive grove, a breeze made its gentle way through fields of lavender. His wife, his two daughters, and his youngest daughter's friend were all still asleep.

The morning was his to enjoy in all its serenity. And he was enjoying it, pacing in shorts and boat shoes, kicking up the gravel.

Now, he stalled in a patch of dappled light and, with a bellow, wrenched the stillness from the summer air.

'Vanessa! Vanessa, they'll be here any minute.'

Birds chirped a non-response.

'Vanessa?'

After twenty years of happy marriage, there was very little that Bruce and his wife could not pretend to agree on. The one exception was the etiquette around guests. To Vanessa, guests were always welcome and always without fuss. To Bruce, however, hospitality was a gift only offered to the deserving: it was a tribute to friendship; a ritual of respect. As such, votive offerings were required. The rules for the host were as follows: he must greet his guests at the door; he must provide refreshments as soon as they crossed the threshold; and, if they stayed overnight, he must always—*always*—be up before them in the morning.

So, although Harry's plane was not due to hit the tarmac until eight, Bruce had been out the front since seven, hoping to spot Harry's hire car as soon as it turned off the main road. Now, he deliberated about whether to go upstairs and wake his wife or whether to remain at his post.

He stayed: a hungry diner unable to tear his eyes away from the kitchen. Harry's arrival could only strengthen what, so far, had been a tenuous success of a holiday.

Skye, who was prone to sneaking out and getting drunk and breaking things, had been uncharacteristically laconic. She had just turned eighteen and apparently believed that mystery and maturity were one and the same. As such, she had taken to lying by the pool—expressionless behind her sunglasses—and only speaking when spoken to. To her credit, it *was* all very mysterious. And it did make her parents wonder whether she had in fact matured in the few weeks she'd spent travelling before meeting up with them in the south of France.

And Anika, their youngest, who was usually such a worry, had been fine to date—happy, even. The friend she'd begged to bring with her had turned out to be a marvel. Cass, the thin-limbed redhead, was remarkably composed for a thirteen-year-old. She could match Skye for watchful silences. And she had a disarmingly sophisticated way of talking to adults: lots of eye contact, and polite, direct questions such as, 'And Bruce, what do you do for work?' Bruce kept telling her that she was 'a delight'. This was more a compliment about Bruce's own splendid judgement than it was about Cass, hence the enthusiasm and frequency with which he delivered it. Two years ago, Bruce had insisted on sending Anika to a public selective school. Since then, every friend she made was proof that he'd been right to do so—the people at selective schools were so well adjusted, while private schools, by comparison, were 'fuckwit incubators'. (Himself and his wife being, of course, two notable exceptions.)

But despite their daughters' new calm and the relaxed surroundings, the atmosphere in the villa remained tense. Neither Bruce nor his wife trusted the peace. In fact, the longer it lasted, the more inevitable it seemed that Anika would disturb it.

Anika did not have her sister or parents' facility for what they called *stoicism* and she called *being fake*. If she was sad, there were tears and accusations, huffing at the dinner table, blank stares into space.

When Anika was a child, Vanessa had always referred to it as *mood-bombing*. 'She's mood-bombed the morning,' she would say, as if Anika had any control over it. Bruce encouraged her to think about it in terms of the weather. 'It's a dark morning.' Or: 'There's a storm coming.' It sounded less accusatory. There was no perpetrator—no one to blame or hold to account—if there was thunder and lightning, or clouds gathered but didn't break.

But recently, even these analogies had become insufficient. They no longer had the words for Anika, not even in the privacy of their marital bed. Even the terms suggested by the counsellor—*depression, anxiety*—seemed insufficient for whatever it was that drove her, shortly after her fourteenth birthday, to cut her inner thigh with a razor.

She had only done it once—Bruce checked, he couldn't help it, every time he saw her in her togs—but the fear was difficult to shake. Especially on holidays like this one, when they were all so flagrantly content. Meanwhile, in the real world, the markets continued to plummet and the word *crisis* was deployed with abandon.

On the horizon, Bruce spotted the black speck of a car. He stood up.

'Vanessa! They're—'

With a turn away from the tree-lined road that wound to their villa, the car scuttled out of sight.

'False alarm.' Bruce spoke quietly so as not to wake anyone.

FROM THEIR FIRST meeting in 1969, Harry and Bruce had been making each other laugh. They met by chance, at a protest in the city. They were both of conscription age, wanting very much not to go to Vietnam. They were also fresh out of school, wanting almost as much to be part of a world larger than the little corners where they'd grown up. With so much at stake, they were absorbed in their marching and might not have noticed each other had one of their comrades not farted. While everybody else ignored it, Harry's eyes, as if by instinct, reached across the crowd to Bruce's.

They were delighted by their own subversiveness—their sense of being at war with the government; with good manners; with conformity of any kind. Bruce was a non-practising Catholic from the city. Harry was a devout Catholic from the country. At the time, these differences seemed so vast, they found each other quite exotic. They were astonished to discover that they shared an identical trove of references. Between Monty Python, The Beatles, and their quick wits, they often arrived at the same joke. Conversation, then, became a game of seeing who could get there first. And although many of their early discussions were deeply misanthropic (their favourite topic was the spiritual shallowness of their peers), they each felt happier, more exhilarated for the other's company. They glowed with the privilege of exemption.

All this was achieved in a matter of weeks. It turned out that they were both studying at the University of Sydney. Tuition was free at the time, which was good for Harry, whose parents would've insisted he stay on the farm even if they could've afforded the fees. It was good for Bruce too, because for the rest of his life he could tell people that he owed his educational opportunities to the state (not to his family's wealth). So, despite their differences, they were relaxed in each other's company. They swapped timetables and spent almost every day together.

Bruce was thrilled. Harry was exactly the person he'd hoped to meet at university: serious about his studies, capable of laughing at almost anything else.

'You know,' Bruce said, when they had been friends for almost a whole semester, 'I think we've seen each other every single day since we met.'

'Thereabouts.'

They had gone to the university gym together and were now sitting in the sauna. Around them were vaguely familiar students and some old professors. Bruce looked at the way their chests sagged around the nipples. It was difficult to imagine ever having a body like that. He, meanwhile, had an athlete's ease. He didn't think about his body except as a tool. Presently, his hips were just two polished hooks from which to hang a little towel.

'I suppose,' Bruce said, 'that's what it feels like to fall in love. Never getting sick of someone, no matter how much time you spend with them.'

In the change room, Harry fumbled with his locker and didn't look at Bruce. He was smaller than Bruce, much thinner, and with terrible posture: a cowering sort of stoop. But with his shirt off, Bruce saw that he had a surprisingly muscular stomach and a confident tuft of dark hair that curled downwards from it.

Bruce pulled his own shirt over his head. Then he took his socks out of his backpack. They were uncomfortably damp. He sat on a bench and was about to bend over to pull them on, when he started.

A hand on his knee, still for a moment, as if it had landed there by accident. Then it started to move.

He'd heard of this kind of thing happening in saunas or in public toilets, but it had never happened to him.

He didn't need to look up to confirm that the hand was Harry's. It was so obvious, it suggested to Bruce that he must have already suspected, subconsciously at least. Maybe that's what prompted the comment about love. Perhaps he had said it to goad Harry, to test him.

Bruce had only ever come across one confirmed homosexual. He was one of the brothers at school: Brother Luke, who taught— of all things—religion. An awful creature with a sweaty upper lip and thighs that rubbed together when he walked. They all said he liked to make passes at boys. His attention was contagion: if he wanted you, then there could be no more class clownery, no more trips to the creek to smoke with the older boys. There would be pity and suspicion. They all would look at you and think: there must have been a reason. Maybe, in some dark, buried place, you had desired it.

Bruce couldn't speak. He felt cold, as if perspiration had been poured over him, instead of emanating from his skin. The rage was exhilarating. He flicked Harry's hand away in one incontrovertible movement and knew, as he raised his arm between them like a threat, that he could beat the other man up. He forced himself to breathe, to feel it fill his lungs. How those skinny legs would writhe.

But when he turned and looked Harry in the eye, he saw only his friend, just as he'd seen him every day for weeks and weeks. His stare lively and unashamed, his smile subtly arrogant. Bruce had seen that smile in class, when Harry made a clever point, or when he was listening to someone else make a dumb one. Triumphant and somehow sad, as if he were bored of being proven right.

Bruce stammered and, before he was aware of forming a thought, or knowing what to say, he heard his own voice. 'I could report you to the police.'

If Harry had cried then, Bruce's contempt may have calcified. But he didn't behave the way Bruce had imagined such men would.

Instead, Harry folded his hands in his lap—slowly, decisively, not with a limp-wristed flinch—and pulled his shoulders back. Without his usual stoop, Harry was noticeably taller than Bruce, even sitting down. Then, in a voice rich with composure, he said, 'I've made you uncomfortable. I apologise, that was never my intention. It won't happen again. I'd be grateful if you didn't mention it.'

For days afterwards, Bruce felt nauseous. He was sick with the need to smash Harry's face in. Or to apologise. He imagined going to his house and asking him to step outside. He wrote letters and tore them up, furious at his own inarticulacy.

To this day, Bruce couldn't remember how, exactly, their friendship had resumed.

And because Bruce *still* didn't know what to say, because Harry had asked it, they never mentioned it again.

'ARE THEY HERE yet?'

Bruce spun around, sending up a spray of gravel. Cass was standing in the doorway. In the soft morning light, her hair was pale orange—almost peachy, like the plaster that flaked behind her.

She had a way of sneaking up on you. Her tread was silent and she held herself with uncommon stillness. It might have looked like poise in someone older. But in a thirteen-year-old, with those alert blue eyes, it was a bit creepy.

Bruce cleared his throat. 'No. I thought I heard them. But they're not due for a while yet.'

Bruce was pleased to see that Cass was holding a book. It looked large and serious: at least four or five hundred pages. Although Bruce wasn't a big reader, he was always telling his children that they should be. And this Cass—this quiet, bookish girl—was surely a credit to Anika, who had chosen her for a friend.

He was about to ask Cass what she was reading when she stepped down out of the doorway and said, 'I heard about Sam.'

Now that Cass mentioned it, Bruce realised he hadn't considered the boy at all. He'd been too busy thinking about himself—about the relief of his old friend's company. It had not occurred to him that Harry might be arriving with complications of his own.

'Oh, yes,' he said. 'I haven't actually met Sam yet. Apparently he's very nice.'

'It's so sad what happened to him.'

'Terrible. To lose a mother at his age. And I don't think the father's in the picture. So she was his whole family, really.'

'Does he have any siblings?'

'No siblings, no relatives. Only Harry, who's his great-uncle. The others are all pretty delinquent, as I understand it.'

'Delinquent?'

'I don't think his mother got on with the rest of the family. Rough sorts.'

'Oh.' Cass nodded, like she understood. 'How awful.'

She looked out across the lavender fields. Harry followed her gaze, wondering if she'd spotted a car.

There was nothing.

'I'm not going to ask him about it.' She said this with such resolve, it was obvious that she was burning to ask him.

'I think that's a good idea.'

'It's all so *tragic*, though. Right?'

'What's important is that we make him feel normal. Not like some . . . patient, or emotional invalid or something.' Bruce spoke with the conviction of someone who had given the matter a lot of thought. In fact, it was only now, in this conversation with Cass, that he was sensitive to the boy's situation. But authority came easily to Bruce. He was a man accustomed to dictating his own emails.

And Cass, who was top in her class and 'a pleasure to teach', was accustomed to taking instruction. She nodded dutifully. 'That's what Vanessa said, too.'

'VANESSA!'

He expected to hear her voice floating through the house—from the downstairs bedroom, or all the way from the pool.

But Vanessa's hearing was better than his (Bruce insisted his ears hadn't yet popped from the flight), so she'd heard the engine before he saw the car make the turn-off, and she was already at her husband's side.

'No need to yell.'

She took his hand. Her face, after almost twenty years together, remained a fresh pleasure. She wore her black hair high and tight to better expose her long neck. And her presence announced itself, as always, with a moneyed tinkle. Even on holidays, Vanessa liked to wear large drop earrings—silver beads fixed in place by little diamonds, and several chain bracelets. Bruce joked with the children that she slept in them.

'Why did you whip the girls up into a lather about Sam?' Bruce said.

'What do you mean?'

'Telling them his whole life story.'

'I didn't!' A chiming sound as Vanessa withdrew her hand. 'I just said his mother had died and they shouldn't ask about it.'

'Oh!' That Cass, Bruce thought, would go places. She had a certain interpersonal genius. With the lightest of touches, she had prodded and prompted, and extracted the whole tale.

At her husband's exclamation, Vanessa grew defensive. 'What?'

Rather than saying he had been deftly manipulated by a little girl just a few moments ago, Bruce matched his wife's tone and said: 'Telling precocious teens *not* to talk about something is the best way to make them talk about it. You know, forbidden fruit.'

'Oh, don't be dramatic.'

'You can't deny, it's an interesting story. The orphan from a rough background, the benevolent, eccentric great-uncle. It's Dickensian!'

'Now who's in a lather?'

'How many people our age have *wards*?'

'You're as bad as the girls. Didn't Sam want to move to Sydney for university anyway? He's hardly Harry's *ward*; he's just staying with him because it's convenient.'

Bruce's intake of breath was sufficient for his wife to pre-empt his next point. 'I *agree*,' Vanessa said, 'it's a very charitable thing Harry's done. He's a saint. But surely it'll make the boy feel more comfortable if we don't draw too much attention to it?'

Bruce didn't have time to concede; a grey car had just appeared over the lip of the driveway. He sprung forward and arrived at the driver's door just as it came to a stop.

Harry emerged, one long limb at a time. Watching him, Bruce became hyper-aware of his own belly beneath his linen shirt—the increasing prominence, from his balding head to his stomach, of curves.

Bruce tried to hug Harry, but Harry leaned in to kiss him twice. After giving Vanessa the same two-cheek treatment, he said, 'Let me introduce you to Sam.'

The boy was standing by the boot of the car, oddly adrift from the three adults who now turned to look at him.

Sam was handsome, and not at all what Bruce had expected. He had imagined someone younger, more downtrodden: a boy whose appearance might at least hint at his tragic circumstances. But this young man looked invulnerable. Average height, brown skin, and such broad shoulders, such an abrupt square jaw that his long eyelashes appeared all the more sensuous for the surrounding toughness. He had now lifted the two large suitcases out of the boot—one in each hand—and his muscular arms bulged with their weight.

He placed the suitcases on the gravel so he could shake their hands, wiping his palms on his jeans before each shake. First Bruce (firm), then Vanessa (firmer).

'How was your flight?' Vanessa asked.

'Hell,' Harry said. 'But worth it. What a villa!'

Bruce smiled. 'What? This old farmhouse?'

He motioned towards it and they began to head inside. On the way, Bruce and Vanessa each succeeded in wresting a suitcase from the boy. Bruce had to surrender his almost immediately—it was too heavy for him to hold by the handle, and he was struggling to drag its wheels through the gravel.

If they had looked up at the villa before they entered it, they would have seen a white face rimmed with orange staring through the upstairs window. Cass watched closely, her face pressed right up to the glass, as if she knew already—although, how could she?—that she would one day want to recall the precise moment when she first saw Sam.

CHAPTER 3

2024

CASS HAD ONLY just taken her seat at Bruce Kelly's funeral service when she began to smell burning.

Dread sharpened her vision as she assessed her surroundings. To her left, a circular side table seemed much closer than when she'd initially taken her seat. And perched precariously on top: a vase, which looked woundingly expensive.

Her last coherent thought was: *It's coming down with me.*

When she arrived at the hospital, Cass's first priority was to get to the bathroom. In the privacy of a toilet cubicle, she lifted up her black dress to examine her underwear. When she'd regained consciousness after the seizure, her dress had been bunched up around her thighs and her legs splayed wide. Now, Cass was able to confirm her worst fears. She was wearing an old pair of white undies. They had the shadow of several successive period stains and a hole just above the crotch, which exposed her brown pubic hair.

How many times in her life had people thought it was funny to ask her—a redhead—whether the curtains matched the drapes?

Nobody would ever tell you that kind of detail after a seizure. They'd say: *We're just relieved you didn't hurt yourself.* They'd never add: *Oh, and you flashed everyone. Have you thought about new underwear?*

It was Anika Kelly, in this case, who had given Cass the incomplete account of her indignities. She had climbed into the ambulance and accompanied Cass to hospital. Cass had protested weakly at first (if any of the Kellys were going to come, she wanted it to be Skye, the doctor) and then more forcefully, when she realised how outrageous it was to pull a daughter out of her own father's funeral. But Anika insisted.

The two of them had only been at the hospital for an hour and Cass had already had her head scanned and an overnight bed allocated. As always, the staff's urgency was distressing, a hospital being perhaps the only place where it's more comforting to have your concerns dismissed than to have them treated with alarm.

The plastic curtain that separated her bed from the neighbouring ones was pulled to its full length, granting a flimsy illusion of privacy. The ward was loud with constant beeping, and further down the corridor someone Cass couldn't see was yelling abuse at a nurse.

The curtain rattled as Anika entered. 'God, I tell you what, it would be nice to do crystal meth just once. You should see that guy over there. He thinks he's a superhero.'

'He's swearing a lot for a superhero.'

Anika threw a paper bag on the bed and climbed on after it, sitting cross-legged at Cass's feet. 'Yeah, but, like, don't you reckon it'd be amazing to know how it feels? When I'm eighty, I'm going to go on a long cruise and do every single drug. Heroin, ayahuasca, the works. It'll be heaven.'

'Sounds scrummy.'

'I kept asking Dad what the morphine was like. He needed it, though, so I think it's different. Like, he wasn't *high*, he was just experiencing not-totally-excruciating pain. Anyway . . .' Anika ripped open the paper bag. Inside it were two large cookies. 'These are *my* crystal meth. Honestly, they're amazing. It's, like, a classic hospital cafeteria down there. Like, you wouldn't come here for the food. But I'm obsessed with these.'

As Anika reached over to offer one to Cass, her silk sleeve slipped up her arm, revealing the white blush of scar tissue.

Cass took the cookie. There were enormous chocolate chunks in it, which melted at the touch.

Anika started on hers, tearing off one crumb at a time, only breaking off the next when she'd audibly chewed and swallowed. With her hunched shoulders and cross-legged position, she might have been a small child, sitting on the ground to pick at her lunchbox. It was exactly how Cass remembered her: always taking up the least amount of space; attracting even more attention as she did so because of the striking shapes she managed to contort.

Now she was prattling away, seemingly oblivious to their circumstances: the ominous beeping, the undignified crepe of Cass's hospital gown. No matter where she was, it seemed, Anika was incapable of stemming her usual flow of free-associating thoughts. 'What's your death row meal?' she was saying now, licking chocolate off her fingers.

'I don't know. Probably pizza or something?'

'Dad had heaps of ice cream in his last few weeks. Ice cream and Scotch, that was all he wanted.' When Cass didn't reply, Anika went on: 'You know, on death row, they used to place the electric chair in front of a glass screen so people—like, victims and gossips and whoever—could watch. Can you imagine? I couldn't cope with the tension. I think I'd just laugh.'

As if Anika had cued it, a cackle erupted from the other end of the ward. They smiled at each other over their cookies. The cackling quickly turned to coughing.

Cass plucked a crumb off her hospital gown and flicked it onto the floor. 'I'm so sorry about your speech,' she said quietly.

'Don't be stupid.'

Cass just kept looking at the crumb, which was petty and obvious against the linoleum.

'It was selfless of you,' Anika said. 'Having a seizure just to spare me a bit of public speaking.'

'Ha.'

Cass was about to ask Anika about Bruce's death—how they were all coping—when the doctor entered and she again became the one to be pitied and examined.

Blond curls and eyes rudely blue against a tanned face. This doctor was so conventionally handsome that his appearance alone could constitute a good bedside manner. He introduced himself—Dr Coleman—and told Cass the results of her CT scan. They had not been able to identify any abnormalities.

'This is good news, of course.' Behind his clipboard, he was unsmiling. 'I know you've already told this to the nurses, but could you please confirm for me, Cass—it's Cass, isn't it? Today wasn't your first attack? There have been events like this before?'

'Yes. I have epilepsy.'

'And when was that diagnosed?'

Cass sat up straighter. She tried to tell her story accurately—not as it happened, or how it felt at the time, but the way Dr Coleman would want to write it down. She was as specific as possible without being pedantic (eleven seizures in two years; the dates and locations of each). And she told him, to the milligram, her first dose of the anti-seizure medication, Keppra, and how that dose had been doubled after her fourth seizure, again after the fifth.

'Right. It all sounds very distressing.' He had stopped taking notes but was still looking at his clipboard, not at his patient. 'And have you found Keppra effective?'

The obvious answer was *no*, hence all the seizures, hence her arrival in hospital today. If it *had* worked, she wouldn't even be in Australia, where health care was more readily accessible than in the UK. At least, that was what she'd told everyone before she left London. It helped to yoke what felt like a personal failure to a broader administrative one. As if her retreat to the country which, for years, she'd been calling 'parochial' was just a matter of practicality. It was a comment about the NHS, about delays and strikes and how difficult it was to get an appointment—not about who *she* was or what she was capable of.

But in Australia, the seizures persisted. Cass had assumed that if she could just get home, where the weather was better and the food was fresher and she could see a GP within a few days of the need arising, she'd soon be back on track. Instead, in her first appointment, her GP was visibly alarmed. Cass was given strict instructions to call every time she had an attack. After a year of increasingly frequent calls, Cass was referred to a specialist. Reading the referral, Cass saw that her GP had described her as 'an intelligent, sensible, successful woman'. The abundance of adjectives aroused her suspicions. It was as if her GP were pre-empting and rebutting the specialist's likely response, as if patients with conditions such as hers were, typically, *not* intelligent or sensible or successful.

That was when Cass realised that medical professionals—people like Dr Coleman—suspected the seizures might be in her head.

Until today, she had thought of Skye Kelly as more friend than doctor. But it seemed that she, too, had her professional doubts.

Skye would have known that epileptics do not need to go straight to hospital after every seizure. And yet, when Cass fell, her first response was to call an ambulance.

Meanwhile, Anika Kelly was still on the edge of the bed, cookie crumbs in the sheets, watching Cass with unabashed, open-mouthed curiosity.

Cass swallowed. 'Yes,' she said. 'The Keppra's been effective.'

'And you've taken it today?'

'Yes.'

'You're sure?'

'I never forget to take it.'

'And that original diagnosis of epilepsy—was that based on anything, or just your own accounts?'

Cass noted the *or*. As if her 'own accounts' were not a legitimate basis for a diagnosis. 'I've had video monitoring, if that's what you mean.'

'Have you?'

This was the only detail she had deliberately omitted. She raised a hand to her forehead and found that her fingertips were cold. 'A few weeks ago, I underwent video surveillance so they could monitor my seizures.'

'And what did they find?'

'I don't know yet. I've got an appointment with a neurologist to discuss the results.'

'When's the appointment?'

'This Wednesday, actually.'

'Well, that's very useful to know.' Dr Coleman was less attractive when he smiled: his teeth were too big for his mouth. 'It will be interesting to see what the neurologist says. I'd just flag that not everybody who has seizures has epilepsy. And if your seizures are caused by something else—if they're psychosomatic, for example—then the drugs won't have any effect. Normally, I'd be encouraging you to pursue that line of inquiry, but it sounds like you're already well on the way. I'd stick to the Keppra, though, in the meantime. Just in case.'

Dr Coleman left quickly after that, saying that he would speak to a nurse about having Cass discharged.

Now that the curtain had been pulled back, and the broad-shouldered figure of Dr Coleman was no longer obstructing it, Cass could see all the way to the end of the ward. In the bed next to her, an elderly man, his hat respectful in his lap, reached a hand out to his wife. And in the bed beyond that was a pair of legs that looked—even from this distance—track-marked and painful.

'What a cunt.'

Cass started. In her moment of contemplation, she had forgotten that Anika was still with her.

She was standing, one hand white-knuckled on the metal rail at the base of the hospital bed, the other at her mouth. With her front teeth, she tore at a fingernail.

'If you were a man,' Anika said, 'he'd have doubled your dose again and sent you on your way.'

'The main thing is, it looks like I'm fine.'

Anika released the bed and, in a vicious, rattling motion, closed the curtain again. She paced across the little cage she had created. 'Doctors! If there's no obvious fix, then it's because you should be trying harder to fix yourself.'

'Anika—'

'You're weak or you're exaggerating or maybe you're just an attention seeker. Maybe you're making it up . . .'

It occurred to Cass that this present performance—the thin arms flailing, tugging at her own hair—didn't do much to buttress Anika's case.

'Or maybe—actually, this is the most likely, this is always a reliable answer—maybe you're a fucking head case.' Her voice broke on that final word.

Cass swung her feet around so she was sitting on the edge of the bed and motioned for Anika to sit next to her. 'I'll be fine. Really.'

With her arm around her old friend, Cass could feel the pull of their childhood dynamic. She would tell her about the strangeness of her illness: how it lay in a marginal place, somewhere between mind and body, beyond the reach of diagnosis and treatment. Anika would probably like this conversation. She knew something about being an anomaly.

Before Cass could speak a loud ringtone made both women jump.

'Oh my god, your phone! Sorry, I've got your bag.' Anika was back on her feet and rustling the sheets at the foot of the bed. The brown paper bag flew onto the floor.

Cass had set her phone to Do Not Disturb for the funeral but the same number had rung so many times a call had finally gotten through.

'Sorry,' she said to Anika as she put the phone to her ear. When Anika didn't move, she said a more clipped, 'Do you mind?'

Anika was careful to close the curtain behind her, but Cass wasn't sure how far away she'd walked. She answered her phone in a whisper. 'Sam, hi.'

'Cass! Are you okay?!'

She had to raise her voice to calm him. 'Yes, yes. I had a seizure at the funeral but it's all good. I went straight to hospital, they've done a scan, there's nothing out of the ordinary. They're about to discharge me.'

'Okay. Okay. So you're okay?'

'I'm fine.'

'That's good. We don't need to talk about it now, but, Cass, you have to tell me.' He said her name with the tenderness that attends disaster: his love clarified by the recent fear of losing her. It was this pleading tone that made her eyes sting. If he'd been angry, she could have fought him.

'I'm sorry.'

'I had to hear it from Harry.'

'Harry?'

'He was there, at Bruce's funeral. He said it was awful to watch.'

'Look, Sam . . .' She was whispering again. There appeared to be a figure moving behind the curtain. 'I'm not alone. Can we talk about this—'

'Of course, you go.'

'I'm sorry.'

'I'm just glad you're okay. I love you.'

Anika poked her head in.

'I . . . yep, you too.'

She had just ended the call when Anika returned to her seat on the end of the bed.

'Was that Sam *Bellows*? Like, Harry's Sam, who was with us in France?' Her smile faltered. 'Sorry, I saw the caller ID.'

'Did Skye not tell you?'

'She said you were bringing a plus-one to the wedding. I didn't realise it was *that* Sam.'

'Yeah.' Cass had known, of course, that a conversation like this was coming—that Anika would have to meet Sam when they both attended Skye's wedding in a few days. But she'd hoped that, in such a context, her own love story might be of little interest. Now, she felt unable to match Anika's excitement.

'Oh my god, that's so cute. You stayed in touch this whole time?' There was something needling, almost self-serving, about

Anika's enthusiasm, as if she might insert herself into their relationship by being its biggest fan.

'No, not at all. We met on Hinge. We barely talk about that summer, actually.'

'Surely it's, like, your origin story?'

'I don't know. We were different people then.'

It seemed unfair, suddenly, that Anika was here. Not Skye, who was a doctor, or even Sam, who was usually by her side. Instead, Cass was required to worry, not about her health, or the fact that Dr Coleman seemed to think she was faking it, but about Anika Kelly's feelings; whether this grown woman felt sufficiently *included* in Cass's life. Cass refused to concede the point: *Yes, you were there, you had a role in our origin story.* What she and Sam shared was irreducible to anecdote. It was private.

THE TRUTH WAS, privately, Cass did think that she and Sam had a compelling origin story.

Cass had only had two boyfriends before, between the ages of nineteen and twenty-five, each lasting about two years. Throughout her twenties, she'd downloaded dating apps periodically when she was feeling unlovable and needed to be reminded that she was single by choice; that she could always settle if she wanted to, that it was only splendidly high expectations that kept her from making such concessions.

Retreating to Australia over a year ago, she had been in need of such a reminder. She re-downloaded Hinge.

The very first profile that appeared made her close the app. She placed her phone on the charger, went to the bathroom to wet her eyes, then rubbed them vigorously, probing until her eyeballs felt gelatinous, until they gave a little when pushed.

Sometimes a coincidence is so stunning, it's easier to understand as design. Cass wasn't religious and she didn't believe in fate. But what occurred naturally, randomly, in the algorithm was such perfect wish fulfilment it would make more sense to say that it was meant to be than that it simply *happened*.

Sam wasn't just her 'type'. It was obvious—and became more so as she scrolled through his pictures—that he was the original: the model on which her tastes had been constructed. In the days leading up to their first date, Cass agonised about an appropriate, not-awkward way to bring up this long-nurtured crush.

Sam's invitation was for a coastal walk. Checking the forecast that morning, Cass had wondered if she should suggest an alternative plan. Not wanting her concerns about the weather to be mistaken for a lack of interest, she said nothing, turned up at the appointed time and left her umbrella at home.

Sam wasn't even wearing a raincoat. Instead, he had opted for a grey jumper, which was already dotted with rain. He kissed her on the cheek, his hand light at her back.

It was a relief to start walking; it meant they didn't need to avoid each other's eyes. In the first few minutes, Cass waited anxiously for one of them to remark that they'd actually met before in that villa in the south of France. Neither of them did.

Instead, Sam gave her the freedom to self-present: she could tell whichever story she liked. So they moved from one topic to the next (work; hobbies; romantic lives), matching each other question for question, with all the civility and passion of tidy, amateurish tennis. Meanwhile, the drizzle—a thin, persistent film—went unacknowledged. Around them, people were sprinting to the car park.

Cass recycled several work-related anecdotes. In London, she had worked for a film production company. The main office was in LA, so her contact with famous people had been limited, but her few brief encounters, between meeting distributors and running specious errands for her boss, had made her a thoroughly palatable first date. Questions were easy. *What movies have you made? Have you met any famous people? Were they nice?* (People always asked whether celebrities were *nice*, when what they really wanted to know was the ways in which they weren't.)

When she asked Sam what he did for work and he said, 'Paramedic,' she felt foolish.

'Right, so a real job. At work, when we had a big release and everyone was stressed, we used to say: *It's PR not ER*. What do you say? *Oh shit, it's ER?*'

Their chitchat had reached a truly aggressive volume when the storm finally broke. Water fell sideways, such was the gale, right into their eyes. Neither of them suggested they stop.

It was only half an hour later, when she slipped on a wet boardwalk and he caught her—one hand deft at the crook of her elbow, carrying her weight like a platter—that he said: 'Maybe we should turn around.'

'Is it still raining?' Cass said. 'I hadn't noticed.'

To her, this was an obvious reference to a film and, given what follows, an obvious juncture for a kiss.

Either he didn't get the reference or he didn't want to kiss her, because the hand retreated from her elbow and they walked back without touching, their conversation continuing down the same careful path.

The ocean was ropable, the rain laced with salt. Now, the weather was invigorating. Cass felt she ought to live up to the drama of her surroundings. She couldn't leave it here: his car pulling out, their voices hoarse from reciting their CVs.

So when they arrived at his car and he pressed his keys to open it, his headlights flashing through the water, she screamed—literally screamed against the wind—her hair sticking to her face in wet, writhing strands: 'Do you want to come back to mine?'

As soon as she suggested it, the invitation took on a new meaning. He gave her a hungry look, swallowed—his Adam's apple moving up and down—and nodded.

In the passenger seat, Cass sat on her hands and gave directions. Salt was stuck to the windscreen, which made it hard to see. Sam sped nonetheless.

They raced from the driveway across the front lawn and were panting at the door. When Cass put the key in the lock, he placed his hands at her waist. By the time she'd turned it, opening the latch, his lips were on her neck.

Where before he had been (for want of a better word) a gentleman, he was shy now, without the codes that might mask his shyness. No car doors to open, no polite requests to make that wouldn't sound stilted: *Might I? Kiss you? There? What about here?* Instead, his hands shook as he tried to unclasp her bra.

'Do you want me to . . .'

'No.' His brow was furrowed. She let him do it. He shook when he touched her nipples with his thumbs.

He lifted her onto the bed—that ease, that grace, like she was a cup he was returning to a high shelf—and went down on her before she pulled him back and guided him inside her. She clenched at the sound he made, and the way he seemed almost to double over with it.

They lay for a moment, with their chests flushed and soaked, her fingers digging into his back, until he began to move. He asked her—tentatively—if it was okay, and she, incapable of words, murmured, then kissed him, taking his face with both hands to prove that it was.

They came together and he fell on the bed beside her, at a respectful distance. He reached out a hand to play with her hair. They lay like that for several minutes—Cass on her front, Sam on his side. They did not look at each other: they scarcely touched. Except for his fingertips, which decorated her skull.

With her previous boyfriends, Cass had found that one of the great joys of a nascent relationship was the self-mythologising. Together, she and her partners would retell the stories of their first encounters: what they thought about the other; the point at which that impression changed. They would luxuriate in this narrative: the union of two perspectives; the nostalgia for a time when they saw things differently and did not know the other's mind. In the security of confessed, requited love, those early days took on a comic light. They could draw shapes on each other's naked backs and laugh at the miscommunications that once upon a time—three weeks, a lifetime ago—were agony.

As weeks passed and she and Sam continued to speak only of the present or the future (their interests; their ambitions; their political opinions; what they would do this weekend), Cass tried to remind herself that these storytelling sessions were only ever a game—a way of formalising and thereby neutralising intimacy: of making a dance out of something as organic and spontaneous as connecting with another human person. It was no more interesting than families telling children the tale of their own birth. They were all the same story (you were late; you were early), and they all said something banal about the child's nature (you've always been in a hurry; you've been taking your time ever since).

Of course, they talked about that summer in France eventually. But it was treated as trivial: a passing coincidence. Cass said, in a self-deprecating way, that she had once harboured a crush on him. Sam just laughed and said, 'I'd like to think you still do.'

WHEN THEY LEFT the hospital, Anika was hard to shake. She insisted on ordering an Uber and dropping Cass off 'to make sure she was safe'. This seemed excessive, especially as it was only mid-afternoon. The whole drama—from the funeral to emergency to being discharged—had taken a little over four hours. On the street, patients smoked while Cass and Anika waited: little white puffs stark against the winter air.

The ride was twenty minutes. Anika questioned her about Sam the whole way.

Cass didn't confess that she actually lived with Sam. Instead, she just kept repeating that Anika would meet him at the wedding, in the hope that she might take the hint and save some of her curiosity until then.

Cass was relieved to find the apartment empty. When Sam came home he would call upon her to recount exactly what had happened at the funeral and then at the hospital. What the doctors said, how they reacted to her, whether she was hurt, whether she remembered anything after that first smell of burning. Then he would ask her the same questions in different ways, until he too could recount the story as if he'd lived it.

Through the living room window, Cass looked out to a tree-lined street. The sun drew clean lines around each individual leaf so that when they shivered and fell the whole world seemed to shake.

It needn't be so fascinating. She and Sam met and then they met again, much later, when they were different people. Only Anika Kelly would fixate on the part of their story when Cass was a child and Sam was an adult. But Cass, too, found herself newly fixated: her thoughts returning to that holiday all those years ago.

She took a shower, very hot, leaving the door unlocked. Steam fogged the mirror, which ran the length of one wall. Her reflection—a blurred figure—watched her, while she stood and looked inwards to the first time she'd met Sam, to the inexplicable import Anika seemed to place on that week in France.

It seemed such bad luck to have had a seizure *today*, in the Kelly home. It was as if, as soon as her body hit the floor—as soon as the Kellys saw—the past reared up, strange and predatory: a crocodile running on its hind legs towards her.

CHAPTER 4

2008

BRUCE AND VANESSA Kelly led their two guests inside the villa. All four paused just over the threshold, their eyes adjusting to the dark. Through half-closed shutters, sunlight fell in strict stripes. To the left, a stone archway led to a kitchen. On their right, a larger room with a fireplace, a mirror, and the shadows of several armchairs.

Harry broke the silence that had risen naturally to accompany the darkness. 'Ooh-la-la!'

Bruce surveyed the room with pride. 'If you think this is good, wait until you see next door.'

'That huge place behind you?'

'We went over the other day. It's exactly what you'd think. Bursting with antiques.'

Vanessa placed a hand on her husband's back. 'Bruce embarrassed himself by trying to sit on a chair.'

Harry gasped. 'You barbarian! You hear that, Sam? The chairs around here are not for sitting. For admiring only.'

'He's a nice bloke, though, the owner,' Bruce said. 'You'd like him, actually. You might even have heard of him. Rupert Tombe? He's a writer.'

'He writes thrillers.' Vanessa's tone suggested that this was a correction, not a clarification. As if writing thrillers and being a writer were mutually exclusive.

Harry frowned. 'I haven't heard of him, no. But they must be very thrilling if they can afford him a whole chateau.'

'It's been in his family for years.'

Although Vanessa's gentle mockery was both characteristic and aimed at Rupert Tombe, Bruce took it as a personal attack. After all, he was the one who'd found the villa online and gone to the trouble of booking it. 'He's hardly a trust-fund baby, though. He went to Cambridge.'

This comment only encouraged his wife. 'Bruce thinks anyone who went to Cambridge must be impressive.'

'Vanessa thinks there's nothing more impressive than being unimpressed.'

'There's nothing to be impressed by! He hasn't written a word since we arrived. He just sits on that balcony smoking.'

'All part of the creative process.'

A cough from the edge of the room broke up this little performance of bickering. Vanessa and Bruce both turned to look. The boy was framed by the doorway. With the sun behind him, his face was difficult to make out.

'Thank you so much for having me.'

It seemed he had wanted to say that when they all shook hands but it had taken this long to work up to it.

Harry put a protective hand on the boy's shoulder. 'Shall we see our rooms then? We can dump these bags.'

'Of course, we'll give you the full tour!' When he was enthused, Bruce moved like a much younger man. Now, he actually bounced on his heels. 'I have to show you the icehouse!'

From the day the Kellys arrived, Bruce had been charmed by an old stone hut at the back of the villa. It was past the pool, by the wall that separated their property from Rupert's, and partly obscured by a large hedge. Skye and Anika had decided straight away that it was dank, Vanessa hadn't thought about it, and Bruce had convinced himself that it was used as a cell, or a hideout, or for some other dramatic historical purpose. When the housekeeper, who dropped by once a week, told him (in broken English, interspersed with mime) that it was for storing ice, Bruce had refused to be disappointed. Now, he began to explain its origins to an amused Harry and a politely attentive Sam. Vanessa, meanwhile, rolled her eyes.

'From a distance, it looks about shoulder-height, like a dog kennel. But when you get closer you realise they've cut this trench around it so you can actually stand up inside. The floor of the trench is filthy—full of pine needles. It looks like a black moat.' (At that flourish, Harry rolled his eyes too.)

'As compelling as this primitive refrigerator sounds—'

'It's *history*, Harry. You'll love it.'

'No, seriously'—his smile was unserious—'I'm busting to see it. But might we shower first?'

'Of course, I'm so sorry. How rude of me. And I haven't even offered you a refreshment. Would you like a drink first? Coffee? Tea? Water?'

'Water would be lovely.'

They passed under the stone arch into the kitchen, while Vanessa hung back.

'The pool's through there.' She motioned with her head. 'If you want to have a look.'

When the boy didn't move, she added: 'Skye's out there. She's close to your age, I think. Maybe a couple of years younger. You're . . . what? Twenty?'

'Nineteen.'

'Oh, you are young.' She looked at his face, from one eye to the other, as if he were a sentence on a page—not someone capable of looking back, or down at the floor, where his dirty sneakers were disturbing the crested pattern on the rug. In the next room, Harry could be heard asking, facetiously, for ice.

THE POOL RAN the length of the house. In front of it, Sam could see the backs of two white sun loungers and, on one of them, a pair of tanned legs. He stood still for a moment, not wanting to creep up on the girl, unsure how to announce himself. It seemed a crystalline moment. The breeze had stilled, the pool's surface was like a pane of glass. The only sound was the turning of a page.

He cleared his throat.

A head poked out on one side of the chair.

'Oh!'

She stood up, revealing a triangle bikini. Her eyes were shaded with sunglasses, and then again with her hand, which she raised to her forehead.

'It's Sam, right?'

He nodded.

'I'm Skye. I didn't realise you were here already. Dad will be furious. He likes us to meet the guests at the door. You'd think we were landed gentry. Not, like, a normal family of four.'

She spoke quickly and lowered her voice on 'meet guests at the door'. Although it sounded nothing like him, it was an accurate impression of her father. Officious, with a stern shake of her head, she'd captured his essence.

'Well,' she said in her own voice, 'it's nice to meet you.'

'You too.'

Skye returned to her seat and lay back with the casual grace—the charity—of beauty. She had a magazine body: slick with tanning oil, a tight stomach, agonisingly large breasts. Her attractiveness was such an obvious and urgent fact, it seemed to demand acknowledgement. It was like talking to someone who had just suffered a great personal tragedy: not knowing what to say, both parties knowing what's not being said.

When Sam didn't move but just kept standing and looking at the pool, she said: 'Is Harry here?'

'Yeah, he's inside. Talking to Bruce.'

'Dad will be thrilled. He finds silence personally offensive.'

'Ah. I can see why they're friends.'

'Yeah,' Skye said. 'Harry never shuts up either.'

It was exactly what Sam had just implied, but it sounded callous when she said it. He was suddenly conscious of the sweat patches under his arms, cultivated over the twenty-four-hour flight.

They both looked at the pool—scattered leaves on the surface that marked the wind's subtle movements—and let the bees fill their silence. It seemed hypocritical now to break it with small talk.

Just when it was becoming unbearable, when Skye was about to offer him a refreshment, someone called Sam's name from the terrace.

'Sorry, I should . . . I think they want to show me around.'

As he turned, Sam got his first proper look at the chateau behind theirs. It was set back a bit, higher up the hill. On the second floor there was a wide balcony where, as Vanessa had predicted, a man sat, white pants and a pink shirt, smoke obscuring his face so that only the black lenses of his sunglasses were visible. They looked like eyeholes in a skull.

Sam was convinced that those dark holes were looking right at him. His suspicion was confirmed when the man raised his fingertips to his brow: a lazy, holiday salute.

Sam did not wave back.

ON THE JOURNEY from Sydney, Harry had brought Sam up to speed on every member of the Kelly family. The way he spoke about them, they sounded like characters in a TV show, not real people with whom he had been friends for decades. There was the patriarch Bruce, who worked constantly, and was 'not your typical person who works in finance' (as if that were a type with which Sam was familiar). Then there were two girls: one was Vivacious and the other Troubled. And it was hard to tell what part of Vanessa's biography Harry most relished: the fact that she was Beautiful, Asian, *Much* Younger than Bruce, or Adopted as a child by a Distinguished Diplomat.

Harry had mythologised the place, too. On their stopover, between spraying himself with expensive perfume and complaining about his swollen ankles, Harry rambled about the villa's long and bloody history (Marquis de This, guillotine that). Sam suspected these details were largely invented. He could always tell when Harry was making something up because it was the only time he seemed absolutely sure of himself.

With his nose for drama, Harry was bored by the very things that Sam most wanted to know. Practical things like: *If they live in Australia, why do they have a villa in France?* Or: *How come they're so rich?*

In recent years, as the chair of the English department at a prestigious university, Harry had just enough money not to worry about it, and not so much that he ever lost sight of the fact that truly wealthy people were, invariably, hilarious—in the way all people are when they start to believe that *their* reality *is* reality. As such, he was an astute observer of what he liked to call 'rich nonsense'. He knew, for example, that rich people downplayed their fortunes: that they had the luxury of thinking it was gauche to go on about money; that there was always someone richer with whom they might compare; that they'd admit to being, at most, 'comfortable'. Which is why he answered Sam's questions in strictly enigmatic terms. *It's not their villa, they're just renting it.* And: *They're not that rich . . . they're comfortable.*

Harry's briefing, however, proved insufficient. There was little that could have prepared Sam to arrive at a house full of strangers, having not slept properly for more than a day.

Now, in his bedroom, which was on the top floor, Sam opened the window and placed both hands on the paint-cracked railings.

He stuck his head out. Purple fields; clouds soft against a pale sky. His room overlooked the pool. If it weren't for the breeze that rippled the water and made the whole day shimmer, he could be looking at a picture on a wall calendar. He took a deep breath. Despite all that lavender, the air was unscented.

In the face of such rampant beauty, he found it impossible to relax. It was like listening to a piece of music, knowing you *ought* to appreciate it, that knowledge preventing you from doing so. He wasn't in the moment. If anything, he was back home, as he had been since he stepped on the plane. It felt fraudulent, somehow, to have stumbled into this life of old buildings and icehouses and storybook fields. Even living with Harry felt fraudulent, in his leafy Sydney suburb, where the water was within walking distance and the houses were called 'workers' cottages'.

People liked to talk to him about grief. But it was guilt that had been his companion lately. It gripped him more tightly with every fresh opportunity; every new place and acquaintance seemed an ill-gotten gain. It was misfortune, after all, that had made this life possible.

SAM WAS EIGHTEEN and in his final year of school when it became obvious to him that something was wrong with his mother. Had he been much younger, he may not have been so quick to notice. But for a few years now, he had been binge-drinking regularly with his friends. A case of beer in the back of the car; a bottle of vodka stashed in the dusty, sneaker-smelling corner of his wardrobe. So he could tell the drunk from the high; could identify that the chemical smell a person emits might not be mouthwash.

That smell was on his mother from ten in the morning. She was forgetting things, too. She would ask him to pick up something from the shop and then look at him, bemused, when she found it in the fridge the following day. Or worse, she'd round on him: 'When did you buy that? Why?' Her exasperation contained the depth of many years. It made him feel like the worst kind of man, the kind women rolled their eyes about: boarish and unwittingly cruel.

He'd always tried hard not to ask his mother for money. Recently, at his request, she'd rented him a suit to wear to his school formal. It was only when he arrived at pre-drinks and all the boys were lining up for photos that Sam realised: most of his friends had borrowed their suits from their dads.

He worked at Bakers Delight two weekday afternoons, both days on the weekend, and full-time over the school holidays. Girls thought it was very witty and alluring to refer to him as Baker Boy—he was always arriving at parties smelling pleasantly doughy and, underneath it, feeling unpleasantly damp, his forehead red-rimmed from the cap. He saved everything he earned to buy a car so that, when he graduated, he could drive himself to Western Sydney for university. Two hours driving each way, over three if he took public transport—it felt like a car would make it all possible.

He hoped—for him and for his mother—that there was a time, not very far away, when he would stop being a burden.

In the evenings, she struggled to hide the traces. A shard from a broken wineglass jutted out beneath the fridge. The kitchen sink purple with what she had managed to pour out.

If it weren't for her new moods, he would never have mentioned it. He didn't mind pulling back the duvet and tucking her in when she'd fallen asleep on top of it, or wiping the rings off the coffee table. He was happy, too, to head out for a run early in the morning and come home late at night after driving around for hours, so they didn't have to go through the ritual of avoiding eye contact. Being so virtuous bolstered him: it felt manly. At school, he didn't mention the development to anyone. He was still able to enjoy the company of his friends while relishing his secret distinction: that life was harder for him, that he was bearing it so well.

But, in light of this spiritual generosity, he found the histrionics hard to take. They were so unlike her. He recorded them once on his phone, so he might play them back and confirm that he wasn't imagining them.

I could just die. You'd prefer it, wouldn't you, if I died?

Eventually, he wrote her a letter. He ripped out a page from a schoolbook and wrote a draft first, then a neater version, on white printer paper, without all the crossing-out. It was long, longer than it needed to be, when the simple thrust of it was: *it's not fair on me.* Several reasons were cited, all of which he would regret later. That his HSC exams were fast approaching. That he wanted to get into a highly competitive course at university so this was a 'particularly critical juncture'. (So intense were his studies that he had adopted the impersonal pomposity of a high school English essay.)

He planned to leave the letter on the kitchen bench before he left for school. He thought it would pack a punch there, among her debris from the night before. But in the morning, it seemed mean-spirited not to tidy up a bit. He folded her unpaid bills into a pile, wiped the bench, and left his letter to wilt on its wet surface. On the way out, he threw three empty bottles in the neighbour's recycling.

That night, he stayed out as long as he could and came home feeling sick. She was sitting on the couch, watching the news, and asked him—in her old, normal voice—how his day had been. Scanning the room, he found it ominously clean.

They ate dinner together—she had waited for him—and their conversation found its old rhythm. He was recalcitrant at first, but soon drawn out by her praise. He told her his recent grades and then, when they were washing up, found himself listing all the people who had irritated him lately, realising, even as he listed them, just how annoyed he'd been.

She offered him a lift into school in the morning. He thanked her, kissed her goodnight, and went to sleep so quickly he didn't have time to reflect that a lift was actually pretty odd.

The next morning, she pulled over a street away from school. They were facing a T-intersection, looking out onto a green sign that pointed two ways. He asked her why she'd stopped and she said he'd find out in a second. 'Just give me one second.'

She locked the doors, which made his heart rate quicken. Her mouth was working, a hard line stretching out at either side—wide but not a smile. She covered her face with her hands and let out a sound that was so low, so animal, it took him a moment to realise that she was crying.

It got worse when he reached out and put a hand on her shoulder. She was thin. Under his thumb he could feel her collarbone, like the flat edge of a knife.

He said all the things she used to say to him when he was small: *take a deep breath, it's okay.*

He kept looking at the clock.

Eventually, when he was fifteen minutes late to school, she told him about the test results.

His mother had been complaining of headaches for months and going to appointments about them. Lately, he'd stopped asking how she was or what the doctors had said. It wasn't because she seemed better—in fact, she'd categorically gotten worse. He'd just been too absorbed in his own life.

The months that followed were made worse by the knowledge that they were fleeting, and therefore, technically, precious. At every moment he was locked in a double torture: he suffered, and he suffered *because* he suffered. His pain was a source of further pain—he flagellated himself for not enjoying their precious time. But it was impossible to enjoy. His mother was understandably outraged—at the universe; at her doctors; at whoever happened to be in the room—that this was all she got from life. She had so much left to do and no time in which to do it, except for a few months in which to catalogue the scale of her loss:

She had given up 'everything', she kept repeating, so she might raise him on her own. The months between that conversation in the car and her passing—three months, thirteen awful weeks—were full of dreams hitherto unexplored, even in her imagination. Now, she indulged in all the possibilities, all the things she might have done. She took a sick pleasure in crafting these plans for herself—the businesses she might have started; the men she might have loved; the countries she might have visited.

During those long months, it was almost impossible to have a trivial conversation. Everything was existential; it all came back to what she couldn't have, all the things she wouldn't do or see him do. They couldn't go to a supermarket without her breaking down at the sight of a child—her children from another marriage; her grandchildren by him.

There was the occasional reprieve. But he was so alert to the need to savour and to treasure that he experienced each happy moment, even at the time, as if it were already over. Her GP gave her a number and she ordered more-than-strictly-medicinal quantities of marijuana. They smoked on the porch together.

When she was high, he asked her questions about his father. She gave her usual elliptical answer: she'd met him while she was travelling and didn't know his name. She repeated the phrase 'the classic one-night stand' so many times he asked if that meant it lasted for a night, or they did it standing up, or both. They were nearing the end of the joint, and they laughed for so long the laughter itself seemed like a joke.

'Do you know what the funny thing is?' she said. 'We definitely used a condom. I know we did, because I remember hearing him flush it down the toilet. You couldn't even put toilet paper in there at that time. I lay awake all night wondering whether the toilet would flood.'

Eventually, she couldn't look at him. One night, a few months after she'd been admitted to hospital, she sent Sam away and told him not to come back. It was too painful, she said. He was glad someone else had said it.

She went quietly in the middle of the night, several days later. The nurse said she'd held on longer than usual.

Then there was the relief and the guilt with which it was braided. Of course he had wanted her to live. But once the diagnosis was final and there was nothing anyone could do, he had been aching for his mother to die. It was cruel to see her so reduced. She wanted to be remembered, he realised, as the woman who had read that petty letter, swallowed the bile of her fate, cooked him chicken satay skewers and listened—with a blankly loving face—to the inanities of his school day.

LOOKING OUT ON lavender fields from his top-floor balcony, Sam experienced the view as a rebuke. He shut his eyes, the sun a blank spot of pressure on his lids.

He imagined jumping straight from this balcony into the pool. From this distance, it looked easy: just a matter of launching himself out a few feet, rather than falling straight down. But it was probably further than it looked. He could hear the thud of a skull on tiles. The others would probably struggle to place the sound amid such peace. A gunshot, perhaps. Or something duller, more summery: a knife thwacked at a watermelon.

He turned to face the room. The single bed with its frame of dark wood, its elegantly curved headboard, evoked another time. A monastery, perhaps, or a castle. Before he set about unpacking or showering, he allowed himself a few horizontal seconds.

Lying on his back, he could still see out the window—not across the fields, but out and up to the clouds and the tops of trees, all of which made the same soft shapes. It was such a still, clear day, he heard Skye's voice intermingled with a man's, floating up from where he'd left her. He was relieved, for a moment, to be lying here alone, not meeting anyone or telling Harry he was fine, not avoiding anyone's eye or shaking hands, or trying to remember a thousand rich-nonsense names—Bruce, Vanessa, Rupert, Skye, Anika, whatever.

His relief was only intensified by the voices out the window, which warned him: this feeling—this peace—was fleeting.

CHAPTER 5

2024

NEITHER OF VANESSA'S daughters was useful in the kitchen: Anika because of her troubled relationship with food (although, relatedly, she loved to bake) and Skye because of her entire personality. It was Skye's charm that, despite her competence in a genuine crisis, she was felled by the slightest domestic challenge. She was simply too fun, too pretty, to organise for her bills to be direct-debited from one account each month or to ever touch an oven.

So on the evening of Bruce Kelly's funeral, his widow was the one fixing dinner—trying to assert, at this late hour, some normality. Most of the guests hadn't lingered to eat. Untouched were finger sandwiches, plus several trays of weepy quince and clammy cheese. Vanessa was doing her best to compile these elements into a more vivacious arrangement. Behind her, the living room walls were lined with folded chairs. And beyond, in the garden, the winter night was dark and prowling.

Anika was sitting at a bar stool, watching her mother work. Skye, meanwhile, was audible in the next room. She had been on the phone to her fiancé since before Anika arrived, discussing wedding logistics.

The original plan was that Skye and her fiancé would be in Italy a week before the wedding so they could complete the preparations. Skye had delayed her flight for the funeral but had refused to let her fiancé do the same.

Now she was speaking very fast and occasionally, when she raised her voice, Vanessa and Anika caught an alarmist snippet, like: '*How* many flowers?!' Or: 'What do you mean "double booked"?'

Occasionally, Anika had to raise her voice so she could be heard over her sister. These fluctuations in volume were the only variation in a monologue about her trip to the hospital—specifically, about what the experience had taught her about Cass Playfair's love-life. Even though Vanessa was really quite anxious to check that the girl was alright, she just let Anika talk. Every now and then, she'd say something encouraging like, 'Really?' or, 'Wow.'

It was a relief, after the day she'd had, to focus on someone else's dramas.

VANESSA'S VISION FOR the Celebration of Life was as follows: Anika would speak first, then Vanessa would act as a sort of emcee while Bruce's friends offered their favourite recollections.

At the start, everyone mingled with an almost manic bonhomie, which boded well. In this mood, Bruce's old friends were unfiltered. As Anika started her speech—halting, yes, but well-expressed— Vanessa even wondered how best to manage a queue for the microphone.

Then Cass had her seizure. By the time she'd been bundled into the ambulance and the audience had resumed their seats, the festive vibe, it was fair to say, had well and truly died. When Vanessa invited them to speak, everyone gazed around, each deferring to the crowd. Their reluctance was palpable. As if they feared that, by taking the microphone, they might cue another disaster.

'Anyone?'

The front row was studying their feet.

'I'll wait.' Her nervous laugh was a needle, inserted into the crowd with no visible effect. There was a moment of panic, in which it looked like she would have to kick things off herself.

While Bruce was sick, she had thought about this moment a lot. Then, it had been a comfort to try to articulate her loss. In her head, she rehearsed her speech with the same repetitious obsession as one touches a mouth ulcer with their tongue. Constantly prodding at the site of pain—feeling it out, testing its scope, controlling it.

As recently as a week ago, she'd had a script. The thesis was: there was no single story—nothing she could say—that could convey a lifetime of subtlety and tact. Her very inarticulacy would count as eloquence. Especially when Bruce's particular gift, always, had been in knowing what *not* to say.

Bruce had, for example, insisted from the very first days of their courtship that their relationship needn't be *explained*. He was a partner then, she a graduate. The age gap, which at the time titillated everyone, seemed to grow year on year. Eventually, it acquired a sinister depth. Whenever Vanessa was at risk of falling into it, Bruce would draw her back from the edge. He would remind her: she could never convince people *not* to pity her; *not* to judge him. It was impossible to explain—undignified to be required to—how they really felt about each other: each one believing the other to be the kinder, the braver, the more faithful partner. And it was this uninterest in summing people up, in putting his finger on what someone was *like* or why, that had attracted her to Bruce in the first place.

Growing up in Canberra, an only child adopted from China by two white parents, Vanessa had been called upon endlessly to explain herself, and pressed, with every follow-up question, to explain *better*, in more lurid detail.

(The answer was that she didn't remember. Her earliest memory, both foggy and vivid, was of a photo of herself and her adoptive father, taken outside the orphanage the day he picked her up. In the memory, she was not standing in front of the camera but sitting on her mother's knee, looking at the photo. At university in the late eighties, Vanessa started making up stories so people would stop suggesting that maybe her memories were 'repressed'. *Before I was adopted, I walked around barefoot—here, see, there's a scar, see it? Beneath my big toe.* She didn't know—couldn't remember—how she got that scar.)

But Bruce wanted to know about the life she *could* remember: what were her parents like (lovely, kind), did an embassy ever feel like a home (for a child, anywhere can be a home: even an industrial kitchen is a place to hide and count to ten), did her father ever speak Mandarin to her (yes, at first, no, once she started school in Australia), how did he become so interested in foreign policy (he was your typical diplomat: curious, clever, a cheerful egomaniac).

When she was pregnant with Skye, at twenty-three, curiosity caught her in a sudden, vicious grip. Who *was* that woman who'd carried her, who'd thrown back her head and, with a leonine roar, torn her own body on Vanessa's behalf? Bruce, just as suddenly, took her curiosity as his own. He did the research. He asked her if there were any identifying details she could remember from that time: the street where she lived, perhaps, or any places she'd frequented. He found a contact at the orphanage and encouraged Vanessa to write.

All this and more she had planned to say at Bruce's funeral: about her husband's remarkable facility to take people on their own terms.

But that was in the weeks before he died. Before Vanessa went to his study to fish out his final wishes and instructions for this very event. Before she found, in the second drawer from the top, other, older correspondence that he'd deliberately kept from her.

The microphone was stubborn in her hand. A cough in the crowd, shuffling, each person waiting for somebody else to volunteer.

She'd betray Bruce if she said nothing. She'd betray herself if she said what she'd planned, when he was still alive, when she hadn't yet gone looking for those Final Wishes, when the facts—or her knowledge of them—were different.

She found herself pointing at the corner of the room where Cass had fallen. 'I'm just sorry Bruce wasn't here to see that vase go down.' Her laugh was ludicrous. 'Bruce hated that vase. It was my father's. He was a diplomat, you see, and he liked to collect things from his postings. You know: vases, me.'

She hadn't made that joke in years. As a teenager, it had been an easy way for Vanessa to explain her parents' house, which was indeed full of vases and shields and masks, and to explain her own presence in it. Bruce, in fact, had been the first person in her adult life who hadn't found it funny. By the time they married, she'd stopped making it altogether.

Such was her fragility after her husband's death. Fragments of her former self, dispersed and rearranging.

The silence that followed was punishing. In the front row, a balding head was bowed and shaking. Vanessa couldn't see who it was.

No wonder he's crying, she thought. It's a fucking funeral. And here I am—Bruce's wife—making jokes about broken vases.

The man moved to cover his face, but this attempt at concealment was revealing: he moved slowly and held his position with the controlled elegance of a pose.

Vanessa had two simultaneous realisations: first, that the man was Harry. Second, that he was the only person laughing.

It got easier after that: she uttered some unmemorable, inoffensive platitudes and other people followed.

Afterwards, when the speeches were over and the hovering by the food began, there was more discussion of Cass than of Bruce. The men Bruce's age and older traded medical stories, of heart attacks and seizures and surgeries. The women of all ages fretted about whether Cass would be okay. It was not what Bruce would have wanted: to be upstaged at his own funeral. But Vanessa was grateful for the distraction. With everyone focused on Cass, they would be less inclined to scrutinise her. Her inability to speak about Bruce—except in this frantic, half-joking mode—would be passed off as a natural expression of her overwhelming grief. That her grief might be confused, that, after almost forty years of marriage, she did not know who he was or how to describe him—all that would go unnoticed, even by her daughters.

'DID YOU KNOW that Cass is dating Sam Bellows?'

Skye had only just hung up from her fiancé. Her phone was still in her hand. Placing it face-up on the bench, she pulled out the stool next to her sister's.

'Yeah,' she said, 'isn't it too good to be true? Although she's yet to re-introduce me, so, who knows, maybe it isn't true. I guess we'll find out this weekend.'

'Is he coming?'

'Allegedly.'

Vanessa passed Skye an empty plate and stood to fetch her a drink. She held up a bottle of white and a bottle of red, and Skye pointed at the white. While Vanessa found a glass and poured, Anika continued her interrogation.

'Apparently, he's a paramedic. Do you know him?'

'Different hospital.'

'So how long have you known?'

'Since they started going out. So, like, maybe a year ago?'

'As if you didn't tell me?'

'I didn't realise Cass's love-life was so fascinating to you. It's not like she's a celebrity.'

As Vanessa passed Skye her glass and the gesture went unacknowledged, it occurred to her that any return to the family home—even as grown women, even for a few hours—was, for her girls, a return to their childhood selves. And she, too, slipped back through the decades, feeling the urge to intercede, to protect Anika and to ask more of Skye, to pick up the weak one and cradle her.

It was obvious: Anika wasn't *fascinated* by Cass's love-life; she just felt excluded. A friendship that had once been her sole comfort in a lonely adolescence had now been overtaken by her sister—her charming, pretty sister, who already had an abundance of friends. And then there was the larger, more pressing exclusion, which Vanessa didn't dare mention, in case naming it made it more real.

Skye was getting married; Vanessa herself had been what her daughters liked to call 'a child bride'. Anika, meanwhile, was thirty years old and yet to have a long-term relationship that didn't end in a court order. So Vanessa's youngest felt excluded, too, from convention, from whatever 'normal' looked like.

In a reflexive attempt to protect Anika by complimenting her, she said: 'It was so good of you to go to the hospital with her, darling. She must have been grateful for the company.'

'Yeah, I think she was. The doctor was a total cunt, too, which didn't help.'

'Anika!' This was the problem with swearing so much while they were growing up: Vanessa was no longer the brashest person at her own table.

'Honestly, he was so patronising. They did some head scan and he couldn't identify an issue so then he started carrying on like Cass had made it up. Can you *imagine* backing yourself that hard? Like, *If I can't see a problem, then the problem must not exist.*'

'So her scans were all normal?'

Anika must have detected a hint of incredulity in Skye's question. She exaggerated accordingly. 'Yeah, and you would've thought she'd faked the seizure. When she explained what happened and her history and everything, he honestly said: *It all sounds very dramatic.*'

'To be fair,' Vanessa said, 'it *was* very dramatic.'

'He basically accused her of being hysterical!'

Skye took a slice of prosciutto—thoughtfully rolled into a cigar shape by her mother for ease of picking up and eating—and began to unravel it. 'I've often wondered that.'

'What?!' Anika finally found a use for her fork, which had been hovering empty above her plate. She brought it down on the tabletop dramatically.

'Not hysterical, obviously,' Skye said. 'But when she told me about her seizures—'

'You knew about the seizures?'

Skye paused to swallow but ignored her sister's interjection: '—and how the drugs weren't helping, I did wonder. I haven't raised it with her. People take that stuff really personally. But one in five people who present to hospital after a seizure end up not having epilepsy. It's super common to be misdiagnosed, initially.'

Vanessa, who had watched this exchange in silence, was impressed, as always, by her oldest daughter's expertise.

Anika, meanwhile, was sceptical. 'One in five?'

'I think that's right. Maybe it's one in twenty. There's some statistic.'

'That's very specific. You and this doctor today must've gone to the same med school.'

'People have fits all the time for all sorts of reasons. Your body is stranger than you realise. It knows things before you do.' Skye kept her voice soothing—a habit formed from talking to patients. 'Once, this woman came into the hospital, she was a nice, healthy mother of three and she said that a few days earlier she'd woken up blind. Like, completely visually impaired. Couldn't see a thing. And she had no illness or genetic predisposition. She didn't even wear glasses. She just went to bed one night and then when she woke up in the morning she couldn't see. Everyone was stumped. Nobody had any idea what to do with her. Eventually, one of the nurses got talking to her.'

Here, Skye might have paused, to create the expectation of a punchline. Unfortunately, she had not inherited her father's gift for anecdote. She rushed to the end. 'And it turned out her husband had just been charged with paedophilia so there were literally things in her life that *she didn't want to see.*'

For several seconds, Vanessa and Anika just looked at her, at a loss for an appropriate response.

A low vibration interrupted their silence. Having tossed off this disturbing story so calmly, Skye now looked at her phone in genuine horror.

'Oh my god. I can't.' She picked it up and showed them the screen. Her fiancé calling again. As she stood, phone in hand, she added,

'If you find *me* writhing on the floor at any point, know it's because of this fucking wedding.'

In Skye's wake, mother and daughter sat in silence.

Anika was staring blankly at the far corner of the room, while Vanessa reflected on Skye's strange story. She thought about all the women she'd known over the years—either personally or anecdotally—who'd found out that their husbands had cheated. *She must have known*, they'd all say. *She knew and, at the same time, didn't want to know.*

Your body knows things before you do, Skye had said.

Vanessa took quiet stock of her own body. A sharp pain in her right knee (but that was just age and imperfect posture—she put too much weight on one side). She hadn't had an appetite for months: she was dry-mouthed and faintly nauseous, not enough to throw up, but enough to stop her from eating. And in the evenings, when she crawled into a bed that was cold on Bruce's side, she was so tired that she couldn't sleep, could only lie there and feel her mind pull in several different directions. Insomnia, surely, explained the near-constant ache just behind her eyes.

Where in her body was Bruce's peculiar betrayal? After he passed, she'd found the incriminating piece of paper so quickly, as if she'd known already where to look. Was that knowledge located in her stomach, or in her head, or in her limbs—all of which, most of the time, hurt?

'I've been thinking today about that holiday in France.'

Anika looked up at her. 'What about it?'

'It's silly,' she said, 'but when Cass had her . . . when she fell today, the first thing I thought of was when we were at that old villa in France and she got trapped in the icehouse. Remember? It was a little hut that your father was obsessed with. Remember how Cass got stuck in there for hours?'

Anika had turned back to the corner of the room. She continued to stare, unmoving.

Vanessa felt the heat of unexpected tears. It had been years since she'd given much thought to that holiday in France. But today, watching Cass writhe, her red hair staining Skye's lap, Vanessa had felt as if she were back outside that icehouse. She could still feel the horror; the gnawing certainty that when they finally broke the door down, Cass would be unmoving inside. And the relief, mixed with terror, when she was discovered alive but bruised. A thirteen-year-old girl splayed out, her body floating on dead pine needles, splintered wood all through her hair.

If Bruce were here she could corroborate these memories: confirm that she hadn't just imagined them. They would remind each other of the order of events; how Cass came to be stuck, the means by which they'd satisfied themselves that nothing too terrible had happened to her while she was trapped in there.

'Anika?' she said. 'Do you remember that icehouse?'

'I do.'

Her daughter's voice was distant, distracted. She turned to see what Anika was looking at so intently. During the afternoon, Vanessa had righted the furniture and swept up the remnants of the vase. But in that far corner—the spot where, several hours earlier, the girl's body had hit the floor—Vanessa thought she could make out several jagged shards.

CHAPTER 6

2008

IN THE VILLA, Skye's room was the smallest. Unlike Sam's, it did not overlook the pool. It was on the other side of the top floor, where the windows were smaller and the corridor had the cramped feel of an attic. Ensconced there, she felt an intensity of privacy that reminded her of being a child. As if nobody else existed, except for when she saw them with her own eyes.

It was there—in that retreat from the real world, in that outpost of the imagination—that she had recently discovered masturbation.

Among her schoolfriends, sex had always been relegated to comedy. At sleepovers, they took turns reading aloud from the sealed section of *Dolly* magazine. Their chosen excerpts always concerned the strictly hypothetical topic of *boyfriends*. (Dolly Doctor didn't print any stories about sexual encounters with girlfriends or strangers. There'd be the occasional stepdad or half-brother, but nobody read those ones aloud: they were a guaranteed vibe kill.) The queries would go something like this:

Sally (15): My boyfriend fingered me while I had a tampon in. Now we can't find the string. It's been a few days and it's starting to hurt.

Rhonda (15): I was fondling my boyfriend's balls after sex and I accidentally pulled too hard. Now one is much lower than the other. Have I broken them permanently?

Alex (13): I recently got my nipples pierced and every time my boyfriend kisses me there I throw up and pass out. Is this normal?

They'd laugh at these until someone's mother came to the door and told them to go to sleep. Then, without the urgent giggles that insisted these were jokes, they'd lie in bed, minds awash with bodily fluids, and worry that maybe they weren't such silly questions. Could a gaggle of virgins—for all the magazines they'd read between them—honestly say that, if they had a boyfriend, they'd cup his testicles with any more dexterity than Rhonda (15)?

While intercourse—the act; the nuts and bolts—was endlessly comic, her friends were always sombre on topics of love and desire. 'Types' were discussed in the breathless tones of prayers.

Skye, naturally, participated in these conversations with the sincerity they demanded. She even acquired the necessary props: she put up posters in her bedroom and read magazines and listened to the same 'favourite' bands as everyone else. What she never talked about—or fully articulated to herself—was that her experience of desire, to date, had been divorced from this performance of teenage lust.

It was only when watching European films—which, inconveniently, she tended to watch with her parents—that she had ever felt those intimate parts (the parts she preferred to ignore) compete with her mind for attention. A king taking a new mistress; a soldier leering at a prisoner—these were more pleasurable to imagine than the hand of a schoolboy beneath her skirt on the bus. She had no difficulty fantasising about a middle-aged duke unfastening her corset, one hook at a time, while she, frightened and aquiver, whispered: 'But, sir, what would my husband think?' All that seemed more immediate—more intense—than the time her boyfriend, Cameron, lifted her school tunic and discovered her Victoria's Secret push-up bra, discoloured and knobbly from the wash.

She had wanted to have sex before she started her gap year. Being a year younger than the rest of the girls at school had given Skye something to prove. She had a mania for milestones. And if those arthouse films were anything to go by, there were no eighteen-year-old virgins in Europe. She did not intend to be the first. Cameron obliged. They made love once in her bedroom at her parents' house. It dragged on for several minutes, with Cameron apologising that he found the banging of the headboard against the wall 'distracting'.

But all that—the sleepovers, the fantasies, the clumsy boyfriend—seemed so obviously a former self, like an old essay, or a school uniform she'd grown out of.

On her Contiki tour, where she was bussed from one European city to another, she'd had sex with three different men. She recorded each incident in the travel journal her parents had given her before she departed. She didn't know their names, so they were represented by three obscurely contemptuous epithets: Ponytail, Canal Boat, and Girthy.

Despite her nightly romps, she was still the first person awake every morning, her backpack laden with fruit from the free hostel breakfasts. She'd walk around museums, reading every word in every display. She thought dour, serious thoughts like: *Even really bad people—even Nazis—wouldn't conceive of themselves as evil*, and, *Isn't history complex?*

And now there was this interlude with her family before backpacking resumed. She had been embarrassed to tell her fellow travellers who she was meeting in the south of France. It seemed adulthood was not a state of being but a pose she was struggling to hold.

Except, when she arrived at the villa, she had found herself unable to regress. She was suspended somewhere between her new and old selves. Around her parents, she was still a child. But when Rupert, that handsome writer staying next door, was talking to her—even when he looked over from his balcony—she felt a newly adult thrill. Despite the sunglasses, she could tell when Rupert's eyes were moving across her body, the way Sam's had by the pool this afternoon. She loved it when men looked at her like that. And she loved looking back—how her boldness could make them all the more uncomfortable. If they sometimes made her squirm, it was only partly because of embarrassment. It was also, in part, to absorb some of the pleasure.

It was Rupert she thought of as she lay there, this warm Monday evening. She imagined telling her friends back home about her wild summer fling with the Famous Writer. They, like Skye, probably wouldn't have heard of him. Successful Writer might be a better story. Or, Mysterious. The Tall Dark Handsome Writer in the Chateau on the Hill. Perhaps Skye could help him through his writer's block. She could be his muse.

She started, as if she had been caught, when she heard her mother's voice in the corridor.

'Skye! It's dinner. Skye?'

'Yeah?'

'Hurry up, it's on the table.'

From Vanessa's urgent tone, Skye could tell that dinner was an Event. Harry did not usually inspire such ceremony. She doubted that Sam would either. They all felt sorry for him, of course. It must be awkward for him to be lumped into this random family's holiday. But Skye knew her mother: her approach to making people feel welcome usually consisted in refusing them special treatment. No, Vanessa's tone could only mean one thing.

Rupert had arrived.

SAM WAS WOKEN by the clink of cutlery on plates and the tinkling of voices. The window was wide open. From the colour of the sky—a soft, pinkish blue, as if the lavender fields had leaked—he could tell it was evening. He must have been asleep for several hours.

He had a quick shower. The water was scalding; the pressure torrential. When he finished, after only a minute or two, the bathroom was so choked with steam that it was impossible to get dry. It didn't help that the clothes he'd left on the toilet seat were wet from shower spray. He might have opened the door to let some air in or snuck back to his room with a towel around his waist. Instead, he changed into damp board shorts and a damp grey t-shirt. Then, his bare feet spongey on the carpet, Sam followed the voices downstairs and outside to the terrace.

They were all there: Harry and the four Kellys, plus a red-headed girl and the man from the neighbouring chateau. He was wearing the same pink shirt from the balcony. His sunglasses were off now, revealing a more youthful face than Sam had expected—at least twenty years younger than Bruce or Harry.

He was telling a story. Sam only caught the end of it—something about an encounter with a French person in town. He spoke nervously but broke off into an impression of the local Frenchman with such gusto (his French, apparently, was fluent) that Sam suspected he wasn't *really* shy of attention; he'd just worked out how to perform shyness to seem endearing. Even his occasional stutters were so perfectly timed that the effect—like a pause—was to heighten his audience's anticipation.

When he finished (in French, which nobody else at the table spoke), they all laughed.

'Oh! There you are.'

At Harry's greeting, the laughter stopped so abruptly it was as if they'd been talking about Sam. All seven diners looked at him.

'Sorry. I had a nap.'

'Naps are for children,' Harry said. 'Siestas, on the other hand, are very Continental. You were acclimatising.'

Bruce stood up and beckoned Sam to the table. 'Sam, I don't think you've met our guest, Rupert.'

Standing, Rupert was even more handsome: six foot two and school-prefect-postured. But Sam took a venomous pleasure in noting his outfit. White slacks and velvet loafers. Sam had never known men to dress like that. Not if they took themselves seriously, or wanted to avoid getting beaten up.

Sam plucked at his own t-shirt—he wondered whether it was obvious that it was from Target—as he scanned the table for a seat. They appeared to be sitting in age order. Bruce was heading up the older end of the table. On his left was Vanessa, Harry to his right. In the middle, Skye was sitting opposite Rupert, leaning forward across the table, as if straining to hear him. Sam chose to sit at the other head, between the two girls. It looked like the safest option: the kids' end.

There was a minute or two of fussing. Dinner was a whole fish and potatoes: unpeeled, boiled, sprinkled with parsley. Sam tried not to look the fish in the eye while Vanessa spooned some of its flesh onto his plate. Eventually, when Sam had both wine and sparkling water in front of him, Harry resumed his seat and the adults started talking again. They appeared to be discussing Harry's work as an academic.

'I don't make anything,' Harry was explaining to Rupert. 'I'm just a barnacle on the ship of culture.'

'I always think, some people make beautiful things, and then some people make things beautiful because of the way they describe them.'

'That's very kind of you, Rupert.'

Bruce treated the dinner table like a desk. He handled his knife and fork with efficiency, poking at his food the way one might smack down on a stapler. Now, he rapped the table with his water glass, as if it were his job to keep them all on topic. The topic, in this case, was himself. 'Which one am I? Do I make or describe?'

'You make money, Bruce.'

Vanessa laughed. 'You walked into that one.'

Harry tried not to look too pleased with himself.

Sam, who had said nothing, just chewed and watched, did not realise that he had started to yawn.

'You know you're meant to stay up all day. That's the trick.'

Her voice—loud, tremulous—had both too much and too little confidence. Sam had been distracted by the adults' conversation, but now he looked up at the girl who'd just addressed him.

He deduced immediately that she was Skye's younger sister. This was partly by elimination: the other girl sitting opposite, with her pale, freckled forearms and red hair, was evidently no child of Vanessa's. But the girl who'd spoken to him—Anika, it must be—had none of her sister's blessings. Puberty, it seemed, had made a swift and savage assault on her body. Her skin was pimpled, her stomach protruded over her shorts, and she sat with a hunch, as if overwhelmed by the sudden burden of breasts. She had her father's face, or a variation on its themes: a strong, arched nose out of place above a pouty mouth.

'The trick?' Sam said.

'To jet lag.'

'Right. I haven't really flown before.'

'You've never been to Europe?'

'I've never been anywhere.'

'Oh, right.' Anika frowned. She looked confused.

'Have *you* been to Europe before?'

'Only once. For skiing.'

Sam laughed at that; he couldn't help it. Before he could ask how old she was when she'd learned to ski, Anika's friend, the redhead, placed a gentle hand on the table.

'I've never been to Europe before either.' She smiled with her mouth closed. It was an oddly subdued gesture in such a young face. There was something melancholy in it, as if she were too world-weary to smile fully. 'I was so excited.'

'Glad someone here is normal.'

She smiled wider, still not revealing any teeth.

Anika said, 'I'm very lucky,' so solemnly that Sam felt bad.

'Hey, I can't talk. Harry paid for my flights.'

'And Harry's your . . . ?'

'He's my great-uncle, technically. He sort of adopted me.'

'Mum was adopted.'

A lull in the adults' conversation, combined with Anika's too-loud voice, meant that the whole table heard this.

The silence was total. Sam looked at the centre of the table: at the fish's impossibly delicate spine. 'Oh.' He swallowed. He hadn't chewed properly: a fuzzy lump of potato caught in his throat.

When his coughing had subsided, Vanessa said: 'From China.'

Another silence, broken by Rupert this time. 'How old were you?'

(Vanessa did not know her exact age. At the time of her adoption, the orphanage had estimated that she was between three and five.)

'I was five.' She turned from Rupert to Sam and, in the exact same tone, as if continuing a single thought, said, 'Tell me, did you like the look of the pool?'

'Yeah.' They all looked at him. Seeing Harry's encouraging smile, Sam remembered their chat when he and Harry had just arrived at the villa: about Rupert's house being too full of antiques; about the chairs that 'weren't for sitting'.

He cleared his throat into the expectant silence—'It was nice, but I wasn't sure if it was for swimming.'

The adults roared with laughter, which made the girls follow suit. For the first time, Sam noticed that Anika's red-headed friend had braces. It was too dark now to make out their colour, but it looked like there was an alternating pattern going on in there.

When the laughter had died down, Rupert leaned back in his chair and said, 'You know, I really should have you all over for a meal. The place is a bit shabby, of course, but there are some real charms to it. Have I told you about the ghost?'

'The ghost?' Skye squealed at a pitch that made her mother and father cringe.

'I never believed it growing up. It's too ridiculous.'

'Please, tell us.'

Rupert feigned reluctance for a few more minutes so he could, inevitably, feign relenting. 'Years ago,' he began, 'between the wars, there was a housekeeper whose child went missing. They never found the body. For the rest of her life, she swore that she could hear the child whispering through the house. Of course, it's very old. Lots of creaky floorboards and loud pipes. Anyway, when I was a little boy, my father had a priest to stay. He wrote to my father afterwards and said: *Thank you for your hospitality, but just letting you know, you've got a ghost in that guest room.*' Here, the rehearsed pause of an inherited anecdote. 'As casually as that. As if he were saying, oh, and by the way, the hot water is patchy. Anyway'—now he turned to face Skye—'on this most recent trip, I saw it.'

Her hand was at her throat. 'You *saw* it?!'

'I can assure you, I no longer sleep in that particular guest room.'

Sam had to admit, Rupert had managed to make a whacky story sound pretty serious. He supposed it was the accent: Rupert had the objective, authoritative voice of a newsreader or the narrator of a wildlife documentary.

Harry, however, was unimpressed. 'And what form did this ghost take?'

'A young woman.'

Harry stroked a finger along the stem of his wineglass. 'I believe that's called a *dream*, Rupert. I have them all the time.'

'This was different.'

'Oh no, my dreams can be quite corporeal, too.'

Before Harry could make his insult any more explicit, Bruce interrupted, rapping his glass on the table once more.

'Well, it might not be so grand, but this house has its secrets, too. As we're learning, aren't we?'

Everybody just stared at Bruce, wondering when, exactly, he had become drunk.

'The icehouse,' he prompted.

If Bruce was guilty of self-importance, it derived, at least, from sincere enthusiasm: a conviction that if *he* found something interesting, other people must.

'It's where they used to keep ice,' he explained, somewhat unnecessarily. 'They used to ship it across the Atlantic. The trick was to get it here before it all melted. I'm not sure when this house was built but it must be at least one hundred years old.'

'So, Rupert's place has a ghost, and we have . . . a super-old fridge?'

Even Bruce laughed at this summary of Skye's. Anika had to shout to make herself heard: 'No, no. It *is* haunted, I swear. I heard noises coming from it the other night.'

Her mother was the only person who paid her any attention. 'What sort of noises?'

'Like, screams.'

Vanessa, who could imbue a single glance with the subtlest disgust, who could ignore someone and make it unambiguously personal, was oddly at her most devastating when she was trying to be nice. Now, she broke into laughter. 'Screams! Oh, darling.'

Only Rupert seemed unamused. His eyes were narrowed, not with their customary good humour, but as if he were formulating a plan. 'I think we should see it.'

Bruce cocked his head to one side. 'What? Now?'

'Why not? We've all finished eating.'

'Oh, I don't know . . .'

'Come on, Bruce. Give us the grand tour.' He placed his hands on the table and pushed his chair back. Trembling wineglasses; the screech of iron against stone.

Bruce stood, Vanessa with him. Harry said he'd also been aching to see the icehouse, which made Sam stand too. Skye and the two younger girls were quick to follow, determined not to be left behind.

IMMEDIATELY, IT BECAME apparent that eight people would struggle to fit inside the icehouse. They piled in one by one, like strangers into a lift. The roof was low: although none of them grazed it, they could sense its presence just above their heads. Bruce was crouching—almost crawling—as he scrounged around for a torch, which he swore was 'just by the door'.

The situation was comic, really. A failed expedition: eight people, some of them basically strangers to each other, in a dirt box with very little to see. But nobody cracked a joke. If it weren't for Bruce's mumbling to himself, they would have stood in total silence. Something about that space—so cool and cave-like—made their little party sombre. Conversation had hushed on entry, as soon as their bodies had started to press against each other.

'I must have left it behind the door.'

Bruce's narration was lost to the dirt walls, which seemed at once to amplify and to smother. His voice—usually so crisp, each word distinct—became a low, nonsensical moan. As they all shuffled to make way for him, each unable to see where he or she was going, their discrete steps merged into one rustling sound.

In the dark, Rupert bumped Vanessa, who stepped on Anika's toe. Anika cried out and fell onto Skye, who ended up with her hands dirty on the floor. 'Anika!'

'What? It wasn't me!'

All of this, too, merged into a single, half-strangled sound.

'Oh, be quiet, both of you.'

As soon as Vanessa had issued her instruction, Bruce reached the door and closed it. What had been dark and even eerie, was now black.

From there, with both hands outstretched, it only took Bruce a few seconds to find the torch and turn it on. But those few seconds, wherein no one could see or be seen, were long and excruciating. Especially when they were measured not by a clock but, upon reflection, by how long they felt and by what they contained.

Anika had been standing with her toes together, so as not to be stepped on. She couldn't see her own feet, let alone who it was she could sense standing behind her. She widened her stance and reached her hands out to gauge her distance from the wall. Moments ago, it had been only a few inches from her face. But with that blackness, she felt untethered, as if she were rubbish floating on the surface of a pool. It was a relief when her fingertips met a coarse dirt wall. She steadied herself against it.

The warmth behind her intensified: someone flush against her back. So she leaned further into the wall. But this movement created no space; the body followed her, until it was not just flush but crushing her. Heat at her back, cold stone against her palms.

Around her, people were murmuring and crying out. Bruce mumbling to himself, Harry trying out a joke, someone apologising for bumping into someone else. But Anika couldn't tell one voice from the other. It was all that same strained sound, as if the icehouse were a living creature and it was out of breath. Then a single voice, distinguishable only because she felt as well as heard it: a tickle in her ear.

First, it shushed her.

Then hands held her firmly by the hips. They pulled her body from the wall. She let them.

She could feel a scream, like a pebble, dropping from her throat through her stomach and down between her legs. The weight of it stayed there, somewhere between fear and arousal, as the hands ran along her body. One went to her mouth and smothered it, fingers digging into her cheek. The other took a breast and squeezed.

The hand on her mouth stayed there, making it difficult to breathe. It was unnecessary—she couldn't have screamed. She was incapable of moving at all. Her body grew even more rigid as the hand that was on her breast passed her stomach and grabbed at her crotch. She was wearing a skirt, so the hand brushed past her underwear, then, with a surprisingly painful yank, it found bare skin.

She was so still now—so apparently pliant—that the other hand relaxed around her mouth. It tilted her head to the side, exposing her left ear.

The breath was warm, trickling all the way down to her eardrum. It said: 'Friday.'

Later, she would wonder whether she had heard correctly. Why *Friday*? What was happening on Friday?

At the time, she was too startled by the rush of sensations—the hands where they had never been before—to formulate a thought, let alone question what was said.

'Aha!'

With Bruce's cry, Anika was released. The hand left her neck so abruptly, she felt a physical twinge, as if something had snapped.

'I knew it was here somewhere,' Bruce said.

Anika was alone and untouched when the light came on. She realised her face had been pressed right up against the wall. She wiped her forehead. It was coarse with crumbled stone.

She scanned all their faces—her parents, her sister, Cass, Rupert, Harry, and Sam. None of them looked predatory. They were quiet, their gazes politely turned towards Bruce, who stood by the door and prattled about the features of the icehouse.

All except for Sam. His expression was taut and pained, perhaps adjusting to the light, as he studied the floor. In the dirt, with the toe of his sneaker, he drew and redrew an X.

They turned then with a disappointed air. As if, for all its eeriness, the icehouse had been an anticlimax. Anika stayed up against the wall and watched them file out, so as not to turn her back on a single person. Her father led the way, then her mother followed. Neither looked at her. Rupert and Skye were next. They approached the door at the same time. He stepped aside and swept his hand to indicate that she should go first, then followed only a few centimetres behind. Sam went after that. Cass, who had hung back and waited, smiled at her.

Anika left the icebox at a run. But Cass started running too, which made it look less like an escape and more like a frolic with her friend.

They all assembled again at the outdoor furniture—the iron weaving sinister shapes in the night. Vanessa went straight to the kitchen to fetch a bowl of peaches and a tub of ice cream. Seated once more around the table, hands hovered over spoons.

This whole time, Anika didn't speak. When she shook her head to indicate that no, she didn't want any sweets, her mother smiled at her encouragingly, like she'd made the right choice.

While they ate and talked, metal clattering against porcelain, Anika stood and walked towards the house. She had already reached the door before her father asked, 'Anika, are you alright?'

'Just going to the bathroom.'

In the bathroom, Anika pulled down her underpants and tentatively touched the spot where the hands had been. Feeling wetness, she withdrew her fingers and braced for the sight of blood. They looked clean but, smelling them, she found them foul.

Then she looked at her face in the mirror.

She imagined what would happen if someone found her. She saw the whole scene. A gentle knocking at the door, her little jump of surprise. The way she'd splash water on her eyes and dry them with toilet paper. How she would compose herself before opening the door. The stoicism with which she would reply when asked, 'Have you been crying?'

But nobody knocked. Not even when she allowed herself a loud, un-stoic sob.

The toilet roll was empty. She wiped her eyes on the handtowel instead. It smelled like a dirt floor and a dark room, which made her wonder when it was last washed and how many hands had touched it since. She dabbed her eyes again: all those hands, touching her face.

TUESDAY

CHAPTER 7

2024

WHEN HIS SHIFT ended on Tuesday afternoon, Sam dropped by Harry's. He wanted to hear about the funeral from Harry's perspective, and to say goodbye before he and Cass headed to Italy for Skye Kelly's wedding. He'd taken the following day off work so they could run their last few errands—do 'life admin', as Cass called it—and then they were flying out on Thursday. Even though 'life admin' included an appointment with a neurologist, which was going to set them back several hundred dollars, Sam was experiencing a freshly clocked-off elation.

He hadn't been to Europe since that summer in France. Driving to Harry's house through the streets of Balmain, which wound gently down towards the water, the concerns of work slid off him. He found that he was looking forward to his holiday. In fact, he was experiencing the tantalising sensation that a mistake had been made—money deposited into his account in error—and that he should enjoy this fortune, falsely borrowed, before it was reclaimed. This simultaneous sensation of fear and liberation—the feeling that he had not only escaped but was now being chased—only heightened his exhilaration.

Within minutes of arriving at Harry's apartment, his mood was ruined.

Having recently retired, Harry was leaning into the tropes of old age with relish. These extended from gardening to fussing about the perceived dangers Sam was forever encountering. As soon as Sam crossed the threshold, Harry turned Sam's sympathies back on him. Well-intentioned questions about the funeral (Bruce was, after all, Harry's oldest friend) were countered with a frenzied interrogation on Cass's health: what she was doing to manage it, how Sam could know—know for sure—that she was safe from further 'attacks'.

Even Harry's apartment felt like an old man's. There was an abundance of knick-knacks (decorative ashtrays, a record player, a paperweight shaped like an animal paw) and stubbornly anachronistic kitchenware. In his fridge, for example, Sam sometimes found a mustard-coloured contraption designed for storing slices of beetroot once they'd been removed from the can.

The only age-related trope to which Harry would not stoop was sitting for hours in front of the TV. Indeed, one of his most passionately held beliefs was that watching TV during daylight was 'unseemly', much like wearing brown shoes 'in town', or being American. So, on these visits, they sat in front of a blank TV, and talked.

'Are you still going to this wedding, then?' Harry said.

'That's the plan.'

'And you think Cass will be okay? On an international flight?'

'She'll be fine. She'll have her pills with her.'

'After yesterday, I must say I have my doubts about the efficacy of those pills.'

'We're seeing a specialist about it tomorrow. If there's any cause for alarm, we can always cancel.'

'Do consider it, Sam. It's a different kettle of fish, having a seizure overseas.'

'I'm sure the Italian medical system can cope with one more tourist.'

'It's not the medical system I'm worried about. Some cultures think epileptics are possessed by the devil, you know. They might want to perform an exorcism!'

Sam hadn't considered an exorcism, but he had certainly been in enough Reddit threads, watched enough clips on YouTube, to be alert to the dangers posed by overseas travel. There was one particularly memorable story, told by a woman from Canada who had tens of thousands of subscribers, about having a seizure in a bazaar in Morocco. According to her account, locals had sat on her, crushing her chest, and wailed—too loudly to hear her family screaming, begging them to get off. But Sam stopped following her when she started suggesting that manifestation, plus niche herbal teas (link in bio), had cured her seizures.

Instead of explaining any of this to Harry, he said, 'She's already stopped driving. Is she supposed to stop travelling now, too? Like, never leave Australia?'

'You're quite right. No, a holiday will be good for you.' Harry paused and contemplated the blank TV. 'Has Cass *tried* an exorcism? It might help.'

'Harry!'

That was just like Harry. At will, he could lower the pitch of his anxiety, giving the impression that he had only ever been semi-serious. Like being a bit dithery and uptight was a joke he played for his own amusement. As if he could hold old age at a safe, ironic distance by meticulously mocking its tropes.

Now, he was looking chastened. But silence wasn't in his repertoire; he resorted instead to patter.

'Where is it, again? This "destination" wedding?'

'Just outside Rome.'

'Is Skye's fiancé Italian?'

'No.'

'Do his relatives live overseas?'

'Nope.'

'Oh. I thought they might have chosen it because they were meeting in the middle. But it sounds like it's not on the way to anywhere.'

'I guess that's why they call it a destination.'

'Ha!'

Sam felt no satisfaction at having made Harry laugh. It felt like a concession. With that dry riposte, he'd yielded to Harry's preferred mode: conversation-by-combat, each party choosing an opposing side, as in a game, just for the sake of winning.

Sam stood to make tea.

Harry's pantry was almost empty—what he called 'bachelor rations'. At the back, Sam found an old box of English breakfast teabags. They were behind a glass jar, the label of which Sam, with his professional eye for medical details, couldn't help but scan. *Viread*. A glance at the fridge confirmed they'd have their tea without milk. There was just a loaf of bread, mould blossoming at its base, two bananas, and several variations of mustard.

Sam had lived with Harry for four years, while he was studying to become a paramedic. That was not long enough, apparently, to grow accustomed to these close-up views of Harry's personal life. It always felt voyeuristic opening his cupboards.

At the start, Sam had felt like a trespasser, not just when he opened the cupboards, but every moment of every day. He felt compelled to apologise when he made a creak on the floorboards, or entered a room that Harry was already in, or placed the toilet seat back down after peeing.

His politeness was excruciating for both of them, and Harry quickly wore it down. Whenever Sam asked for permission—*Do you mind if I take a shower? Do you think I could borrow your car, Harry?*—Harry would make such an excessive show of granting it that Sam could only laugh: *Make yourself at home, pee in the shower! Oh, write it off! Run someone over. Wrap it round a tree!*

Looking in his near-empty fridge, Sam recalled the lengths to which Harry went to cater for him. He wasn't a proficient cook. But every morning, Sam would wake to find three types of cereal and several condiments spread out on the kitchen bench. At the time, he'd felt like an imposition. Now it was obvious: how nice it must have been, after all those years alone, to have someone to look after.

Sam brought two steaming cups to where they were sitting. They rattled in their saucers.

'Now. Tell me about the funeral.'

'It was fine. Until Cass—'

'Yes, apart from that. Was it a good send-off?'

'Fine.'

'I'm glad you got to see him before he died.'

Harry didn't meet Sam's gaze. Instead, he made a study of the floor.

Harry was an old man now. His hands were wrinkled and delicate where they held his teacup. His eyes had lost some of their colour and were now a murky, fading brown. It occurred to Sam that, within a few years, he would have known Harry for longer than he knew his own mother. His throat caught then, as it did occasionally when he looked back and realised how far he'd travelled from the place where she stopped. How far he had come with Harry.

'Bruce loved you. You know that, Harry.'

For a moment, Harry yielded to an uncharacteristic silence. Then he leaned across and rapped his knuckles on Sam's armrest. Near to his hand but not touching.

'You're a good boy.'

HARRY DID NOT, in fact, see Bruce before he died—not quite. Several months before he passed, a mutual friend—acquaintance, more like—who had bumped into Vanessa at the hospital told Harry about Bruce's diagnosis. Bernard Owen was perhaps the worst person to break the news. For one thing, Harry had always been suspicious of people with two first names. It was a mark of loyalty to Bruce Kelly that Harry never held this against him. (Kelly was more of a girl's name, so it didn't count. And Vanessa Kelly was the exception that proved the rule. Skye was a noun, so that was fine. And Anika Kelly . . . well, some people did find her suspect.) And Bernard Owen was one of those corporate types who liked golf and stocks but had decided, as his hair thinned, that he'd better start caring about wine or else nobody would find him interesting. He had seen Harry in the supermarket and said (assuming, of course, that Harry would already know): *I'm so sorry about Bruce Kelly.*

The problem with being friends for decades and decades is that, in moments of legitimate grievance, there is a treasure trove of resentments upon which to draw. It was easy for Harry to buttress his hurt with prior slights. Shock and grief quickly cauterised and became, instead, *offence*.

All the parties Harry hadn't been invited to, the fact that he wasn't chosen as godfather to either of the children, Bruce's total lack of interest in his personal life, how he'd never tried to get to know any of Harry's boyfriends—all of these formed a familiar picture. That Bruce was more important to Harry than Harry was to Bruce. That Harry had never been fully integrated into Bruce's life or his family. That he was just an addendum. The entertainment.

Then, a few weeks after the bump in, Vanessa had called to relay the bad news. Harry feigned shock when she told him about Bruce's diagnosis, as if this was the first he'd heard of it. But his shock, when she went on to recount Bruce's recent heart attack, was genuine.

'Oh god, will he be alright?'

'He's not really up to visitors. But he'd love to see you.'

When Harry didn't say anything, she added, 'He . . . we thought we'd have more time.'

Harry's visit took place on a typically bright Sydney autumn day. Bruce was in a private hospital. Through the windows on the top floor, the coloured terraces of Paddington were stacked like toy blocks. Vanessa met him in the corridor and pointed him to Bruce's room. She was going to go for a walk. She looked like she could do with some sun.

For several moments, Harry hovered on the threshold. Bruce was sitting on the edge of his bed, his back to Harry. His hospital gown was tied at the nape of his neck, revealing bare mottled skin. At first, Harry thought that his friend was admiring the view. Then, as he was about to announce himself, Harry noticed that Bruce's arms were shaking. He waited, deliberating about whether or not to rush in and help. Bruce was trying to stand up.

But it was becoming increasingly obvious, as he stood there watching, why Bruce hadn't told Harry—told anyone—about his condition. It was there in that open-backed gown, in the food tray and the plastic water bottle with a straw built into the lid, as if for a baby. Bruce didn't want his friends to see him so reduced.

With a clatter, he stood, revealing his bare bottom, his skinny little legs, and the entrails of a catheter. Quietly, while Bruce caught his breath—before he had enough energy to take a single step—Harry turned away.

At the time, he told himself that he was respecting Bruce's wishes. He was affording him the dignity of privacy. He would come back another day.

But as ten days passed and Harry kept finding excuses not to return, his reasons became clear. It was his own frailty—not Bruce's—that had frightened him. They had been boys together, then middle-aged, and now had reached this new phase, which Harry was reluctant to enter. To look at Bruce was to look into the future—or, worse, at a reflection: to admit that he had already arrived. Harry saw, in that flush of sagging flesh, the dwindling years, the funerals attended, the inevitable sparseness of his own. He turned from it all.

Walking away from the hospital, Harry headed down Oxford Street, past men who did not look at him—or if they did, looked only for a moment and saw only an old man.

'DID HARRY SAY anything about yesterday?'

Sam had anticipated this question. Cass always wanted to know what other people said about her seizures. In fact, the opinions of bystanders seemed to concern her more than those of the medical professionals.

'Not really.'

They were in the bathroom brushing their teeth. He leaned forward to spit. She was yet to place her toothbrush in her mouth. In the mirror, their eyes met.

'What does that mean?' she said.

'He asked after you. Like, checked that you were okay. But we didn't really discuss it. We talked about Bruce a bit.'

'Oh my god, of course. I'm sorry.'

'No, it's fine.'

'They were so close.'

Her toothbrush hung limp at her side. Sam had meant to change the subject, not to reprimand her for thinking about herself. Sensing a melancholic slide, he said, 'Hey,' and smiled at her, foamy-mouthed, in the mirror. Then, with a swoop, he kissed her cheek. The foam dripped towards her chin. She shrieked as he tried to grab her.

It was a favourite game of theirs: cooking together, brushing their teeth together, eating together, he would try to smudge her face. She would shriek and giggle as he chased her around the apartment with a wooden spoon or a toothbrush. They discussed it sometimes, in their sombre adult voices, when they lay together, heads on pillows or making pillows of each other. What was this need that they had to act like children?

They agreed it was the ultimate marker of maturity, to make a gift of innocence.

AFTERWARDS, AS THEY lay in bed, Sam heard a tapping sound. He moved his arm from under Cass's neck and stood up. Before going to the bathroom, he covered her naked body with a sheet.

He knew already what he would find. Above the sink there was a round window like a porthole. For weeks now, a bird had been flying into it. Headfirst, its beak making the same futile *tap* where it hit the pane.

Sam turned the light on, revealing the white scratches on the glass. He thought of Cass's account of her trip to the hospital yesterday: the shock of Anika's scarred arm.

It must be a cruel trick of evolution, Sam thought, that cute creatures were those who needed us and whom we felt we could protect. Babies in the cold, animals with big eyes, anything small enough to bundle. But when a living thing was technically old or large enough to help itself—to be possessed of dignity—then all we felt was pity.

He thought, as he had many nights before, about covering up the window. Perhaps it would help if the bird could not see through to the other side.

By the sink sat their two toothbrushes and a cardboard box of Cass's anti-seizure medication. Sam had pulled it out while they were brushing their teeth. Now, with mounting alertness, he started to replay the rest of the evening. They'd talked about Harry, then he'd chased her, trying to plant mint-foamy kisses on her cheek. Then they'd had sex and Cass had dozed off at his side. He didn't recall her taking her pill.

Before frustration, or even anger, came exhaustion. He couldn't be bothered having another version of the same fight.

Cass complained about her anti-seizure medication often: she said it had a flattening effect on her moods, made the world seem distant. He believed her. But he also thought about those side effects, whenever she 'forgot' to take her pill. In light of her complaints, these frequent omissions looked deliberate.

And they *were* frequent: at least once or twice a week. If he worked late and she was in bed before him, he would ask her whether she had taken it. Often she would say 'Yes,' only to get out of bed, minutes later, and say, 'Sorry, no. I forgot.'

Once, he asked her why she felt compelled to lie and she said that her first thought, always, was to tell him what he wanted to hear.

He couldn't articulate *why* at the time, but it filled him with rage, that she might take the pill—or say that she had—to please him. He'd brought his fist down on a pillow. They'd had the fight in the living room, sitting on the couch, so it was a decorative pillow, one Cass had brought when she moved in. Now, he couldn't look at it without feeling ashamed. It had mocking orange tassels at the corners.

It just seemed outrageous that she might construe a medical instruction as some kind of whim. As if it mattered what he wanted. As if she had a choice! It was doctor's orders: every night before bed, she had to take her pill.

He was still standing by the sink, trying to calm down before he woke her. He told himself to be more generous. He couldn't imagine how hard it was for Cass: trapped in a body that insisted on randomly, publicly, betraying her.

But it was hard for him too. A falling object, a door slamming; a call from an unknown number—these were enough to weaken Sam's legs and fill his head with sirens. It was agonising to live, always, with the intensity of two equally possible worlds: one mundane, the other catastrophic. Every phone call was as likely to be a summons to the hospital as: *I'm at the shops, do you want anything?*

Cass thought that his work had made him paranoid. True, as a paramedic he spent a disproportionate amount of time dealing with calamities. Even before he met Cass, he had seen more seizures than most people would in a lifetime. And he knew how to handle them, how to sit astride the patient, pinning their thrashing legs with his own so he might inject benzodiazepine, an anticonvulsant, into their thigh.

But statistics, as well as personal experience, fuelled his fears. He knew, for example, that seizures became more frequent and more intense until, eventually, they were so violent as to send the sufferer into cardiac arrest. He knew that there was a correlation between epilepsy and sleep apnoea: that even when she *wasn't* having a fit—even when Cass was seemingly peacefully asleep—her breathing could just stop, perhaps for long enough to reduce her oxygen to a life-threatening level. He knew that one in every thousand people with epilepsy died, for no particular reason, every year—so many that there was a term for it: SUDEP, or Sudden Unexpected Death in Epilepsy. And those were just the risks posed by her own body. There were external dangers too, depending on where a seizure occurred. Bodies of water (drowning). Roads (collisions). Public transport (the high step onto a bus, the steep drop onto train tracks—all places where skulls might crack).

At work, he saw his own fear in strangers' faces. Not in the patients, but in their carers, who would stand back while he checked blood pressure or administered CPR or said, *Describe your pain from one to ten, ten being unbearable.* The eagerness they all displayed to cede to his authority, the palpable relief when he arrived. And at the same time, the hovering, the straining, the way they wrestled with their own helplessness: wanting most of all to reach out and be a comfort to the one they loved.

He gripped the edge of the sink, the porcelain cool beneath his palms. A pill was such a small thing. The horror of another fit reduced to a matter of milligrams. It wasn't much to ask. How many times had he hoped, as a boy, that there might be a pill for his mother?

'Cass?'

Through the open bathroom door, he couldn't hear her stir. He went and knelt by the bed.

He forced himself to whisper. 'Cass?'

'Mmm.'

Gently, he shook her.

'What?'

Still half asleep, she was not quite aware of her surroundings. She looked to him for guidance: the only real thing in the room.

He couldn't help the note of accusation. It was his inflection that did it: phrased like a question, but expressed with an incurious, disappointed certainty.

'You didn't take your pill, did you.'

CHAPTER 8

2008

VANESSA WOKE IN the villa on Tuesday morning, as she did every morning, fearing for her children. Before she opened her eyes—before she knew who or where she was or that she was no longer dreaming—she thought: I'm worried about Anika.

She worried about Skye too, of course: worried that her appetites were stronger than she knew, that she was possessed of beauty, which she did not yet have the wherewithal to manipulate. A lion cub yet to grow into her paws. But Skye was, for all her curiosity and her risk-taking, her endless pursuit of her own ever-stretching limits, happy. Bruce always said it was because she wasn't as smart as her little sister—as if the world really *was* an awful place, but only those who were clever enough noticed.

Although Vanessa agreed Anika was very smart (it wasn't really a matter of opinion), she thought her youngest daughter might put her intellect to better use. Her greatest passion in life so far seemed to be for concocting games.

Sometimes these were charming: she'd have her friends over and, rather than watch TV, they would re-enact Anika's favourite shows.

The shows were always *her* favourites, never her friends', so Anika could be both writer and director and could chastise anyone who remembered wrong.

Other games were oddly upsetting. A mother called to say that, at a sleepover, Anika had insisted on playing with tarot cards and had told each of the girls when and how they would die. Each of them was murdered by a lover.

'I just thought it was odd,' the woman said—*odd* carrying the full weight of pity and implication—'that someone so young would think of that.'

Vanessa didn't know why Anika had thought of that, or where she got any of her ideas. Before becoming a mother—and a mother to Anika, specifically—the problem of human subjectivity had never really troubled her. She had always thought that reality existed, objectively, basically as it appeared, and that reasonable people could be relied upon to see it the same way. Now, multiple times a day, she would have paid almost any sum, sacrificed any comfort, if she could just crawl inside Anika's head and, even for a minute, see the world the way she did. She often felt a physical urge to grab her by the ears. As if shaking her head, like a piggybank, might make the thoughts fall out.

Even when she was a newborn, Anika's state of mind was an impenetrable mystery. She cried constantly. After Skye, who slept as soon as she was swaddled and whom her mother would proudly bring to coffee with her friends (she was no more obtrusive than a handbag), Vanessa had thought that babies weren't that onerous and the trials of motherhood had been exaggerated. Then, as if to punish her for her hubris, Anika had screeched without rest for the first six months of her life. The sounds she made were more animal than human—harsh, scratching noises that were agony to hear.

What's wrong? Vanessa used to whisper into that tiny marshmallow ear. *What's going on in there?*

It was always when Bruce left for work that the crying started—as soon as he closed the door behind him, as if father and daughter were in a conspiracy to drive Vanessa insane. At those times, Vanessa could have killed her. She never made a malicious move but she imagined it. Smothering with a pillow was what she always visualised. It would be soft: cries muffled, the application of pressure, and then blissful, permanent silence. Her baby made her abhor her own imagination. It must reveal something about her, she thought—that she was, in some way, evil, that something inside her was lacking or broken, perhaps by her own biological mother.

Then, when Anika first spoke, it was in a whole sentence. As if she'd been capable all along but been too bored or too amused or too cynical about the capacity of language to communicate truth to bother making the attempt.

She seemed to demonstrate, from an early age, a will to power. It was an interpretation Vanessa couldn't quite shake. Anika seemed always to want to expend her intellect, creativity, and energy on making others do things for her.

First, she had taken all her mother's time. Before Anika was born, Vanessa had never contemplated becoming a full-time parent. There was never a conversation around her giving up her career, never a moment of decision, merely days in which smaller decisions— *not now, not yet*—accumulated. Just as someone driving a familiar route does make, at every intersection, a decision *not* to deviate. It was only natural that Bruce should be the one to work. He was successful. Whereas Vanessa, at twenty-six, was already married with two children. Her 'career' was only putative. It's not a sacrifice if you have nothing to throw away.

In Vanessa's mind, the ultimate expression of this particular character defect was Anika's refusal to play sport. She wouldn't exercise on her own because, unlike schoolwork (where there were occasional prizes), she was never going to be the fastest or the strongest. And she certainly wasn't going to join any kind of team: that would require participating in a game where she hadn't written the rules.

And yet, last night, when Anika declined dessert, Vanessa had felt her throat ache with pride. It was only the fear of embarrassing her in front of Cass that stopped Vanessa from throwing her arms around her little girl and telling her she was brave and perfect. Her brilliant youngest daughter, who was so perceptive. Even if she used those gifts not to get closer to other people, but to bring them under her control.

As Vanessa woke and thought of all this, her reflections crystallised, as always, into guilt. It was out of character for Anika to forgo dessert. She was still a child—it was unlikely she was having a spontaneous flowering of willpower. Vanessa regretted now that she was not kinder, more attentive, that she had not asked what was wrong.

By the time she sat up, she was determined that today would be different. Today, she would make amends.

Bruce had already woken up, eaten breakfast, and was just getting back to bed. Determined as ever to rise before his guests, he had allowed for jet lag and set his alarm for four thirty am. After breakfasting with Harry at five (Sam appeared to have slept the night through, which they attributed to youth), he crawled back to bed, defeated. It was this return that had roused his wife.

'I think we need to talk to Anika,' she murmured.

'Anika?'

'Your daughter.'

'Oh. What?'

'I'm worried about her.'

Bruce sighed. Like a hypochondriac, his wife could generate daughter dramas just by worrying about them. Sometimes, Bruce could find it in himself to sympathise (after all, the hypochondriac's pain *feels* real). Not at this hour.

'You're always worried about her.'

With that, she lost him to sleep.

The sunlight was still tentative as she made her way down to the kitchen. It was just past six.

There was something deliciously on-holiday about being barefoot in another person's home. As she passed the front door, she poked her head out the window and saw a cloudless sky: the shy promise of another perfect day.

So total was her sense that this morning was, for now, her own, Vanessa jumped when she entered the kitchen and found someone else sitting there.

With its exposed stone walls, the kitchen was the darkest and coolest room in the villa. On the right, upon entering via the archway, was a ceramic white sink and wall-to-wall cupboards painted pale blue. To the left, the door that led out to the laundry and then on to the terrace. And in the centre, an enormous wooden table, above which several copper pots hung low.

Anika was sitting at the head of the table on the right, closest to the fridge. Vanessa immediately noted that she'd left the fridge door ajar. She was wearing a grey singlet and unforgiving cotton pyjama shorts. On the table in front of her was a white bowl filled generously with brightly coloured cereal. Bleeding food dye had turned the milk a bluey grey. For a moment, Vanessa hovered at the archway, watching her teenager eat a child's breakfast, the fluorescence of the open fridge incriminating behind her.

'Morning!' Vanessa closed the fridge door without comment.

Anika sighed with an air of having been interrupted. She did not look up from her bowl, not even when Vanessa reached over to touch her lightly on the shoulder.

'You're up early.'

Anika shrugged.

'How long have you been awake?'

'I dunno. Not long.' Anika took a heaped spoonful and slurped. A drop of milk fell on the table.

'Anika!'

'Mum!' Anika pulled her singlet up and used it to wipe the counter. As she did, she exposed a pale flash of tummy, lighter than her tanned arms. 'It's fine.'

'Where's Cass?'

'Asleep?' She used the teenage inflection that turns an answer into a comment on the stupidity of the question.

'And is Harry around?'

'No?'

'What? Has he gone back to bed too? Dad just had breakfast with him.'

'It sounds like you're the authority on their whereabouts.' She returned to her bowl and—slower now, with more care—she took another mouthful.

A final clink of metal on ceramic signalled that she was done. Anika rested her head on her right hand and, with her left, placed a finger on an ant which was making its circuitous way across the table.

'Where's your necklace?'

Anika raised both hands so they cradled her neck.

For her recent fourteenth birthday, her parents had given her a silver necklace from Pandora. Bruce thought it was ridiculous but Skye had a similar one (a boyfriend had given it to her) and Anika was fixated on it. Upon unwrapping it, she had shrieked with pleasure and immediately put it on. Since then, she had worn it every day. And every night, she removed the daisy-shaped pendant from its delicate chain and polished it with the cloth that Bruce used for cleaning his glasses.

For a moment, Vanessa thought her daughter was about to cry. Her eyes were wide and watery and her grip on her own neck seemed punishingly tight.

She's lost it, Vanessa thought, and took a step towards her. It was unlike Anika to lose something. She wanted to give her a hug.

Then Anika swallowed, and her hands retreated to the tabletop. She sat up straight—chest out, head rigid, chin up, looking just like her older sister. 'It's in my room,' she said. 'I just didn't feel like wearing it this morning.'

'Why not?' Vanessa tried to sound genuine and not like she was cross-examining her.

'Don't freak out. I still like it.' Anika stood and went to the bench where the milk and cereal stood open. She reached for both.

'You know, it really won't help if you eat that crap.'

For a moment, Vanessa wondered whether she'd just imagined saying it out loud. Then Anika turned to look at her.

She knew, immediately, that she had ruined the morning. Perhaps even the whole holiday.

'I'm sorry, darling,' Vanessa said. 'That's not what I—you should eat what you want. I just want you to be healthy, that's all.'

'Right.'

'You're beautiful, you know that.'

When Anika spoke, it was with none of the force—the theatrical flair—that she usually expressed hurt. Her voice cracked, and her words seemed to be directed inwards, as if to wound herself alone. 'I really don't want to talk right now.' And then she added, even more meekly, 'I'm sorry.'

'Okay. Okay, darling. Sure.'

Vanessa kissed the top of her daughter's head, realising as she did it how clucky that must seem. Then, not knowing where to go, she walked straight back to her bedroom. As if she might start the day again.

The house—the villa—felt suddenly ridiculous. It was too charming, too old-fashioned, too sophisticated for her family. She felt foolish for trying, even for a few days, to claim it as her own.

No matter how far she travelled, she always seemed to bring this smallness and meanness; always lugging around her fallible, predictable self.

WHEN SHE RETURNED to the room she shared with Cass, Anika found her friend sitting upright on the bed, reading a book. Cass was already wearing her swimmers.

Anika crawled back under the covers without speaking. She wondered how long Cass would sit politely before she grew hungry or bored. And how much longer still before she admitted to either.

Eventually, Cass asked if Anika wanted to go for a swim.

'I don't feel like it.'

'Are you sure?'

'I've got a sore tummy.'

'Oh no. Can I get you anything?'

'I'm fine.' Hearing herself, Anika thought she sounded very brave.

'Anika?'

She was curled in the foetal position, facing the wall. What looked like a clump of hair was floating up towards the ceiling. She tilted her head to stare, baffled by its gravity-defying path. Then she made out a pattern of legs. It was only a spider: fine-limbed and friendly, not like the ones back home.

'Anika? Are you crying?'

She shuddered at the hand on her shoulder. In silence, Cass had crossed to Anika's bedside. 'I'm *fine*.'

'If you're in pain, maybe we can get you a Panadol or something?'

'No it's not that. It's—' She sniffed, in an attempt to pull back the tears, but this only made her cough.

Only an hour or so ago, she'd been excited by the possibility of telling Cass what had happened last night in the icehouse. She'd actually woken up feeling exhilarated, high on secrecy. The brazen touch, the mysterious suitor—it made for a salacious tale. Anika had entered a world Cass couldn't hope to experience, except second-hand. And once she let Cass in, then *she* would be the wiser one, the one who'd done and seen and felt more than her friend.

That was what she'd thought about as she ate her Froot Loops in delicious solitude: how she'd wake Cass up and blow her mind with this wild, adult-tasting story.

But then her mother had pointed to her bare neck and she'd realised her necklace was gone. Immediately, the feeling from last night had crept back: that weighty, throat-achy sense that Anika had done something wrong.

'I've lost my necklace.'

'Oh.' Cass sounded relieved. The shoulder-patting resumed. 'I'm sure we'll find it.'

'I just need to go back to sleep for a bit.'

'Okay.'

Anika didn't hear her move but, from the occasional rustle of a turning page, she deduced that Cass had returned to her own bed.

It took several more minutes before Cass said, with an unconvincing air of spontaneity, 'Maybe I'll go for a quick swim, if you're okay here?'

'Have fun.'

Cass left quietly, and Anika felt solitude settle on the room. She stayed in bed for a few more minutes. Then, pausing by the window to confirm that Cass was indeed at the pool, she got up and went to their shared bathroom. There was no mirror in the bedroom and she wanted to study her neck for scratches.

Last night, Anika had definitely been wearing the necklace at dinner. She remembered touching it—a nervous habit—when Rupert told his story about the ghost. And she wasn't wearing it when she went to bed, otherwise it would be on her side table, where she always placed it before she went to sleep. She knew—had known, since her mother pointed to her bare neck—that she must have lost it in the icehouse. Her stomach tightened at the thought. It seemed violent: perhaps he, whoever he was, had gripped her neck too hard, yanking at the silver chain until it broke.

But Anika's neck, in the old and spotted mirror, was unblemished. No blood, no bruises. No evidence of her body's edges.

There was a window in the bathroom, high up on the wall. Through it, Anika could see an uncomplicated blue sky. Laughter from the pool wafted up—Cass's, shrill, Sam's lower and harder to discern. Together, they bounced off the tiles.

It seemed suddenly embarrassing, instead of mysterious, that Anika didn't know who had reached for her in the dark. It could have been Sam or Rupert or even Harry. She let out a single sob, realising that she didn't know for sure, and that she didn't want to make the requisite fuss to find out. Without clarification, it might as well be all of them.

As she walked back to her bed, she imagined that she was like a ghost, or like Cass, moving in supernatural silence. Nobody would notice her, or disturb her, until the time came to make her presence known.

SAM SPENT THE day by the pool. At first, he was tense, putting his t-shirt back on almost as soon as he came out of the water and saying very little. Eventually, when it became apparent that the others were just lying there and reading and occasionally splashing each other, he convinced himself that he couldn't do it wrong.

It was only when Cass and Skye started talking about Anika that he started to feel uncomfortable. He, too, had wondered where she was all day. Rather than ask, he lay his towel flat on the far end of the pool under the guise of chasing the last of the fading sun. He closed his eyes. Cicadas thrummed and overtook the girls' low voices.

He might even have nodded off because it seemed, when he moved to swat away a fly, that silence had fallen very abruptly.

He sat up and saw that only Cass remained perched on a sun lounger. It was late afternoon: still warm, but the sun had lost its strength. Cass sat with her knees up and her towel draped around her shoulders. Her index finger was in her mouth, picking at her teeth, while she concentrated on her book.

'Everything alright?'

'Hmm?'

'You and Skye looked serious.'

'Oh, yeah. It's nothing. Anika's just lost her necklace.'

Propping himself up on his elbows, Sam squinted through the pine trees. It had been another sparkling day. The clouds were hilariously fluffy. They were in France, of all places. They were young and their parents were alive and rich. But: *Anika's lost her necklace.*

'I'm really sorry about your mother.'

Sam looked at her. 'Thanks.'

The word *mother* had sounded oddly formal, especially in such a young, high voice. He appreciated that she had probably been working up to that comment. Also, nobody else had said it, not since he arrived. 'Harry's been very good to me.'

'So he's your . . .'

'Great-uncle, I guess.'

'On your mum's side?'

'Yeah, so she was his niece.'

'What about your grandparents?'

'What about them?'

'Are they still alive?'

'My granddad is. As in, Harry's brother. But he's a piece of work. And Mum's always loved her gay uncle Harry, so . . .'

She laughed. 'Is that what you call him?'

'Not to his face.'

'And what about your dad?'

'I've never known my dad.'

'Wow.' She nodded slowly. 'I didn't realise you were an orphan.'

He had to laugh.

'No offence!'

His laughter must have sounded crueller than he intended, because her hands flew to her cheeks—her fingers, he noticed, were perhaps the only part of her that was unfreckled—and she mumbled something about never having met an orphan.

'No, that's fine,' he said. 'I guess I am one.'

There was a protracted silence before Cass said, very quietly, 'How did she die?'

'Brain tumour.'

'I'm so sorry. How awful. My mum gets headaches. It's different, obviously. Hers are psychological.'

'Like, they're just in her head?'

'Yeah. They started right after I was born.'

'How old was she then?'

'She had me at twenty-eight.'

Sam's mum was twenty-three when she had him. He looked at Cass, her hair in a wet knot at the base of her neck. One single strand had fallen out and was dripping onto her shoulder. She couldn't be much older than thirteen. Their mothers, if they were both alive, would have been about the same age.

'Right.'

'Then she had a bunch of miscarriages and the headaches and stuff got worse after that.' She spoke with detachment, as if reading aloud.

'So you're an only child?'

'Yeah.'

'Me too.'

She moved her book from her lap to the cushion so both her hands were free for a pair of exaggerated bunny ears. 'Do you always get: "You're such an only child"?'

'Not really, to be honest. Maybe I'm good at sharing.'

'You know the shortest, saddest story ever written in the English language is: *For sale, baby shoes, never worn?*'

He laughed, taken aback by this apparent non sequitur. 'Did you make that up?'

'It's Hemingway.'

'Hemingway! Jesus. How old are you?'

'I'm turning fourteen next week.'

'That's big only-child vibes.'

'What?' Her smile was wide now, her braces on full display.

'You know, being a voracious reader. Lunchtimes in the library.'

'Hey!' In the pitch of her giggle, he heard how young she was. 'You're an only child too.'

'And an orphan, as you keep telling me.'

She looked up at him with such gratitude—for taking her guilt, which might have pushed him away, and fashioning it into a joke that brought them closer—that he couldn't help but smile back.

HIS FEET SILENT on the carpeted stairs, Sam let out an involuntary cry. Rupert was walking down from the first floor, his hand possessive on the railing.

'Have you seen Vanessa?' Rupert asked.

'No.'

Rupert slowed his pace, descending a few more steps. He was moving with the sinister aimlessness of a prowl. From his wry smile, Sam could tell that he had a joke in mind, probably at Sam's expense. That was Rupert's style: saying inappropriate things, testing the bounds of what you would tolerate. Sam understood that it was meant to make him feel special: Rupert was taking the time to annoy *him*, to do it in a personalised way. But Sam was tired. It was only his second day in France and he was still erratic with jet lag.

In fact, he felt suddenly furious at these people—all of them, Harry included—who could make a home anywhere. Who could fly to France and drape themselves by a foreign pool and saunter down a stranger's staircase.

When there was only one step separating the two men, Rupert stopped. Sam couldn't get up without squeezing past.

'I see you've made a friend.'

It occurred to Sam that Rupert's charisma had a mocking edge. As if the confidence that propelled him were comparative, his lack of self-doubt based not in the judgement that he was *good enough* but, rather, *better than*.

Yet it wasn't Rupert's teasing tone or the intimacy it presumed which annoyed Sam. It was his perceptiveness. Sam felt he'd endeared himself to Cass, outsider to outsider. Their conversation, brief though it was, had somehow made him feel less crazy. As if the villa and its surrounds were not a dream but were, in their heightened, unrealistic way, tethered to the world.

All Sam could manage was a grunt.

'How old is she?'

He had a visceral desire to throw Rupert down the stairs. It wasn't difficult to imagine. Although Sam had the disadvantage of standing on the lower step, he reckoned it would only take one punch to knock Rupert backwards. He could climb up then, until he was standing with his feet either side of Rupert's head, grab him under the armpits, and—with some effort, but not an impossible amount—send him hurtling down. He'd hit people before. He felt, for a moment, the memory of that rush.

'She's thirteen.'

'No! At least fifteen, surely.'

This time, Sam was better prepared for Rupert's teasing implication. He managed to keep his voice flat and calm. 'She's turning fourteen next week,' he said. Then he did shove past, making sure to give Rupert a good knock with his shoulder.

Sam didn't turn around, so was denied the satisfaction of seeing Rupert rub the spot where it hurt.

'Aren't you good, knowing a thing like that?'

Sam pretended not to hear. Pretending involved continuing his ascent, his fists clenched, and closing his bedroom door behind him, so nobody would hear him cry out as he lifted a pillow, squeezed it like a human neck and brought it crashing down into the bed.

He lay atop the mattress and counted how many nights he had left in this mercilessly beautiful house.

WEDNESDAY

CHAPTER 9

2024

EVER SINCE HER GP referred her to a neurologist, Cass had been dreading the appointment. It wasn't just that she was wary of what Dr Anand might reveal about her condition, it was that—without having met the woman—she already resented her.

When Cass called Dr Anand's practice to make the appointment, a medical secretary had said that she would first need to undergo video monitoring. This required Cass to stay in a private room at the hospital for several nights. For the duration of her stay, she was filmed by CCTV cameras. Perhaps even more invasively, she was attached to an electroencephalograph recording machine by hundreds of coloured wires, which were taped to her skull. The aim was to catch a seizure both on camera and on the electroencephalograph simultaneously. The first would allow Dr Anand to see what happened to her body during a seizure; the second would show what was occurring in her brain.

Cass told her manager she had a 'family emergency' that required her to leave Sydney and asked if she could work remotely for a week. The whole exercise would be useless unless she had a seizure, so she wanted to leave the largest possible window.

It was a relief when the attack occurred on the morning of her second day. The whole process was an assault to her dignity—from the probing ceiling cameras, which rendered her a suspect, to the wire-riven crown, which made her feel like a specimen.

But from the moment Dr Anand introduced herself on Wednesday morning, only five minutes after the appointed time, Cass warmed to her. She shook hands with both Cass and Sam, and ushered them into her office with a brusqueness that suggested she had many more important things to do that day.

Her dark hair was pulled back into a tight, no-nonsense bun, and she wore no make-up, save for brown lipstick. High cheekbones hid the insults of age. It was only the lipstick, in fact, which was webbed in the wrinkled skin around her lips, that suggested she was well into her sixties. Her office, too, was bare. The walls were unadorned: no family photos or children's drawings, not even a framed wedding picture. Just two leather-bound chairs, which faced her at a lower vantage, across the barren slab of her desk.

She sat down, clapped her hands and said, 'Okay, Cassandra, let's get to it.'

'Please, call me Cass.'

'Right, Cass. The good news is that the test was a success, in the sense that we were able to catch an event on camera.'

In the chair next to her, Sam's knuckles whitened where they were clenched at his knees. Evidently, he found Dr Anand's lack of preamble rather pitiless. Cass, however, was grateful for it. It made her feel that her predicament was as unremarkable as a common cold. In fact, she felt compelled to match Dr Anand: to show that she, too could be rational and businesslike about a medical phenomenon that other, less sensible women, might find distressing. So much so that when Dr Anand turned her computer screen, showing the results of the electroencephalograph recording and said, 'This is your normal brain activity,' Cass leaned forward and said: 'Oh! Interesting,' as if she were being prompted to look at a headline about some minor celebrity—not a physical rendering of the infinite mysteries of her own consciousness.

Dr Anand moved her mouse across the screen. It looked like a blank page of sheet music: a white background with black lines across it. 'So this is what "normal" looks like. This is what it was before you had your . . . event.'

'And this'—Dr Anand paused to move her cursor to a different timestamp—'is your brain activity during the event.'

The black lines remained parallel. There was no change at all.

'And *this* . . .' Dr Anand paused to open a new tab. She touched her top lip with her tongue and took slow deliberate clicks of the mouse. 'This is what brain activity looks like during an epileptic seizure.'

The lines shuddered. No longer straight, they were now violent and chaotic, row after zigzagging row.

Cass was suddenly very conscious of her posture: of sitting up straight and giving the appearance of polite interest. Dr Anand continued with the same efficiency, apparently ignorant of Cass's rising panic.

'This is helpful,' she was saying, 'because it means we can rule out a physical cause. It appears that the cause of your seizures is psychological. It's what we call a functional neurological disorder. Now, our bodies articulate emotions without the mediation of our conscious will all the time. When we're sad, our tear ducts fill. When we're stressed, the adrenal glands flood the body with hormones.'

'Right.' Cass said, and hated the sound of her voice. 'That makes sense.'

'Normally—that is, when the brain is functioning normally—these physical responses will be immediate. Cause and symptom are almost instantaneous. But in some cases, the emotional cause and the symptom that expresses it occur at different times.' Dr Anand placed her palms together and moved them apart. 'This is what happens when someone has a functional neurological disorder.' Her hands still spread, she kept her face grave so as not to remind anyone of a phallic joke. *Say when.*

Sam supplied the laugh. It was without amusement. 'So because you weren't able to find anything, we're expected to believe that there's nothing wrong with her?'

'I'm sorry—Sam, was it?' Dr Anand smiled at him: an empty smile, a shadow of his derision. 'This is the tricky thing with functional neurological disorders, Sam. A diagnosis of FND is usually a last resort. The burden of proof, if you will, is on the medical system to show that everything else has been ruled out. Obviously, that's difficult, but in your case, Cass, we can rule out any physical cause.' She raised a hand and started to count on her fingers. 'You have no unusual growths in your brain. There are no signs of a neurological disorder, like multiple sclerosis or Parkinson's. And your seizures are definitively not caused by epilepsy.'

Cass reached across their chairs and took hold of Sam's arm. Partly to prevent another outburst, partly to let Dr Anand know that she didn't endorse his first one.

'And it's not just a process of elimination,' Dr Anand was saying. 'You display all the hallmarks of someone with a functional neurological disorder. Medication is having no effect. In fact, your seizures are increasing in length. Some of them, as you've reported, are several minutes in duration. And'—Dr Anand consulted her notes—'you've never had a seizure in private.'

'Excuse me?' Cass hadn't meant to speak so loudly. 'What do you mean by *private*?'

It was Sam's turn to reach out. He shuffled his chair so he could place a soothing hand on her knee.

'One of the greatest challenges for epileptics is the risk of having a seizure when they're alone. Most can never live independently. If they fall in the shower, for example. Or in the middle of the night. Often, they're wary of locking themselves in a room, even to go to the toilet. Their case histories tend to involve a lot of broken-down doors. Your seizures, however, have always occurred in front of an aud—' Dr Anand corrected herself: 'When there are other people around.'

'Dr Anand,' Cass paused to clear her throat. The idea that she might perform her seizures to an *audience* was so offensive, she had actually scoffed out loud when Dr Anand said it. But she was wary of overreacting. Any sign of emotion—the slightest whisper of histrionics—could only support Dr Anand's case. When she finally responded, it was with careful rigidity.

'I can assure you, having other people around is hardly my preference. They're not exactly helpful. I've woken to strangers' fingers in my mouth, for example. They're trying to stop me choking, I guess. But try *not* choking when you've got random fingers rammed down your throat. I've also had people straddling me, crushing me.' She moved her hands over her chest to demonstrate and realised they were shaking. 'And more than once, I've woken to phone screens.'

'Phone screens?'

'People filming me.'

Dr Anand sighed and with it, her whole body seemed to droop. As if those high cheekbones had caved, her face collapsing into sympathy. Her little shake of her head was slow and sad. 'One in five people who present to hospital with seizures are not suffering epilepsy. That does not make their condition any less real.

The impact on your life and your relationships is real. The pain you suffer is very real. The cause just happens to be . . .'

'In my head.'

'Exactly.'

Perhaps feeling that they had reached a tenuous understanding, Dr Anand reached for a pen. 'Do you mind if I ask you a few questions?' With Cass's nod, she went on. 'Anything particularly stressful in your life at the moment? Anything unusual?'

'My seizures are overwhelmingly the biggest cause of stress in my life.'

'Understandably.'

'And any major or unresolved stresses in your past?'

'No.'

'And when did they start?'

'A little over two years ago. The fifteenth of June, 2022.'

Dr Anand raised an eyebrow at Cass's precision. 'Not a date you're likely to forget.'

'It's my birthday. Hilariously.'

At last, she put pen to paper. Leaning over, Cass noted that her handwriting was small and pedantic.

'My mother is mad,' Cass said. 'Do you want to make a note of that, too?' Sam's hand was still on her knee. He squeezed until it started to hurt.

Dr Anand placed her pen down. 'Cass, in medicine, a symptom just means: something you experience. All symptoms—whether they derive from cancer or from a paper cut—occur at the level of perception. Your symptom happens to be seizures. I know that functional neurological disorders are not widely understood, and people might treat you like you're "mad". But *I* certainly don't think that. I'd be surprised if anyone who's met you could think that. You're evidently a . . .'

Cass braced for a borrowed phrase. She expected Dr Anand to quote from her GP's referral: *intelligent, sensible, successful woman*.

'. . . you have this natural grace. This whole ordeal must be especially hard for you.'

Her phrasing was disarming. Having natural grace was such an incongruous choice: hardly the opposite of *mad*. Because it was surprising, Cass allowed herself to be flattered. More than flattered, she felt that Dr Anand had put her finger on something that Cass had been wrestling with, unable to articulate herself. She *did* aspire to grace, if that meant being someone for whom the way was always smooth, who smoothed the way for others.

It was impossible, under the glare of such perceptiveness, to keep pretending that everything was okay.

Dr Anand reached over to the box on her shelf and pulled out a tissue. While Cass wiped her eyes and Sam rubbed her back, she afforded them the dignity of looking away, making a study of her bare walls.

For the remainder of the consultation, Cass was so focused on trying not to cry again that she did not really listen to what was said. Dr Anand recommended a course of therapy, adding that they might want to seek a second opinion and, seemingly abruptly, they were standing, shaking hands at the door. Cass's grip was weak.

In the corridor, she asked Sam to wait. 'I just need to tell her one more thing.'

Dr Anand hadn't had time to sit back down. She was standing behind her desk when Cass walked back in without knocking.

Hovering just behind the two armchairs, Cass suddenly felt absurd. All she wanted was for Dr Anand to like her; to be impressed by her. Parting with tears, all fumbling and broken, had seemed unbearable. But coming back in like this, closing the door behind her (which made Dr Anand reach for a pen) was hardly reasonable or impressive behaviour.

'I just wanted you to know . . .' Cass tried to keep her tone impersonal, as if she were delivering a speech written by someone else. 'I thought it was important to make it clear . . . In case I do undergo therapy, I want to make a note of something before I start.'

'Of course.' Dr Anand still didn't sit. 'Go on.'

'I want you to know that I've never been abused. You know, sexually.'

Dr Anand took a deep breath through her nose. 'What makes you say that?'

'It's what people will say.'

'Have people been saying that?'

Cass touched the back of the armchair. Just lightly, for something to do with her hand, not leaning on it for support. 'It's what I would think. If this was happening to someone else.'

Dr Anand stood and came around to the front of her desk. Instinctively, Cass took a step back. 'With some patients, there is one particular event, usually from childhood, that they need to work through. But with others—with most, I'd say—it's much more complicated. It would be easier, in some ways, if one event could explain everything. Admittedly, most of my patients have suffered a lot. They haven't had easy lives. But I've also seen patients with debilitating functional neurological disorders who by all accounts lead charmed lives.'

'Well, I'm definitely in the latter camp. Nothing like that—' She quavered on *that*. 'Nothing has ever happened to me.'

Dr Anand appraised her silently for what felt like several seconds.

'I'm pleased to hear it.'

When they shook hands again—firm this time—Cass met Dr Anand's eye. Her clinical demeanour was back. There was no way of knowing whether the doctor believed her.

IN THE LIFT on the way out of the hospital, Cass and Sam stood apart to make room for a patient in a wheelchair. As they descended towards the ground floor in silence, Cass felt almost exhilarated, as if the doors had opened and she had stepped into an empty shaft, into a free, easy fall.

In their consultation, Dr Anand had opened up a new territory. She had created space between sick and insane. It occurred to Cass that her strangely intense desire to impress Dr Anand—her instinct to return to her office and make claims as to her own invulnerability—might be a form of gratitude. It seemed possible, now, in a way that it hadn't when she and Sam rode the same lift up less than an hour ago, that her seizures might be in her head, and that she might have a serious . . . what was the phrase Dr Anand had used? *Neurological disorder.*

That was why Cass had made the comment about her mother. Previously, the fear that she might become her—that madness might be her inheritance—had been so pervasive, she wasn't able to see it clearly. It was the air she breathed, the temperature that coloured every mood. Now, that Dr Anand had clarified Cass's condition—not derangement, but *disorder*—Cass was able to say with confidence: I am not my mother.

As liberating as this mantra was, Cass felt, too, the stirrings of regret. If only she hadn't mentioned it in the consultation.

It was normal—enigmatic, even—to be a girl with Daddy Issues. Wayward fathers, abusive fathers, absent fathers: they confirmed a worldview in which women were shaped by suffering at the hands of men.

But a bad mother? There was no narrative for that. There was no familiar story arc that could normalise the following facts: that her mother was a hysterical presence in the home, insecure to the point of insanity, that the divorce, when Cass was eighteen, was long overdue. That she had been the one to cut Cass off, vowing never to speak to her daughter again if she 'chose' her father.

Motherhood was nurturing. It went to the root of the concept. To say that your mother was incapable of caring for anyone more than herself—to call her 'mad', as Cass had done—was to say, in a way, that she hadn't mothered at all. Most people struggled to believe her, and she doubted Dr Anand would be an exception. The problem wasn't with the mother's mind, people seemed to think; it was with the daughter's attitude.

All the evidence that might make her appraisal seem rational and not at all unfair was simply too personal, too revealing, to be relayed. To tell almost any true story about her childhood was to command pity for herself and invite judgement of her mother. And Cass had no interest in being seen as her mother's victim. So she kept them to herself—all the anecdotes that might prove her point.

There were the minor instances of social paranoia. Several times in her early childhood, Cass's mother dropped her at a friend's place for a play date, only to pick her up and carry her away from the threshold if the doorbell wasn't answered in the first thirty seconds. They weren't wanted, she'd say, sometimes growing so enraged, she'd accuse Cass of lying about having been invited in the first place. And Cass would admit that she'd lied, just to calm her down—a false confession the only way to wipe away the tears, make all the spit-flecking and finger-pointing go away.

She hated nothing more than to see her mother cry. Sometimes at night, after hours of yelling and breaking things, her mother would come into her room, cheeks scarred with mascara, and shake her awake. '*You* love me, don't you, Cassie?' she'd say. And it was the best feeling in the world to wrap her little arms around her mother's neck and say, 'Yes, Mummy. Of course, I do.'

By the time Cass was about fifteen, the paranoia was no longer a slow predator, yellow eyes blinking from the corner of the room. It was rabid. She was forever threatening to sue people, to sue the government. She was rarely where she said she'd be, and, if she did turn up, she was never on time. This was because she opted for meandering routes on the conviction that she was being followed, sometimes abandoning her destination entirely. She spent days at a time in bed, insisting that the chip in her mobile phone had given her headaches. Their house was especially filthy then. It had always been filthy—her mother reserving the right to throw whatever she wanted and leave the target to clean it up. But now things grew in it. Slices of bread were stashed under mattresses and left to rot, dirty plates spread from the usual spots (the sink or the kitchen table) to the strangest places. Cass found bowls alive with maggots everywhere from the lid of the toilet to the back of the wardrobe. If Cass or her father moved anything—even to wipe it and put it back—her mother would shriek and cry conspiracy.

Cass had spared Sam these stories. She had explained that she didn't get on with her mother, wasn't on speaking terms with her, hadn't been since she was eighteen. She had whispered it, nervously, as if it were a confession. He'd swallowed and drawn his mouth into a thin, pained line. Immediately, she'd felt guilty. How dare she not speak to her own mother when he had lost his so young. But when he was able to respond, Sam had said, in a voice that quivered with emotion: 'How could anyone not want to speak to you?'

It was enough—it was more than enough—that he believed her, without the need for these illustrative anecdotes. And even if she did tell him stories of her childhood, she doubted her own ability to convey what it felt like at the time, or how she felt about it now. What mattered, she thought, wasn't her past, or Sam's. But the people they were for each other.

With a ding, they touched the ground. The lift doors opened. The patient in a wheelchair went out first. Cass took Sam's hand and hoped that her mother, her mistake in mentioning it, might be left behind at the hospital.

ON THE STREET outside, Cass passed the exact spot where, just the day before yesterday, she had waited with Anika Kelly for a cab. Today, winter was wearing its more predictable coat: the sky was grey and threatening. Sam was a few steps ahead of her, walking to the car in long, hasty strides.

Before she'd closed the passenger door, the wind still harsh at her cheek, Sam slammed his.

'Well,' he said. 'That was a fucking waste of time.'

Cass was hesitant to contradict him. It wasn't like Sam to swear or even raise his voice, let alone slam a door for emphasis. So, for several minutes, they drove in silence. Sam gripped the steering wheel in both hands and worked his jaw, straining against his rage. Even his speed—abrupt acceleration at every green light—felt hostile.

When he had calmed down enough to speak at a more conversational volume, he described Dr Anand as, variously, a moron, a hack, a fraud, and a fake.

She knew what he was doing. Indeed, it was exactly what partners were supposed to do. Because he loved her, he was trying to crawl inside her mind and furnish it with his ideas. He was making sure that they had seen and heard the same things, that they each gave Dr Anand's words very little weight. He described Dr Anand's brusqueness as 'dismissiveness' and her note-taking as 'superior', as if her pen had been a gavel. Cass knew, already, the genre of the story he wanted to tell. *Remember that time we went to that hack doctor, and she was horrible to you?*

It felt easier—while the streets rolled past and she thought, idly, that she hadn't paid attention to them for several minutes, couldn't retrace their route if she needed to—to let him talk. She nodded and said 'mm-hmm', even when he became cheap and a discredit to himself, calling Dr Anand a bitch.

Now he was talking about the underdiagnosis of women's health issues—about how women aren't believed by the medical establishment.

The thought occurred to Cass that this was mostly true of working-class women, of women of colour.

Silently, she took his hand and squeezed it. The least she could do was be the patient Sam could cope with—the one whose ailments were real and not imagined.

All she said the whole ride home was: 'I love you.' By which she meant: *It will be okay. It has to be.*

CHAPTER 10

2008

EVEN THOUGH ANIKA had chosen not to tell anyone what happened to her in the icehouse—not, at least, until she had a better handle on the story, until she knew who was responsible—she felt increasingly indignant as the days passed and nobody asked her what was wrong.

Even the weather was indifferent. Lying by the pool on Wednesday morning, the constant exclamations by the other guests at the villa seemed to mock her: *It's so hot! I still can't get over that view! Another perfect day!*

The sunlight was shameless, the breeze gentle, the clouds decorative. The insects, too, were without menace. Bees roaming lavender. Spiders so small you couldn't see their fangs. Anika looked out for a mouse darting across the tiles or the odd cockroach, dead and belly-up—anything, which might lend her internal drama some resonance.

'Did you find your necklace, then?'

Anika sat up. She'd been lying flat on her towel, her forearm shielding her closed eyes from the pressure of the sun. Now, she scanned the scene. Cass was a submerged blur, holding her breath at the deep end of the pool. Sam, meanwhile, had shuffled to the end of his sun lounger. His feet flat on the ground, he leaned forward with his elbows on his knees and tried again.

'I thought you lost your necklace or something. Yesterday?'

When he'd first spoken, Anika thought she'd detected something mocking in his tone. But his eyes, blinking at her now through those heavy lashes, revealed his interest to be genuine.

'Oh, no. I mean, I did. But I was just feeling sick yesterday.'

'That sucks, I'm sorry.'

Anika, like Cass, and like her sister before her, attended an all-girls' school. Which meant that the only men she'd ever had meaningful interactions with fell into the following categories: relatives, teachers, her friends' parents, and her parents' friends.

To have a boy a little older than her—old enough to resemble the men in their twenties who tended to portray 'boys' on screen—ask after her health made her feel, in a sudden, sunny rush, quite giddy. It seemed that yesterday's skulking indoors had been effective. Her absence was noted. People were starting to care.

'Have you retraced your steps? My mum used to always say that.'

'I'm pretty sure I left it in the icehouse.'

'Oh. It was pretty creepy in there, hey?'

Her laugh was meant to sound chill and casual. Instead, it caught in her throat and came out choked. 'I guess.'

'Really? Were you scared in there?' Cass, apparently emboldened by the laughter, was now inserting herself into their conversation. Her arms were folded at the edge of the pool, her legs kicking out behind her. 'Did Rupert's story get to you?'

'It wasn't even that good,' Sam said.

Cass pulled her goggles up to her forehead, making an unwitting nest of her hair. 'I know he's a writer, but I honestly reckon we could make up a better one.'

'Well, *you* could, maybe.' Sam's first smile of the day—and it was for Cass. 'All those lunchtimes in the library.'

Cass splashed him. Because she was lying at the foot of his sun lounger, it was Anika who copped most of it.

The existence of a private joke between Sam and Cass was devastating. Where only moments ago Anika had felt satisfied at the attention she'd garnered for being 'sick', now she wished she could give it all back. There was, apparently, a whole day of banter to catch up on.

She lay back down on her towel: on her stomach this time, her cheek pressed up against the damp. For a moment, she indulged familiar frustrations.

Cass wasn't quiet or polite, like all the adults seemed to think. She was stealthy. Everybody, even Anika's own mother, liked Cass more than Anika.

At school, where all the girls divided into cliques, Cass spread herself across an unnatural jumble of friends. Anika knew this because they had recently started using Facebook and Cass would often fail to respond to her, despite being active for hours at a time. Then, in class, Cass would reference a joke that had been made the night before, while Anika, too, had been online, waiting for someone to message her: a ghost hovering behind the screen.

In times like these, of rising bitterness, Anika sought comfort in an equally bitter conviction: that she was smarter than Cass. Admittedly, her marks weren't as good, but Cass exhibited an ease in the world that must have something to do with obliviousness. She was too satisfied by conventional achievements, by praise for something as banal as Obeying the Rules or Being a Good Sport.

Unmoving, her face buried in her towel, an onlooker would have seen in Anika's prostrate body a picture of relaxation. Instead, she was in the throes of self-flagellation. If she were nicer, like Cass, and less cynical—if she saw the world differently and didn't find it so trivial and pointless and easy to mock—then maybe Cass might like Anika best of all her many friends. Maybe, if she were a better friend to Cass, and cheerier, less prone to making comparisons, then her own mother would prefer her too.

At the sound of fresh feet on the stairs, Anika sat up, blinking against the sun. Skye was approaching the pool, plucking at the strings that tied her bikini. With petty satisfaction, Anika noted how Sam sat up at the sight of her sister. At least Cass couldn't hold his attention either.

Skye dropped her towel on the lounger next to Sam's. In the same motion, without even pausing to say hello, she walked to the edge of the pool.

A wolf-whistle stopped her in her tracks. Skye froze—her tensing shoulders the only movement—before deciding not to turn around. She sat slowly, placing her feet in the pool. Only when she was settled did she raise her left hand and give whoever had whistled the finger.

Cass, however, stood up with a splash. She was in the shallow end now: the water stopped just above her bellybutton. She looked over her shoulder, then pointed to herself with one hand, touching her cheek with the other. The whole thing was an exaggerated mime that seemed to say: *Who? Me? Well, I never!*

In so doing, Cass performed a kind of social alchemy. Where they'd all been silent and feeling complicit by their silence, now they were laughing. No longer reluctant enablers to something weird and leery, but happy participants in a well-intentioned joke.

Skye turned to see who had catcalled. Rupert, waving from his balcony, was smiling. His kneecaps were white and sunny, spread wide in his shorts. She waved back.

Sam, meanwhile, pointed at Cass. 'You're good,' he said.

Although Anika had been thinking just the same, she stopped laughing abruptly.

Skye was looking up at Rupert, her hands on her hips. 'Why don't you join us?'

Leisurely, he took a drag on his cigarette. 'I will. Shortly.'

With this brief interaction, Anika realised something so obvious her first response was self-recrimination: *How stupid of me not to see it before.*

When Sam had said that the icehouse was 'creepy' and looked at her with such kindness, an idea had occurred to her—not even a fully-fledged thought, composed of words, just the colour of an idea, a blood-bubbling nervousness. She thought it might have been Sam who reached for her in the icehouse. That's why he was so anxious to know how she was feeling, why he broached the topic of the icehouse's *creepiness*. He was trying to assess the damage he had done.

Already, that seemed delusional. The vain hopes of a silly little girl. This new scene, which Anika was observing play out at a yell between the pool and Rupert's balcony, made much more sense. It was Romeo and Juliet inverted: this time, the suitor was on the balcony, the object of admiration looking up.

It was Rupert who had touched Anika in the icehouse—and he had been reaching for Skye all along.

With this thought, Anika felt not only embarrassed by her own stupidity but a deeper shame. Rupert was *old*. He must be almost forty. Anika had not been beckoned into an exciting world just beyond her years. Instead, she had been stained by something she didn't care to understand.

She stood up and slipped into the pool. It was shallow at this end so she had to kneel to get her head under. It felt clumsy but she did it anyway. It was the only way to disguise the fact that, as she'd lain belly down on her towel, her cheeks had grown wet.

SKYE FORCED HERSELF to wait several minutes after Rupert had vacated the balcony—flicking the end of his cigarette over the edge as he went—before making a move herself. It was never a good idea to appear too keen.

After ten excruciating, sun-baking minutes, she took her towel, wrapped it around her waist, and followed a man's voice around to the front of the villa.

She was devastated, then, when she picked her way across the gravel—harsh under bare feet—and saw her mother standing by Rupert's car. It was obvious that the vehicle belonged to Rupert, not only because of his proprietorial lean on the bonnet but because it was bright red and polished to such a shine she had to squint to look at it.

Upon seeing her, Rupert's smile spun webs around his eyes. 'I'm heading into Saint-Tropez. I thought I'd see whether anyone wanted to join me.'

'I'll come.'

Skye looked from Rupert to her mother. The car seemed to radiate heat in the space between them.

Vanessa crossed her arms. 'Are you sure? It's almost two hours away.'

'Depends who's driving.'

Rupert flashed a smile but Vanessa didn't let him get away with it. 'Oh, for fuck's sake.'

Now Rupert had admitted to speeding, Skye exhaled, as if at a blow. It was slipping away—the afternoon she'd only had a few seconds to imagine and yet had already imagined in exhilarating detail.

She was about to say something pleading when her mother spared her the indignity.

'Go on then.'

Vanessa had almost whispered it, her arms still crossed, as if provoking Rupert or issuing a challenge. But the subtleties of Vanessa's manner didn't interest Skye. Surprised by her good fortune, doubtful that it might stick, she turned and ran into the villa. Behind her, she could hear Rupert directing polite protestations at her mother. *Are you sure you don't want to join us?*

She sprinted upstairs and pulled on a pair of strappy sandals and the same white cotton minidress that she had been wearing every day. Near the hem, there was a blot of olive oil.

SITTING IN THE front seat of Rupert's car, Skye had the perfect vantage from which to inspect him while pretending to admire the view. She marked the clean slope of his nose in profile, the surprising length of his thumbnail, where it rested against the wheel. Her bikini, still damp, was soaking the cotton and, although it was difficult to look without drawing attention to it, she suspected that the hard bumps of her nipples were poking through.

Last week, there had been a family excursion to Saint-Tropez. It was before Harry and Sam arrived at the villa, while Bruce was still looking beyond its walls for entertainment. Skye had not enjoyed it. Hotel balconies that jutted out of old facades like coins in a slot machine. Boats with fragile masts overburdened by seagulls.

Slim women who walked around with large men, wearing caftans and never appearing to sweat. And amid it all, the embarrassment. In every shop window, Skye saw her own reflection and the crowd to which she belonged. Tourists, dragging their children behind them, spending money on ice creams and cappuccinos—luxury without leisure, just heat and complaints and the pain of the expense. She was among the gormless hordes: the ones who had been invited just to look, who left smudge marks where they pressed their faces to the glass.

They took a series of family photos, like all tourists do. Cass was very obliging about being their photographer. Anika didn't smile in any of them.

Skye knew it was cheap and selfish to look at all that beauty and see only her own inadequacies. But that only added to her sense that the excursion was a failure—that, and what happened at the cafe.

At some point, Anika said that she felt sick. Vanessa took her inside a cafe to ask about the facilities. Cass followed without complaint. Bruce and Skye, meanwhile, sat at an outside table, overlooking the Place des Lices. Her father ordered an espresso and Skye was about to tell the waitress that she'd like the same—at last feeling tolerably adult!—when the waitress said to Bruce: 'And for your wife?'

It took him a beat but Bruce got there before Skye did. 'No, no,' he said. *Non, non.* 'This is my daughter.'

Skye didn't end up ordering anything. That had never happened to her before. It would happen increasingly as she grew older: that people would confuse the white father of the Asian woman for her much-older husband. At the time, she and Bruce both laughed about it, but neither of them said anything to Vanessa or the girls when they returned. This made Skye feel obscurely guilty, as if that waitress had interposed, between her father and her, a secret—as if she really were her mother's replacement.

With Rupert, however, Skye felt glamorous already, her hair flowing in the breeze from the open car window. She thought about the clocktower she'd seen above the rooftops of Saint-Tropez, its hopeful yellow face. Maybe they would sit again in that same square and she could order a drink. An alcoholic one, this time. She could almost hear the sound of ice cubes acquainting. Or they might go into the church to cool down. It would be dark in there and they could speak in whispers.

Rupert turned his eyes from the road so he could look at her. 'Have you been to Saint-Tropez before?'

'No,' she lied, so she wouldn't have to talk about that dismal day last week, when she was a younger, more awkward version of herself. She stretched her legs out, her thighs unsticking from the leather seat. 'You speak French, I imagine?'

'I imagine you don't?'

Skye shook her head.

'And what about your mum?'

She didn't like how naturally he turned to *your mum*. Like talking to a child. 'Just English.'

'Not Mandarin or Cantonese?'

'Australians are bad like that. We only speak one language. Well, a version of it.'

'Ha.'

She'd intended that last part to be charmingly self-deprecating, but his was a laugh laced with recognition. As if her accent really were an aberration, the poorer version of his own. She turned her head, making a conspicuous study of his face. 'Maybe you could teach me some French.'

Skye continued to stare—at the silver hairs around his ears, at the stubble that carved up his jaw. Beneath it, she could make out a single throbbing vein. Eventually, Rupert moved his eyes from the road. They exchanged smiles.

As they rounded a bend, she noticed something flash on the floor of the car, just by her feet.

'Oh, look!'

Reaching down, she pulled from the carpeted floor a necklace: a silver chain, with a silver daisy for a pendant.

Rupert turned to see what she had found. His gaze was accompanied by the sudden lurching of the car. Skye cried out. He snapped his head back and placed both hands on the wheel. At the same time, he slammed the brake and they were both thrust forward, their backs off their seats.

'Skye!'

He sounded furious, as if she'd done something wrong.

'Sorry. I thought . . . we've been looking for this, is all.'

Skye could still feel the frantic flicker of her own heart. He had swerved so violently, she hadn't yet registered that they were safe, back in the centre of the lane.

'Oh, yeah. I've been meaning to give that back to Vanessa.'

It bothered her, the way he pronounced *yeah* like *ja*. There was something strained about his casualness, which prevented Skye from telling him that it was Cass's necklace, not Vanessa's. Having caught the whiff of a lie, her instinct was to chase it.

'Where'd you find it?' she asked.

Rupert removed one hand from the wheel to rub the back of his neck. 'It was on the floor at my place. It must have fallen off when your parents came over the other day.'

Now she knew he was lying. Vanessa had visited Rupert's house several days before Cass's necklace went missing—there was no way he could've found it there. She tried to keep her voice devoid of suspicion. 'We thought it might've been in the icehouse.'

For a moment, Rupert said nothing. Then he took his eyes off the road so he could give her a smile, which, five minutes ago, she would have found winning. 'I'll have to apologise. Vanessa will think I'm a thief.'

He held out his hand.

Instead of placing the necklace in his expectant palm, Skye clutched it tighter. 'Don't worry,' she said. 'I'll give it to her.'

Although the car's path had straightened, she felt no calmer. There was the growing awareness that the car was flimsy, that their speed was climbing, that this man at the wheel, this person she barely knew, was not necessarily someone she could trust.

THURSDAY

CHAPTER 11

2024

AS SHE PACKED for Skye's wedding, Vanessa found that, for the first time all week, she missed her husband. Of course, he had been in her thoughts constantly but always as the object of her anger. It was almost a mode of denial—to think incessantly upon the letter she'd found in his top drawer, to imagine the confrontation they might have about it. It was a way of keeping him alive.

The letter was from Vanessa's orphanage. Bruce had written to them right after Skye was born, inquiring after Vanessa's biological parents. Apparently, the orphanage had written back. Since his death, Vanessa had been scripting their argument.

First, she would want to know why he hadn't showed it to her when he first received it. The timing of her discovery made the point for her. Bruce had the letter since Skye was a newborn. And now, over thirty years later, Skye was about to be married. There was no better, more dramatic measure of the span of time than their daughter's *entire life*. Second, she would ask him why, having decided to keep the letter a secret, he didn't just throw it out.

And third, whether he had left it in that drawer, right next to his final wishes, because he *intended* her to find it.

Before his death, Bruce had tied up several loose ends. He had summoned Harry to his bedside, for example. He had insisted, in the days leading up to Harry's visit, that he 'had things to say'. The vagueness of 'things', to Vanessa's mind, only emphasised their significance. She saw Harry come in but didn't see him leave. From Bruce's watery eyes, and his plea that she not ask about what had happened, Vanessa assumed they'd talked about the very things they had always found so difficult to discuss.

So Bruce's passivity in relation to this letter enraged her. He'd been up for tough discussions. Just not with his devoted wife, apparently.

By having this fight with him—organising her thoughts; gathering her evidence; making her case—she could, at least, speak to him. He was furiously present.

It was when she packed for the airport that she realised how totally he was gone. Her mind was full of *his* possessions: reminders about his socks and his cufflinks and his anti-fungal cream. It felt paltry to pack one bag, to sit by herself in the back of the cab. If they had been together, setting out might have acquired a sense of adventure. But she was—would be, from now on—travelling alone.

AT THE AIRPORT, Anika was startled by her own irritability. Mostly—and most unfairly—her grievances were directed at her mother. Vanessa was late to meet Anika at Departures and didn't apologise when she arrived. Instead, she told Anika how she'd liked her Uber driver so much, she'd taken down his number. She said, 'We can call him and he'll pick us up when we get back,' as if that were any more efficient than just using the app as it was designed.

Then, because of her own lateness, Vanessa began to fret that three-and-a-quarter hours (she'd planned for three-and-a-half) wouldn't be enough time to make it to their gate. Anika repeated that they had an abundance of time: 'You could call your favourite Uber driver, go for a joyride, and *still* have enough time.'

In the queue to check in, Vanessa kept zipping her passport into her overlarge leather travel wallet, only to pull it out again every few metres. She was not yet sixty. And yet, as she moved through the world, the friction was increasing. Perhaps age accounted for this hardening and cautiousness; this need, always, to be in control. Or perhaps it was the fact that, without Bruce, the world really was a scary place.

When they made it to the front, Anika's sympathies began to shift. An airline employee was greeting them with an inhumanly delighted smile. She spoke slowly, with exaggerated mouth movements, as if hoping that someone in the back of the queue might be able to lip-read what she was saying. She continued in this manner, even though Vanessa made it apparent that her English was perfect, and even after she saw the surname Kelly on the two passports. All of which forced Anika to conclude that she hadn't made any racial assumptions: she just spoke like this to everyone. Oddly, this made Anika feel even more contemptuous.

'Also,' Vanessa said, zipping her passport back into her travel wallet, 'there was someone else on the booking. I just thought I'd let you know he's not coming.'

'Oh, okay. Let me just check the booking details . . .'

Her typing sounded plastic: fake nails hitting the keys.

After several seconds, and increasingly frantic tapping, Vanessa supplied the answer. 'Bruce Kelly.'

'Oh, okay. So he won't be flying with you today?'

Her smile actually looked painful.

'He's dead,' Anika said.

Remarkably, the smile didn't falter.

'Oh, I'm so sorry for your loss. But I'm afraid at such late notice we're not able to refund his ticket.'

Vanessa stepped forward. 'I wasn't expecting a refund. I was just letting you know. In case you couldn't take off without him, or it was a security issue or something.'

'I understand,' the woman said, then immediately offered proof that she hadn't: 'The best I can do is a food and drink voucher. You can spend it at any of the restaurants in the departure terminal.'

Mother and daughter leaned forward to look at said voucher. It was on a slip of white paper, and they both laughed at the price.

The flight attendant thought their laughter was delighted. She let her smile drop and said, with real satisfaction, 'Is there anything else I can help you with today?'

LATER, ANIKA WOULD reflect that the setting had misled her. Had she not been in an airport bar, she might never have brought up the topic of Cassandra Playfair's seizures. But international travel imposes a sense of unreality.

On a long haul, with over twenty-four hours of flying still to go, the traveller is without context. The airport, wherever it is, has no character, just a neutrality of luxury brands and food courts and toilets where people brush their teeth. The information boards display so many clocks, in so many different time zones, none claims any particular authority.

And the bar, where Vanessa and Anika had chosen to spend their twenty-dollar voucher, reminded Anika of a showroom or a set. Especially sitting where they were, in a booth at the perimeter. In a real-world pub, these booths would line the walls. Here, a rope separated them from the rest of the airport. The futility of the whole structure was masked, however, by the conviction with which people used it. At the entrance, people queued for a seat as if at a real door. Those walking past averted their gaze, as if the pub were a private space, and not just another corner of the cavern that was International Departures at Sydney Kingsford Smith.

In such a timeless, spaceless place, it seemed possible that the past could be reassessed: old narratives, like bad habits, shaken off.

ANIKA HAD SPENT the days since her father's funeral thinking about Cass. Even when she wasn't consciously thinking about her, there she was, writhing in the background.

Anika had googled 'seizures caused by trauma' and read the Mayo Clinic webpage about non-epileptic seizures. There wasn't much information. The first, blunt sentence set the tone: *The cause of functional neurologic disorder is unknown.*

So she'd resorted to YouTube and Reddit and TikTok. There, she found personal accounts, which were more compelling. She read about a woman who'd been abused as a child: her seizures started when she bumped into her abuser decades later. Another woman, who was medically epileptic, forgot to take her anti-seizure medication once and found that her attack brought out such a change in her otherwise uncaring partner that she started having non-epileptic seizures, too. Another woman had a seizure on the same day every year. It was only after extensive therapy that she realised: that was the date on which she'd had an abortion in her early twenties. As far as Anika could tell, it was always a woman.

How often, in Anika's life, had she known, without really knowing, that something had happened to another woman? She'd see her at work, walking into the shop, or socially, or even just passing in the street, and there'd be something about her expression and mannerisms . . . Anika couldn't pinpoint it, couldn't even describe it to herself—there was no word for it—but the woman would display a sort of resolve, a steeliness, and, beyond that, a kind of inward-looking distractibility: an internal retreat, a turning away from the world towards a private pain. Anika would see this woman and think: *survivor*. It was as if they all had a mutual understanding, all these women showing the subtle signs of damage—perceptible to those who shared them, who knew what to look for.

Anika had long been convinced that it wasn't just fellow victims who had an instinct for the signs. It was predators, too.

When she was in her first year of university, Anika met her first and only boyfriend. He read sensitive books and wore combat boots, which only underscored his total lack of toughness. At the time, Anika was especially thin. Her arms had started to become hairy and she was always cold. One night, she pulled her hair up into a high, tight ponytail—the way her sister often wore it—and applied some lipstick. She thought the red looked striking against the black turtleneck she'd taken to wearing daily, even in the warmer months. In the mirror, she thought she could see a sophisticated, bookish girl: just the sort of person her boyfriend would like to be seen with. Of course, when she arrived at the pub, he leaned over to kiss her cheek and, while all her new friends watched, he whispered: *What's with the lipstick?* She ordered a burger, which she didn't eat. With the paper napkin, she wiped the lipstick off.

He waited until they were alone later that night to justify his comment. *I just thought it looked cheap.* She hadn't asked him to explain—she'd understood him perfectly. In fact, she'd felt immediately foolish for inviting his derision by thinking that she could dress like a person other than herself.

They went out for several more months, his comments growing steadily more explicit. Eventually, at a club one night, they had a huge fight out on the street, which ended in him pushing her against the wall. But the wall was a fire door, and she fell right through it. She laughed—several people inside the club had spilled their drinks when she fell onto them, but, remarkably, she hadn't cut herself on any glass. She smiled at the onlookers and apologised for making a mess. In the bathroom, a stranger asked her if she was okay. *Oh yes.* She smiled. *Just a bit sticky.* The stranger grabbed Anika's hand. She was drunk but there was something else about her manner—something difficult to pinpoint. *I was outside*, she said. *I saw him push you. Do you want me to get security?*

Anika hadn't had a boyfriend since. She'd had her fair share of one-night stands. People always seemed to want to choke her but she gathered that was a generational thing. Once, when travelling, she'd contracted a UTI from one such stranger. Going to a foreign medical centre, she was dismayed that the only appointment she could get was with a male doctor. At the start of the consultation, she told him, using Google Translate on her phone, that she had a urinary tract infection. He asked her to lie down so he could examine her properly. A cold hand pressed down on her stomach. She could tell, even without the translator app, that he was asking her whether it hurt. Meekly, she nodded. The hand, as it was always going to, ended up sliding from her stomach, down beneath her underpants. In English, she asked him to please stop. Then she said, *Ow, ow, that hurts*, until he stopped.

Things like that—they happened to women like her. They had happened too many times in her life to attribute it to coincidence. It was embarrassing to admit the thought. She'd never confessed it, even to her loved ones. But, privately, the conviction was unshakeable: there was something wrong with her. Anika was—in a way that her sister and even her mother weren't—*marked*. It was as if men knew: if they reached out through the dark and touched her, she could be relied upon not to scream.

But Cass had never been one of those women. She'd always given an impression of blissful stability. Even at school, she was the one with the polite, proportionate responses, the one whom teachers respected and parents wanted to adopt. Cassandra Playfair, who was good at everything, even at coping.

Cass was the last person, whom anyone would suspect of harbouring a buried, unresolved secret. Yet, that very unlikelihood was what propelled Anika to believe it. It was terrible to think that Cass might have been hurt as a child and haunted well into adulthood. But Anika was drawn, irresistibly, to the idea that such things really *could* happen to anyone, and not just to women like her—the ones who, without knowing how, seemed to invite such treatment.

'I'VE BEEN THINKING about Cass.'

Anika was halfway through her (free) prosecco, while Vanessa played with the stem of the one she'd paid for. (Twenty dollars only goes so far.)

At her mother's blank look, Anika took another sip for courage. 'Remember, after Dad's funeral, you said that Cass's seizure reminded you of that time in France when she got trapped in the icehouse?'

'Oh, that.'

'I've been thinking about it. I think—actually, I've thought for a while now—that something might have happened to her in there.'

'How do you mean?'

'I'm no expert, obviously, but I've looked into it and it turns out it's not uncommon for people who've been abused as children to have medically unexplained symptoms in later life. You know, like Skye was saying. Often chronic pain or irritable bowel syndrome or even seizures can be a symptom of, like, unexamined trauma.'

The sound that came out of her mother was worse than she'd expected. Anika had entertained the idea that she might be patronised, that Vanessa might imply, as she so often did, that her youngest daughter was just being dramatic. This thought had taken shape not so much as a judgement about her mother but as a yearning for her dad. Over the past few days, Anika had been fantasising about having this conversation with Bruce. With the painful, straining futility of the freshly bereaved, she wished that he was still here. It wasn't the same with Vanessa.

However, Anika had never imagined that she would actually laugh at her.

Vanessa covered her mouth as if she, too, couldn't believe the sound. 'I'm sorry,' she said. 'It's really touching that you're so affected by it. And I agree, of course, it was distressing to see Cass like that the other day. And it did remind me of that holiday, as I said. I'm sure it wasn't fun being trapped in there, but I doubt it was *traumatic*.' Vanessa couldn't bring herself to say the word without a stir of parody. 'She was in there for . . . what? Two, three hours?'

'That's a long time.'

'Sorry. Even if you're right, and you may well be, that she is having a delayed reaction to something she hasn't processed, the odds are pretty slim that it'd be something we witnessed. Imagine if the worst thing that's ever happened to her happened in the one week she was on our watch.'

Anika's voice was very quiet. 'I'm not blaming you.'

'In fact, if being stuck underground for a few hours is the worst thing that's ever happened to her, then I'd say she's had a pretty great life.'

'But what if she wasn't just stuck there for a few hours? What if someone locked her in there on purpose?' Anika paused, hearing herself. *On purpose* sounded juvenile. She should have said *intentionally*. It was as if, in talking about that time, she was reverting to her teenage self: that sulky child who felt perennially misunderstood. She swallowed and forced herself to go on. 'What if they did something to her, then locked her in so they'd have time to get away?'

'Who? Who's "they"?'

'Rupert.'

Where her mother had been sitting with her arms crossed, facing inexpressively out, she now turned to Anika. In the intensity of her gaze, Anika thought she could identify fear.

'Remember? That posh guy in the villa next to us? Dad loved him.'

'Of course I remember Rupert. He's a writer, Anika, not a paedophile. He wrote thrillers, for fuck's sake, not *Lolita*.'

'But he and Skye were flirting the whole time, don't you remember?'

She ignored her mother's scoff.

'What if they'd planned to meet in the icehouse—you know, like, away from everything but still on the property, so nobody would notice Skye sneaking out—and instead of Skye, he found Cass. It was dark in there, don't you remember? It's not impossible that he might have done something to Cass by . . . by mistake.'

Vanessa took Anika's wrist. 'Anika'—her grip was tight—'I really think you should let this go. It's not fair on Cass. It's not fair on your sister, either.'

Anika identified, in the invocation of Skye's impending wedding, a familiar criticism. Not wanting to be a burden, she bowed her head and said nothing.

She felt suddenly silly for thinking that she might have—in this airport, of all places—a moment of reckoning. It was as if she'd treated her own life like a play. People didn't just randomly reinterpret the past. Moments of epiphany weren't easily conveyed to others; guilt and blame weren't divvied up by way of a serious chat. What had she expected to get out of her freshly widowed mother? A Catharsis? A Breakthrough Moment?

Talking about it couldn't change the past, or even change Vanessa's present impression of it. The very reason Anika believed that Cass was abused in that icehouse was also the one thing she could never discuss with her mother. If *Anika* had not been abused in that icehouse too—if Rupert hadn't touched her a few days before he got to Cass—she would find it more difficult to imagine. But drawing as she was on her own experience, it was all she could see. Anika had no intention of telling her mother about the icehouse. She had been tempted many times throughout the years—when Vanessa begged her to eat, when she encouraged her to move home so she could be 'better looked after', when she sighed before saying something nice, as if each compliment were a great effort of will. Her mother always seemed to be asking: *Why are you like this?* Or, more to the point: *Did I make you like this?*

The icehouse was the obvious response. But Anika didn't want Vanessa to take all her usual maternal doubts and fix them on a single event, the vague shadows of guilt solidifying into a specific, unbearable regret. So no matter how desperately Vanessa asked the question, Anika knew she would never supply the answer. *It's because I'm marked, Mum. Because Rupert marked me.*

Instead Anika said: 'You're right.'

Vanessa released her wrist and put an arm around her youngest daughter. 'It's been a big week.'

They sat in silence for a few moments. Then Anika picked up her phone. Vanessa followed, eager to mark the end of their conversation and proceed with the normal, boring business of waiting.

But Anika had not moved on. She was drafting a text to Cass:

Hey, sorry this is a bit random but I was wondering when you're going to get to the hotel? Basically, I was hoping we could get a drink or something before the wedding? I think I might have something that can help with the seizures. And, at the very least, I owe you an apology. I doubt you'd have them at all, if it weren't for me.

The exchange with her mother, while not at all what she'd hoped, was nonetheless useful. There are some thoughts so personal, so difficult to face, that they only appear in conversation. It takes a question or some external prompt to turn your mind to the places it has become accustomed to avoiding.

In Anika's case, it was not until she said to Vanessa, *I'm not blaming you*, that she was able to confront, in her own mind, the question of responsibility.

Now, she deleted *for me* which appeared, on a second, more considered reading, cowardly in its ambiguity.

Before pressing send, she changed it to:

. . . if it weren't for what I did.

CHAPTER 12

2008

IT WAS ABOUT eight in the evening: the end of another pleasantly uneventful day at the villa. The breeze had stilled, the pool's surface was cleanly reflective, even the cicadas, in all their thrumming, sounded sleepy, and Harry and Bruce were sitting by the pool, fighting. They were smoking cigars, which felt very chic, and drinking beers straight from the bottle, which seemed, in France, cheerfully loutish: the perfect accompaniment to their argument. The ferocity of their insults was complimentary. *Idiot, moron* and *madman* were their terms of endearment: it was only because of their great mutual esteem that they could treat each other with such disrespect.

What a relief it was, to talk to someone you knew so well and had long since stopped judging, so you could get on with the friendly business of judging everyone and everything else.

Bruce liked talking to Harry because, unlike most of his colleagues and contemporaries, Harry had all the clarity of a genuine eccentric. There was no group to which he belonged.

Neither left- nor right-wing, all he ever asked of an argument was that it be reasoned, that it make sense.

Today, Harry had flitted from the words he could no longer use in his classroom to the denigration of the Western canon in favour of postcolonial narratives and, without even appearing to jump ship, he had found himself in a long-winded lament of the government's use of the term 'boat people'.

'*Boat* comes first, Bruce. *People* is emphatically second. It doesn't get more dehumanising than that. *Refugee*s, *asylum seekers*: these are words of action. They imply subjects. You know what's hard to empathise with?'

'Queue jumpers? That's an action.'

'A *boat*, you miserable bastard. A boat.'

Up on his balcony in the adjacent villa, Rupert stood, stubbing out a cigarette, and retreated inside. Presumably, their bickering had disturbed his peace.

Harry's whisper was low and contemptuous. 'Doesn't he read the news?'

'What?'

'I read an article the other day about British people on balconies—'

'Slow news day?'

'It was interesting, actually. Tourists keep getting drunk and falling off them. Four Brits dead already this summer. The government has had to launch a campaign.'

Because Bruce had started to laugh, he grew louder. 'I'm telling you, it's a national crisis! Have you been to Ibiza lately? Corfu? It's a bloodbath! You know what you should do?'

'What should I do?'

Harry motioned to Rupert's villa with his cigar. 'You should call the police.'

Bruce made a study of his beer bottle. To Harry, the phrase appeared to have no particular resonance. But even at the distance of several decades, Bruce could hear in it an echo. *I could report you to the police.*

It was only because he thought about these words often—because they'd been enshrined by regret—that they came to him verbatim.

Bruce studied his friend's face, so familiar that it was difficult to see. The lines were new, of course, but they didn't obscure the boy he'd been, at once tentative and precocious. There were hairs in his ears, and at some point he had acquired jowls. Presently, Harry had his eyes closed, his face tilted to the setting sun: blissful repose. It was possible that he, unlike Bruce, never thought about that day in the university sauna.

Harry never mentioned any of his boyfriends to Bruce, let alone introduced one of them to him. He had navigated the AIDS crisis with a silence that claimed no particular dignity, even when he was called upon (always clumsily) to be a sort of spokesperson. When asked, 'What do you think, Harry?' he would ignore the emphasis on *you*, denying the implication that he had any special investment in the issue.

Vanessa had often wondered over the years whether he was asexual. 'Plenty of people are.' Bruce, meanwhile, always countered that it was rude to speculate, while speculating that she was wrong and didn't know Harry like he did.

Then, recently, he and Vanessa had gone to the movies one night on Oxford Street. It was about midnight when the screening ended. Adopting the old marital post—waiting for his wife to finish whatever complex conjuring trick, whatever impossibly lengthy operation seemed to take place in a female bathroom—Bruce stood by the window. On the street, across the road, two men exited a bar. One was Black and (although it was hard to tell at this distance) young. Probably in his twenties. The other was white, much older, tall and thin, with a stranger's gait and Harry's face.

Weeks later, Bruce and Vanessa were at a dinner party with Vanessa's friends, all women her age and older, whom she'd met through the girls' school. One of these women lived in Harry's building. Did Bruce know, she asked, that Harry had a boyfriend? From South Africa, apparently.

Of course Bruce knew, he said. Harry was his closest friend. He could see in their faces that his vehemence had betrayed him.

He knew they meant well. Or that they weren't malicious, at least: they were all clever, career-minded women, as fond of gay men as they were of their own tolerance. But it struck him, in that moment, that Harry was the most private person Bruce had ever known. And that tolerance was intolerable if it required—for gossip, for conformity—that Harry turn his private self outwards.

If Bruce were less secure in his worldview, this episode might have undermined his confidence in his own perceptions. He might have wondered what he didn't know about the love-lives of his own wife or daughters, for example. Instead, he took his unease and blamed it on Harry. He interpreted Harry's choice to withhold as a deliberate effort to conceal. As if *his* Harry, his oldest friend, were fake, and some other, more private version were real.

It didn't occur to Bruce that notions of performance and reality might be too binary, that Harry's personality was multifaceted, and that all were real at all times, even if impossible to express at once. Because Bruce's unmediated, unfiltered self had always been socially acceptable, he had the luxury of conflating consistency with integrity.

Bruce's thoughts were interrupted when Harry sat up abruptly. He'd just seen Skye hurrying down the stairs. She was on the other side of the pool: the water between them so pale and sunset-streaked it was almost yellow. Harry called out to her to join them. She shook her head. It looked like she was in a rush.

If Vanessa had been sitting beside him, Bruce might have asked his wife what she made of it: where could that girl possibly be heading? But Vanessa had complained of a headache straight after dinner and hadn't been seen since. So it was Harry by his side, his shorts belted high up his waist, his boat shoe relaxed on one knee. Bruce could remember the first time Harry held Skye: his discomfort, the charm in how terribly he disguised it. Now, he was offering her a cigar.

As the slap of Skye's sandals faded away, Bruce became aware of the juncture he and Harry had reached: that point of relaxation and inebriation at which talking about their feelings—or what was really troubling them—became a possibility.

Vanessa would say they'd been shyly working towards their troubles all along—that the conversation which came before was just emotional procrastination. But in Bruce's experience, the serious stuff had a way of slipping out only and especially if you were thinking of other things, like the lovely thickness of the cigar, or the complex smell of its smoke, or what a perfect evening it was, and how lucky to have old friends with whom summer could still feel so full of promise.

'He seems to be doing well, don't you think?'

Although Harry hadn't said his name, Bruce knew at once that they were talking about Sam.

'He does, he does. It's an amazing thing you've done, Harry.'

'The problem is . . .' Harry tapped his cigar on the ashtray. 'What I worry about is that he's so difficult to read. He's so mild-mannered. Polite. I don't know that I understand him.'

'I'm sure—'

Harry shook his head. His point would be made. 'He was very agitated before his mother's funeral. It's the only time that I've seen him—*break down* would be too strong—seen him lose composure. He was distracted during the service, and I assumed it was the effort of keeping it together. I thought, maybe he's trying to mentally absent himself so he can get through the eulogy. You remember me when my mother died. I was fine, until I tried to speak. I got up and went to jelly. So I thought, he's wise. He's keeping himself at a distance. He delivered the eulogy well. Not *unemotive*, but it was still a bit detached, like he was just reading aloud without really thinking about the words. And he was distracted again when we stood outside. Everybody wanted to talk to him and he kept looking over their heads. Then, in the car on the way to the burial, he wouldn't stop crying.'

Harry took a sip of his beer and cleared his throat.

'I gave him, you know, a little speech about grief. I was very careful to keep God out of it. Did you know this YouTube thing has turned his whole generation into a pack of scathing atheists? Anyway, I said that people really do go and they don't come back and that it's very cruel. But I said the only thing we can do when we lose someone—the only way to keep them—is by osmosis. You know: you forget eventually how their voice sounds or their exact expressions, but they can become part of you, if you let them. I got quite emotional delivering it. I spoke softly'—he was speaking softly now—'and my hand was on his back . . .' He stretched his hand out in the space between him and Bruce. 'You know, I really thought: Thank god he has me. I had this profound sense that I could help him. And then I realised later that night when I got back to my hotel . . .'

It was an effort of will for Bruce not to prompt him, but he was convinced that Harry had never told this story before.

There was a fledgling delicacy to the moment: to interrupt would be to snuff it out.

'It was so obvious, I realised it in this great clarifying rush, all at once. It really was an epiphany. He wasn't sad about his mother. I mean, he *was*, obviously. But that wasn't why he was so distractable.'

Harry couldn't help himself. His narrative instincts were too good. He took a long drag on his cigar, drawing out the tension of the moment.

'He was looking for his father.'

Bruce let out a low groan.

'He's never met him,' Harry went on. 'I don't know that he even knows who he is. Nobody in the family does. And I could see what he was thinking. Even if Sam's mum never said that she was pregnant—even if this man didn't know that Sam existed—he must have known Sam's mum, however briefly. So of all the events he might attend, in the course of Sam's life, it would be her funeral.'

'Have you spoken to him about it?'

'What's the point? I always knew my father. Much to my disappointment.'

Bruce was not ready, yet, to joke. 'I admire you, you know, Harry.'

'Don't talk rubbish.'

'I'm serious. It's a brave thing you've done. It shows real courage.'

'Well, as they say'—Harry adopted the stilted cadence of a recitation—'*Neither fear nor courage saves us. Unnatural vices are fathered by our heroism. Virtues are forced upon us by our impudent crimes.*'

The longer Bruce stared without comment—not even to say, 'Where's that from?'—the more the recitation acquired the quality of an incantation. It seemed to shiver in the fading light.

Harry's decision to open up about Sam, and the years of friendship to which that decision attested, had created an uncomplicated closeness. For a moment, Bruce was convinced that this Harry—his Harry—was the real one. He had an urge to reach out and touch him. Just a gentle hand on his knee to show that he was here, to show how much it meant to be at his side.

But over the years, they had traded shames. Where once, Harry had been disgraced for reaching out, now it was Bruce's turn, for having batted him away.

Bruce knew that even a platonic touch—a hand at a knee—was a clumsy grope for the past. It would highlight just how wildly Bruce had overreacted all those years ago, how weak he was for never mentioning it since.

So he expressed this unexpected onrush of affection using the only language they'd developed.

Averting his gaze from Harry, Bruce looked at the pool, his cigar half-raised to his lips: 'You're full of shit, mate.'

WITH AN INTENSITY that embarrassed her, Cass was fascinated by the human body. She knew that growing up and becoming a woman involved acquiring a repulsion for your own physicality. Obviously, you had to be hygienic; you couldn't always be a child picking your nose and eating it. One day, you would stop being like a dog, running around sniffing absolutely everything, even your own vomit. You would have loftier things to care about. Then, it would genuinely be a surprise whenever you were confronted with incontrovertible evidence that this mind, this soul, this creature of insight and perception was also a physical thing. But for now, Cass was fascinated by the sight of blood. Too fascinated even to register horror.

In the bathroom she shared with Anika, streaks of red were corrupting the porcelain.

A used sanitary pad lay soiled-side-up to the left of the white sink.

Cass leaned closer and marvelled at the texture. When she imagined her period, she'd always pictured blood as if from a wound. But this was thicker and browner. It had shadows and texture, like a scab.

A knock at the door yanked her attention back to herself and how she must appear: her nose only centimetres away. She straightened up.

'Cass! Let me in. I think I . . . I just need to check . . .'

'What?'

'You've been in there for ages.'

This was embarrassing for both of them. A joke was the only way to neutralise the situation.

In her head, it was self-evidently funny. As soon as she saw Anika's face, she realised that it was behaviour which, if described to an adult, especially through tears, would be a prime example of bullying.

Cass picked up the pad, holding it between her thumb and forefinger by a clean white tip that appeared to have no blood on it at all, and she shook it as she opened the door, saying 'ew-ee'. Later, she would console herself with the fact that she hadn't said 'ew'. *Ew*, a single syllable, was judgemental. But *ew-ee* had a singsong quality to it—it was a parody of revulsion, not an expression of it.

Almost immediately, both girls were in tears. Anika because she was humiliated, and Cass because she was, apparently, capable of humiliating a friend. It was difficult to know who was the more abject.

'I'm sorry,' Cass kept repeating, even as she turned her back on Anika and ran back to the bathroom. There, she dropped the pad in the bin and covered the wound in scrunched-up toilet paper. She tried not to think about what would happen—how awful it would be, the kind of trouble she might get into—if it adhered to the base of the bin.

'I'm sorry,' she said again, when she re-entered the room. 'It's gone. I threw it out.'

Anika had raised both hands to cover her face. She wasn't making a sound, but her shaking shoulders were unambiguous.

'I thought it'd be funny,' Cass said. 'I didn't mean—I didn't know . . .'

Anika lowered her hands so she could look Cass in the eye. 'You were holding my pad.'

'No, I mean obviously I realised it was yours. But I just—I didn't know you'd got your period.'

In response, Anika just blinked at her. Her face was red and blotchy, her eyes full of challenge.

Cass had the uncomfortably uncharitable thought that Anika was an ugly crier. 'I'm really, really, really sorry,' she said again, more tenderly because of the callousness of her own observation. She was trying to be better in the real world than she was in her head. 'What's it like?'

'It sucks.'

'Yeah? Is it really painful?'

Anika seemed to think about this. 'Yeah, I get, like, stomach cramps.'

Anika always perked up when treated like the older, wiser one. And all Cass wanted, in that moment, was to be someone who was capable of making other people happy. So they spent several minutes discussing the pros and cons of tampons and whether they thought it was true that people had literally died from leaving them up there too long. They agreed that it was a possibility, but the probability was exaggerated.

'You're more likely to die in a car crash,' Anika reasoned. She was dry-eyed now and sitting cross-legged on the bed. Cass, sitting on the floor, mirrored her.

There was a brief silence, which Cass filled with another apology. She wanted to forget the whole thing, but she also wanted to wring out this stomach-twisting guilt. 'I'll make it up to you. I'll do anything.'

Anika thought for a moment. Then, as she occasionally did when she was excited, she spoke too loudly, almost shouting: 'My necklace!'

'Yes! I'll find it.' Cass jumped up, as if she'd been given an opportunity, not a punishment. 'In the icehouse, right?'

She went to the window. Outside, the sun had set. The dust mites that had glowed a moment ago were invisible again. 'It's too dark now. I'll get it tomorrow.'

Anika forced a smile. Cass, seeing how halting it was, assumed that she wasn't yet forgiven.

'I'll find it,' she said. 'I promise.'

STILL SEATED ON the bed, Anika imagined taking her friend's place by the window. She pictured the view. From up here, the icehouse would be easy to spot, even as the sun set and the shadows stretched and yawned. All those fallen pine needles carved a thick black line around the structure.

She shivered.

Cass turned around, and said again, with whispering intensity, 'I'll find it.'

'Thanks,' was all Anika could manage. In her mind, another whisper echoed louder, and almost drowned Cass's out. Anika's thoughts had returned to a dark room and a dirt floor, to a voice thick with wine. *Friday*, it had said.

And although that word echoed, it was so clammy, so densely resonant, that its more quotidian significance escaped her. The girls had been in the villa for over a week now. Without the structure of school and weekends, the days relaxed into each other. So it did not occur to Anika, even as the plan was laid and she agreed to it, that today was a Thursday and that therefore tomorrow—the day Cass had vowed to go into the icehouse—must be Friday.

FRIDAY

CHAPTER 13

2024

'HARRY WANTS A word.'

Cass took the phone from Sam. They were standing on either side of an open suitcase. With his hands now free, Sam bent down and started to unpack.

They'd only checked into the hotel a few minutes ago. As soon as they got on to the wi-fi, Sam had wanted to ring Harry to tell him that they'd arrived safely.

In fact, the flight had gone as well as could be expected: a bit of sleep, no seizures, not even a whiff of burning. Upon landing, Cass and Sam fell immediately into that pleasant leisure mode: always occupied, but never with any urgency. A train to catch, a hire car to collect, check-in from two.

Because they had no intention of spending an exorbitant sum on the best day of someone else's life, they were staying at Skye's wedding venue for the minimum number of days, after which they planned to spend two weeks driving around Italy.

They had also booked the cheapest available room. The hotel was a converted monastery and they were on the top floor of one of its towers. There was no lift access, no air conditioning, and only just enough room between the bed and the wardrobe to open their shared suitcase. But the balcony more than made up for any discomfort.

A tiny space had been cut into the sloping roof. Accessible from the room via a pair of French windows, it was large enough to accommodate a round table but too small for chairs. Instead, a wooden bench had been pushed up against the low back wall. Two could sit on it, their legs touching. To the left and right, the roof continued for several metres. At their backs were a few rows of baking hot roof tiles, then a sheer drop.

If they leaned over the edge and looked straight down, they could see the chlorinated blue rectangle that was the hotel's pool. It was easier to stand and look straight out: to the soft sky and the lazily undulating fields.

Here, Cass stood to take the call. She was jet-lagged—they'd landed just after five that morning—so the afternoon sun felt clarifying.

'So it's all going well?' Harry said.

'So far so good.'

'And how's your hotel room?'

She glanced at it over her shoulder. Sam, still unpacking, was lifting her toiletries bag out of the suitcase and taking it into the bathroom.

'Yeah, it's nice. There's a nice balcony.'

'Does the bed face the door?'

'No. Why?'

'Italians think it's bad luck to sleep with the bottom of the bed facing the door. Because corpses used to get dragged out feet-first.'

'Is that true?'

'It is, actually. They also don't put hats on beds, because priests performing the last rites used to take their hats off.'

From the ensuite, she could hear Sam calling out to her.

'Sorry, Harry—one sec.' She poked her head through the French windows. 'What's up?'

But Harry was on a roll now. 'Is there a hat on your bed?'

'What was that?'

'There is, isn't there?'

Through Harry's prattle, Cass couldn't make out what Sam was saying. 'No, Harry. There's no hat.'

'Good. Keep it that way. When in Rome!'

'We're not in Rome.'

'When in the vicinity of Rome!'

'Sorry, Harry. I think I have to go.'

After his effusive *arrivederci*, Cass hung up.

When Cass entered the room, Sam's back was turned. He was a silhouette in the doorway to the bathroom. He was still—so still he looked like a figurine in a model set, placed in the room at random. She was almost afraid to disturb him.

'Sam?'

'Is there something you haven't told me?'

His back was still turned towards her. Although she couldn't see his face, the quiver in his voice did not bode well.

She sat on the edge of the bed, both hands flat against the mattress to steady herself.

'About what?' she said.

He turned then, revealing that he was still holding her toiletries bag. It was open.

'Sam? What's wrong?'

'If anything happened to you, when you were younger or whatever . . . I don't know, something bad, something you haven't processed . . . you know you can tell me.'

She tried to grip the cover. But it had been pulled too tight, like a hospital bed. Her hands slid over it, forming empty fists.

They had been together for over a year now. Sam had known about her seizures for at least twelve months. She'd had to cancel one of their early dates after she had a seizure on the train on the way over. And ever since then, she had wondered when he would put this question to her. When Sam would start to think—as all people seemed to, as *she* sometimes did—that she was making it up.

'I know I was rude about that doctor the other day,' he was saying, 'but you can tell me, if you think it might be . . .'

A neurological disorder. That was what Dr Anand had called it. When she'd used that term, it had seemed possible, for the first time, that Cass's seizures might be psychological *and* that she might have a legitimate, medically recognised condition.

But she didn't let him finish his sentence. Where he paused, she interjected with the most unflattering—most combative—interpretation of his concerns.

'Do *you* think it's in my head?'

'I wasn't going to mention it, but I saw that message.'

He didn't need to clarify—she knew at once what he was referring to. But she remained expressionless, so he went on: 'From Anika Kelly. She seemed to have something specific in mind. Like, it sounds like she knows what happened to you.'

Cass knew at an instinctive level—like knowing how to swim when trying not to drown—that the best defence was outrage. So she stole his tone and made her own accusation.

'I can't believe you read that. It was private.'

'That's beside the point.'

'Is it?'

'It came up! I was looking at Maps. Sorry, but if you have messages on your phone that you don't want your partner to read, I think I have grounds for concern.'

'Anika Kelly's crazy, Sam. Like, she's actually unstable. I don't know what the fuck she's talking about.'

'Then why didn't you bring your pills?'

He was still holding her toiletries bag. He shook it as he spoke. It was a large item she'd had for years: white with lurid pink spots, an accumulation of ambiguous filth in the white inner lining.

He shook it again, as if for emphasis. 'If you had even a shadow of a doubt about Dr Anand's diagnosis, you would've packed your pills, just in case she was wrong.'

'I did pack them.'

He shook his head. 'No you didn't.'

'That's not true.'

Cass stood up off the bed and snatched the bag from his hands. Unable to find the packet of Keppra, she upturned it onto the bed.

As she picked through the debris of make-up and tampons and nail clippers and tweezers and Nurofen packets, Sam, at her back, kept talking.

'You know, I was going to remind you, but I deliberately stopped myself. The night before we left I seriously lay in bed saying to myself: *Don't be a nag. You've got to trust her.*'

Abandoning the bag, she turned to the open suitcase.

'Don't bother,' he said. 'I've looked.'

In her frustration, Cass started to throw things over her shoulder. Sam asked her to stop. But Cass couldn't stop. She was her mother, kneeling down, frenzied now, sending the room into increasing disarray. At the same time, she was also her childhood self, watching on, helpless, wondering when it would stop. Neither mother nor daughter could hear Sam, much less respond to him, when he said, 'please' in such a measured tone.

'Stop! Would you stop, please?'

She tried to swat him away, but his grip on her forearms was too tight. He yanked her up until she was standing, then stepped around, kicking the suitcase behind him, so he could stand in front of her.

He didn't let go of her arms. His frown lines were deep. But he didn't look angry. His tone was pleading. 'Cass, you have to be honest with me. If you think it's in your head, then that's okay. Let's go with that.'

His grip was almost violent; she was sure she would bruise. But he sounded calm. He was better at this than her. While Cass doubted herself even as she spoke, her accusations ringing false in her own ears, Sam argued with all the reasoned confidence of his best self. Now, squeezing her so hard that it hurt, he was almost motionless—just his jaw working, as if swallowing his outrage. He made her look all the more tempestuous for the obvious efforts he exerted to remain calm. A man who, despite his baser nature, refused to be goaded to extremes.

Cass rose to the challenge.

'Sure,' she said, 'let's go with that. Let's go with *I'm fucked in the head.*'

She tried to wriggle out of his grasp, but he held her even more tightly. 'I'm not saying that.'

'Of course you are. You're the one who decided Dr Anand was a hack. You're always on at me about those fucking pills. Which clearly *don't work*, by the way. I'm surprised you haven't noticed, with your professional eye.'

'That's not fair. You thought it was epilepsy, too.'

'I *wanted* it to be epilepsy because *you* wanted it. I was trying to be this perfect little patient, because you like it so much. We probably wouldn't even be together if I wasn't sick.'

She winced at her own forced emphasis—the *even* was excessive. She knew she was exaggerating: it was true and it wasn't; it felt truer in the moment for being convenient.

'It's not normal, Sam, to meet someone on Hinge and then move in with them four months later.'

His grip went slack. 'That doesn't mean I want you to be sick.'

'Well, you can't save someone unless they're in danger, so . . .'

'Do you really think that? That I have some kind of saviour complex?'

'It's not your fault.'

'That's generous,' he said.

But she was unfazed by his sarcasm. She was looking over his shoulder and out the window. She'd closed it behind her, when she came back into the room, so she couldn't say for sure whether the smell was coming from outside.

'It's not my fault either that—' She couldn't finish her thought. It smelled like charcoal, like something was burning.

After several seconds, Sam managed a whisper so strained, it contained the promise of a shout: 'Not your fault that *what?*'

She looked at him. Later, she would console herself with the idea that she was distracted—that the smell had destabilised her. But when she said it, at the time, it was to wound him.

'It's not my fault that you couldn't save your mother.'

Sam released her and she realised—the pain clarifying where his hands had been—that she had been relying on him to stand. She took a few faltering steps to steady herself.

'Can you smell that?'

'Oh, come off it . . .'

'Can you smell it? It smells like burning.'

'Okay, now you're faking. That's such a fucked thing to say, Cass.' His voice was raised now. 'You can't just have a seizure to get out of it . . .' As he said the word *seizure*, his hand moved in a wild motion. In its manic energy, it looked suspiciously like an impersonation of a fit.

Except she saw it as if from a distance. As if she were up in the ceiling looking down on the scene. There were thoughts forming which she wanted to speak, the words pushing up against her skull; a physical pressure, like screaming underwater.

She didn't want this, the evidence that would prove his point—that it was all in her head, that she was a faker. The timing was cruelly apt.

He lunged at her as she fell. From the swiftness of his movements—a continuation, it seemed, of that same vicious performance—it felt like he was going to hit her.

CASS WAS SITTING on the floor, her back propped up against the bed. Her knees were bent. Clothes from the open suitcase were all over the carpet.

Sam stood by the window, which was open now. His arms crossed over his chest, he said: 'Put your head between your knees. You need to get the blood back to your head.'

She did as he instructed. 'Did I—?'

'No. You just fainted.'

She knew before she asked that this was true. There was no loss of consciousness: just a moment of wooziness—not so much a *fall* as a sudden inescapable need to sit. And Sam hadn't lunged *at* her but past her, so he could open the window. She understood now what he was trying to show her. The smell was unmistakable: nicotine.

Of course. They were not at home in Sydney; they were in an Italian hotel, where every room was filled with guests. One of them must be smoking.

Lifting her head from her knees, she saw that Sam was still standing by the window. Although the room was small, and the distance between them only a few paces, it seemed significant. It was as if she were contagious.

Cass opened her arms, reaching for him.

He didn't move. Instead, a sound came out of him: a high whine. At first, she didn't understand what was happening. Then he raised his fists to his face. Without uncurling them—just using his knuckles—he rubbed at his eyes.

Cass realised then that he was crying, with all the shame and awkwardness of someone whose body was betraying him.

'I'm sorry,' she said. 'Sam? I'm so sorry.'

He nodded.

'It was an accident. I just forgot. I promise. What was I going to do? Lie to you about taking Keppra for the whole trip?'

'I know, I know. I should have reminded you.'

'No, it's not your—'

'No.' He looked up. His eyes were swollen, but his voice managed to maintain that same infuriating calm. 'I shouldn't have freaked out. That message from Anika made me spiral. I hated the idea that you were hiding things from me, after . . .'

'I'm not hiding—'

'I'm not saying that you are.' With a few steps, he was by her side. He slid down until he was sitting on the floor next to her and placed a hand on her knee. 'Sorry, I meant that's what it *felt* like when I read that message. I knew it was paranoid, and I wasn't going to mention it to you, but then the combination of that and the pill thing . . . I just spun out.'

They still hadn't addressed her comment about his mother. Even so, she put her hand over his, as if to seal the reconciliation.

It terrified her, how cruel she could be. And without much provocation. As much as she didn't want to burden Sam, she had to confront the idea that she was terrified, too, that he might leave her—that she might be abandoned with this 'neurological disorder'.

But she had done it. She'd said the worst thing she could imagine. And he was still here, his hand on her knee, apologising.

'I'm sorry,' she said. 'I'm not hiding anything from you. Not like that.' She squeezed his hand. 'I think sometimes I hide how angry I am. Or how scared that there's no cure. I just don't want you to ever think I'm . . . I'm too hard.'

'However hard it is for me, it's much harder for you.' He lifted his hand off her knee and pulled her into a hug. 'I mean, I'm not the one who has to have a drink with Anika Kelly this afternoon.'

Her laughter was muffled, her face buried in his chest. 'True. And hear her deranged theory.' Cass sat up so she could look at him. 'You know Anika's not well, right? Like, her whole life she's always been this drama magnet.'

'You've mentioned.'

'I know. Coming from me!'

At last, one of his rare smiles. It was always an achievement to extract one.

'You did just tactically faint,' he said.

'That was a bit nineteenth century of me, wasn't it?'

'It worked, though.'

'Shame I forgot to pack my smelling salts.'

They were both laughing now, both amazed that they could already laugh about it.

With one arm still around her, he raised the other hand to her face. His thumb lingered at her throat and she felt the unbidden tightening of desire: a knot between her legs.

He turned then, so he might kiss her, his tongue deep and unambiguous.

IF IT WERE up to Cass, their fight would not have ended here: her lying facedown on the bed, him pinning her left leg with his left hand, spreading her right with his right.

That was not to say she didn't want it; her desire was an ache. But her desire wasn't entirely her own. He had willed it into being.

She cried out when he thrust inside her. There was no foreplay and it hurt. He held her head into the cushion, squeezing where her neck met her hairline, a forefinger and a thumb at each ear. She moaned, silenced by the pillow, as she tried to wriggle and absorb the fullness of him, and he squeezed her tighter, holding her in place.

Turning her face to the side, she released another cry when he paused between thrusts and kissed her back. It was slow—his lips pressed to her skin for a prolonged moment—and reverential. This teasing dance; now shoving, now worshipping. Soothing an animal to better slip the knife in.

He whispered—breath clammy in her ear—that he was almost finished. When he gasped, her head was buried in the cushion. Her nose had started to hurt.

Afterwards, she rolled onto her back. The room was painfully bright.

'Sam,' she said, feeling suddenly cold everywhere he was no longer touching her, 'I'm scared.'

CHAPTER 14

2008

BRUCE STOOD BACK so the girls could peer into the kitchen sink. Anika held her nose as she leaned over the rim. Bruce, looking over her shoulder, resisted the urge to do the same. It didn't smell salty, like the ocean. It was complicated and private. A smell to be ashamed of.

At first glance, the contents of the sink looked orange. Upon closer inspection, the colour was subtler, with gradations fading to a fleshy, blushing pink. Each creature reached two enormous claws up and out. Together, they formed a nonsense of Y-shapes. Polished and armoured, they looked like they were made of plastic. It was only the whiskers that were fragile enough to suggest they had ever been alive. Now, one such tendril began to move.

The girls shrieked.

'Langoustines,' Bruce said, savouring the *ou*. 'I got them at the market.'

'They look like prawns.'

'With claws.' Cass reached into the bowl to pick one up and shake it in Anika's face.

Bruce had taught Anika how to peel prawns years ago. The head first—that was the worst part; she preferred to rip it off from lower down so as not to see the brains—then the little legs, then the translucent shell. Finally, he'd showed her how to peel off the spine to remove the thin brown cord. When she couldn't get it all out, she'd scraped the rest with her fingers. It was Skye who'd broken the news: what she was removing, what was caked beneath her nails, was the prawn's 'poo line'. Bruce remembered that incident now as he watched his daughter's face turn a humiliated, prawn-coloured pink.

'Don't worry,' he said. 'I'm going to cook it. Garlic butter langoustine for lunch.'

Even Cass couldn't muster a polite *yum*. Anika shivered.

'They're a delicacy.'

Bruce felt childish for sounding so hurt. He only cooked when he was on holidays. Because his efforts were so infrequent—because he had been spared years of weeknight dinners and untouched lunchboxes—he still cared what his daughters thought. Praise, or lack thereof, meant something.

Determined to garner a more appreciative audience, he said, 'I think I'll invite Rupert.'

'Rupert, really?'

Bruce turned to see Vanessa leaning against the stone archway at the entrance to the kitchen. She was wearing that brown dress he liked, the one with the scooped back. The fabric had thinned over several successive summers. When the light was behind her, he could see the shape of her legs through it. This morning, however, Vanessa was in shadow. 'We've had him over a lot,' she said.

Bruce knew better than to argue. It was another perfect, sunny day. 'Fair enough.'

'He probably needs a break from us,' Vanessa went on.

'Sure.'

'And besides, that'll leave more for us.'

'I'm not arguing with you!'

She gave him an inexplicably wounded look.

'What? We're in vehement agreement. I won't invite Rupert. Awful bloke. Why would anyone invite him anywhere?'

The girls giggled but Vanessa remained stern. Without looking at him, she crossed from the kitchen to the laundry room.

'Right.' Bruce clapped his hands together. 'Who's coming to the shops?'

'I'll come, Dad.'

'Excellent.' All Bruce wanted in that moment was to throw his arm around Anika and pull her close. Whenever his wife was being haughty and confusing—whenever her mood gestured to some failing on his part which was supposedly 'obvious' yet always impossible to divine—it was Anika he turned to. His littlest one, whose head still fit nicely at his shoulder. The one who needed him the most.

But he didn't move. He had already pissed off Vanessa; he didn't need to alienate Anika as well by embarrassing her in front of her friend.

'Cass,' he said now, 'would you like to come?'

'It's okay. You guys go.'

'You're sure?'

She nodded slowly, not breaking eye contact. It was as if she understood. 'I've got my book and stuff.'

As Cass padded silently out, it was Anika who threw her arms around her father. His throat struggled: at the spontaneity of her hug, at how tightly she clung on.

—

IN THE SAME way that the smell of food can trigger hunger, the suggestion that Anika might leave with her dad made Cass suddenly, achingly aware of her craving for solitude. Now they'd left, she had the bedroom to herself for the first time since she'd arrived at the villa. Freedom! What a relief it was to be safely tucked away inside her own head, to sigh and stare out the window, not to have to check out of the corner of her eye to see how Anika was feeling. It was in this relaxed mode, lying back on the bed with a book unread on her lap, that her irritations finally had the space to bloom.

Travelling, she had to admit, was difficult. She had imagined it would be like school camp or a sleepover: talking and laughing long into the night, sharing secrets and holding competitions to see who could stay up latest. But if she learned anything about Anika, it wasn't in confessional whispers but in their long, frequent silences.

Cass had never thought of herself as patient or even as particularly sociable. There was her mother, who retreated from the world. And then there were people like herself, like her father, like Harry and Bruce and Vanessa and Skye—functioning, normal people—who participated in it. They smiled and they made jokes and, when there was nothing to say, they asked a question or made an observation.

I wonder what we'll have for dinner. It's hot today, hotter than yesterday. Isn't it beautiful? Cass, what subjects do you like at school?

But Anika, she was realising, was a different type of person. Unlike Cass, she was not perennially aware of her relation to other people: attending to them, asking questions, thinking of the right thing to say, waiting for the right opportunity to say it.

Anika was stubborn. She had opinions on everything, most vehemently on things that didn't matter. Like the correct way to slice a tomato, or whether sunscreen should be applied first to the palm and dispensed across the body or squirted straight onto the back.

Cass relented and apologised, even when she disagreed. She could think of very few principles she wouldn't sacrifice if it meant that everybody could just get along.

Sometimes, Anika would withdraw right in the middle of a meal or a conversation without even a suggestion of embarrassment—as abrupt and unashamed as a computer switching off. Ever since Sam and Harry arrived, for example, she had been sullen and removed. She had rolled over and gone to sleep without saying goodnight and had woken up in a mood so surly it felt personal.

Even this morning, Anika had barely been awake for more than a few minutes and her sullenness was already infectious. The first thing Cass had done when she opened her eyes was go to the window, draw back the curtain and look down at the icehouse. From up here, she could see its square roof, framed by pine needles. A black moat, Bruce had called it.

Cass would have gone down to get the necklace right then, if she hadn't seen Skye sitting just outside. Her hair was pulled into a high ponytail. It swung: a pendulum marking her impatience. She looked like she was waiting for someone.

Skye's presence was obstructive. Cass didn't want to have a conversation: to explain what she was doing, first thing in the morning, running errands for Anika. It was not the promise she'd made Anika but the incident that had prompted it which embarrassed her now. She'd been cruel. She didn't want to think about it, let alone talk about it, until she'd made amends: until the story had a happy ending.

Just as Cass had stood there, cloaked in morning guilt, wondering how long Skye's vigil could last, Anika had called out from her bed: 'Can you not? It's so bright.'

She had managed to lace those words with real hatred.

And then, just now in the kitchen, when Bruce had asked Cass to join them on a trip to the market, Cass had seen yet another mood approaching. This time, however, she had managed to fend it off, she'd read the room, she'd left Anika alone with her father.

And as she lay in bed and reflected on that decision, she thought how good it felt to make someone happy, even if you didn't understand—and never really could—why they were sad in the first place.

With that thought, another scene came to her. She imagined greeting Anika in the driveway upon her return, the lost necklace in hand. Anika would roll down the window, revealing a face full of gratitude and relief.

Cass sat up. She'd been alone for about half an hour. Already, solitude was seeping into boredom. She resolved to head down to the icehouse as a matter of urgency. But first, she had to finish the chapter of the book she'd started last night.

MEANWHILE, BRUCE AND Anika were, after much dithering on Bruce's part, almost ready to leave. At the front door, Bruce gave Anika the car keys and told her to wait for him. He needed to double-check his shopping list with Vanessa.

Anika proceeded out to the gravel drive, the keys feeling pleasantly heavy in her hand. She loved holding her parents' car keys: a talisman of adulthood. Was there anything more sophisticated than pressing that little black button and hearing, at a distance of several metres, the locks click?

But she couldn't hear the click properly. From the other side of the drive, Skye called out to her. She was running around the side of the villa. Her gait was silly: she looked like she was doing a parody of speed-walking, her arms pumping at her sides, her legs stiff and chicken-like. Looking down, Anika noticed that she was barefoot, and hopping on her heels across the gravel.

'Ow, ow, ow.' When she reached the car, Skye leaned on it so she could stand on one leg, brushing off the soles of her feet. 'Dad said you're going to the shops?'

'Are you coming?'

'How long will you be?'

'No idea.'

Skye looked over her shoulder, back towards the pool. A moment ago, when she had been hopping strangely towards her, Anika had been full of an incongruous dread. As if this absurd, chicken-like approach were predatory. Skye was coming to steal her perfect morning. But the youngest child always has a keen—almost rabid—nose for plans from which they are excluded. Skye's quick glance over her shoulder was sufficient. Anika knew, as soon as she saw it, that Skye had no intention of getting in the car. There was something at the villa that she wanted to do. Preferably while her father was out.

'You don't want to come?'

'Nah. I can't.'

Having sniffed out her prey, Anika now sunk her teeth in. 'Why not?'

'I'm busy.'

'Are you and Cass doing something?'

'No? She's *your* friend, freak.'

'Sam then? Or Rupert?'

That did it. Skye, who had been bent over, cupping her foot in both hands, now snapped upright. 'I don't want to come to the fucking shops, alright?'

'Alright.' Anika couldn't help but smile. 'Calm down.'

Skye was quick to exaggerate her irritability, as if it had been a joke all along. She waved a dismissive hand. 'I'm busy, okay? I've got to, like, lounge around. These skin cells won't traumatise themselves.'

Anika laughed at that: she recognised the phrase from the ad campaigns that had been everywhere in the Australian summer. Dire warnings from the government about the dangers of the Australian sun. *Tanning*, the authoritative baritone declared, *is skin cells in trauma.* All those ads had done, in Anika's mind at least, was put tanning in the same category as smoking: it was all the more tantalising for promising to slowly kill you.

Now, she opened the car, climbed into the passenger seat and watched through the window as her sister hobbled off. Leaning her arm on the window ledge, Anika studied its colour. She wasn't as tanned as her sister but she was well on the way, much darker than Cass. Just the other day, Skye had showed them both her Tumblr, where she shared mirror selfies, or bits of her body (white nail polish against a brown hand; her feet hanging out a car window) with incongruous quotes like, *Stars can't shine without darkness,* or, less incongruously, *Nothing tastes as good as skinny feels.* Looking at her arm now, Anika noted with pride that she was probably tanned enough to accent it with white nail polish.

When they arrived back at school, Anika would take off her watch or unbutton her school shirt and yank it aside to reveal the point at which her skin abruptly changed colour: proof of a holiday in the sun. All the girls would make the same comments: that she was lucky, that they wished they tanned like she did. But she wouldn't instil in them quite the same envy as those lucky few who were both blonde *and* sprayed the exact same shade as her—the Pretty Girls, who were all friends and carried themselves with confidence and were in the top sports teams but never the top classes. Anika wondered sometimes whether they planned their little synchronicities of appearance: they all wore the same socks and pulled bits of hair out of their ponytail to frame their faces. *Slut strands,* they called them. Although they didn't invent the term, they owned it by using it collectively.

She was distracted from these familiar themes by the accumulating heat inside the car. The window was open but the day was breezeless. Her thighs were wet where they touched the leather seat. She sighed—a sigh nobody heard—and contemplated turning on the aircon. Running the engine in a stationary car was—like leaving lights on or eating in her room, or opening the fridge just to see what was inside—one of the things sure to enrage her father.

She thought of the babies that died back home every year because their parents left them in hot cars. How long, she wondered, would she have to sit here, before she passed out? How long before anyone would notice she was missing?

Just when she was about to place the key in the ignition, her father opened the driver door.

He smiled at her. 'Good to go?'

Anika didn't smile back. She just nodded.

One of the things Anika loved most about spending time with her father was that, unlike her mother, he didn't think that a bad mood was a problem to be solved or that a good one could be acquired by example. So as Bruce drove away from the villa, neither of them spoke.

In their continuing silence, Anika took in the great expanse of lavender that carpeted their route. For the first time in several days, the thought occurred to her that what she was looking at was beautiful.

SIGNS OF DAMAGE | 195

—

THE GRASS WAS long and it itched Cass's calves. The afternoon heat made her aware of her skin: the back of her neck, her shoulders. She touched them in turn, checking she wasn't burned.

She tried to adopt a businesslike efficiency as she fumbled with the latch. In case anyone was watching—perhaps Rupert from his balcony, or Sam from the top floor of the villa—she wanted to give the impression that she had a job to do.

Inside, it was cool, with a dirt smell that was oddly clean, like grass after rain. She left the door ajar: a slab of light across the floor. At its edge, she found the handle of the torch.

The door creaked behind her. The slab of sun was now a needle squeezing between the door and its frame.

She walked to the far end of the icehouse and shone her torch in the cavity at the back wall. The light was dull and the dirt monotonous. Undeterred, she turned, knelt on all fours and started to scan the floor.

If Cass were less focused on her task (torch moving left to right, like eyes across a page), she might have noticed when the door swung shut behind her. With her nose almost grazing the dirt, she didn't see how the light in the icehouse darkened. And there was no slamming sound that might have made her jump or turn around. It was absorbed, like a sob caught in a throat, by the surrounding dirt.

Cass looked for the necklace thoroughly and for about twenty minutes, until her own uncleanliness started to irritate. Upon a quick inspection with her torch she saw that her hands were filthy.

Turning, she expected to find the door ajar. But the darkness where the wood met the wall—where the sunlight ought to have shone—was resolute.

She couldn't find the handle, so she pushed the door with both hands, then with her shoulder. It didn't move. She ran the torchlight across it until she found the latch. It was a brass square with a keyhole. There was no visible handle, not even a knob. Beneath her probing fingers, the metal was bumpy with rust. She tried the door once more, shoving it with her shoulder. It didn't move or even rattle, the pain in her upper arm the only evidence of any impact.

Because her heart felt like a clenched fist, and because she knew from horror movies that the tone always changed irrevocably when the young women started to scream, she crouched in silence and tried to think.

She started with the worst-case scenario: what if she screamed and nobody heard? What if the day dragged all the way into evening before the Kellys realised she was missing? As far as she knew, nobody had seen her come in here. Maybe they would go out into the fields to look for her. Maybe they would notify the police and start scouring the nearby town for convicted child abductors. It would be a good plot for one of those horror movies, Cass thought: the child starving to death at home while the responsible adults looked to the world outside for predators.

Then came the self-dramatisation. Sylvia Plath had not been so much older than Cass when she buried herself in a cellar beneath her house. (Cass hadn't read *The Bell Jar*, but it was among the books she felt confident referencing in conversation.) Did the dirt smell the same to that young poetess? Was it suffocating or cocooning? Plath, Cass thought, would at least have had the comfort of achieving her own ends: she *intended* to stay down there.

Following a well-trodden route, her thoughts turned naturally from Sylvia Plath to her own mother.

CASS WAS TEN when she first began to make sense of her mother. She was away at the time (in hospital, as Cass was about to discover) and Cass was lying in her parents' bed, where it smelled the most of her.

Although Cass could recall the scene with great clarity, she could never remember how it began, why she'd climbed into her parents' bed that day. It might have been because of the telephone, which her mother kept on her bedside table. That was usually why Cass went into her parents' room: to have long chats with her friends and relive, in multiple perspectives, the intricacies of the school day.

As always, the lights were out but the sun was insistent behind the curtains. Her father found her there. She must have been off the phone by then, because he didn't leave her to it. Instead, he sat on the edge of the bed and held her feet through the duvet. The weight of him felt unnatural, like they were on a boat and the sea was turbulent.

'Your mother,' he said, and then passed his hand over his eyes, 'she loves you very much. But . . . you see . . . she's . . .'

For a long time, she would remember the way he struggled through that speech. Pausing for long periods, looking over his shoulder as if expecting her mother to interrupt them. He had small eyes and a very thin mouth. When he smiled, his cheeks were rounded like a child's. Today, his face drooped; his chin, where he bent his head to stare at his lap, sunk into his neck.

From his long, fumbling speech, Cass retained a single phrase, easy to recall because it stood out from the rest for having a borrowed quality. It was more clinical and, at the same time, more elliptical than the way her father usually articulated himself.

Sometimes, in Cass's experience, learning a word or a concept meant that things you'd never noticed became suddenly apparent.

Like learning what a sanitary bin was and then seeing it in every public bathroom, right there beside the toilet.

And sometimes, words were a way of confirming what you already knew. Of taking the thoughts and the feelings and organising them into a phrase. A phrase like *mentally ill* could clean up the mess inside her head, put everything in piles.

On that pile now was the game she and her mother had developed when she was a very young child. (The rules were: whenever Mummy was wearing her bird-shaped brooch, which Cass loved for its real, grey feathers, Cass had to keep very quiet and not speak until spoken to, not even to ask a question.) On the pile, too, went the times when she had woken in the night to the sound of her parents fighting. Or the time she didn't eat the lunch her mum had packed for school and the Tupperware container hit her on the head. (It was Cass's fault, admittedly, that the container was heavy enough to cause her to bleed. She was the one who'd left an uneaten apple inside.)

Everything that had felt awful at the time—that had made her blame herself—now made sense. Cass was not her mother: they were separate entities. And there were things her mother experienced which Cass did not. Things which Cass could nonetheless identify and understand, even explain to other people.

Since that day, Cass tended to think of her mother with a mixture of pride and hurt. On the one hand, her mother was too clever for this world. Like Sylvia Plath, she had a poet's depth of feeling. On the other hand, if she loved Cass more, like Vanessa loved *her* children, she would surely find a way to pick Cass up from school or cook her a meal without crying or needing to go to sleep for several hours. And if she really *was* mentally ill, couldn't she be like that all the time so Cass could get on with resenting her? Instead, she turned it on and off, occasionally bruising Cass with tenderness, pulling her close, stroking her hair, telling her, through misty eyes, what a good girl she was.

But in the icehouse, Cass thought of her mother as she used to when she was a child. Not as the mentally ill woman, the complicated character, the person in her own right. Now, her mother was an ache—as much a part of Cass as her own appetites. As she scanned the icehouse's dirty walls with the torch and took in the scope of her entrapment, Cass's thoughts collapsed into a single, straining refrain: *I want my mum.*

BUT CASS DID not indulge the ache for long. That way lay despair. And she simply refused to stoop to her mother's level: to meet each challenge with self-pity and tears. No, she would not be bested by this really old fridge: buried alive in an anachronism. That phrase cheered her somewhat—she had only recently learned about anachronisms in history class.

With a keen awareness of her own ridiculousness, she knocked on the door. 'Hello?'

The walls were close and thick; they absorbed the word, reducing it to its vowels. She said it again, and heard another long: *Oh.* In the same voice—not quite a scream, more an authoritative shout, like she was a teacher calling for quiet—she tried a few variations. *Is anyone there? Can you hear me? Anyone?* She would not say *help*. It was too clichéd.

Each cry folded in on itself. She might as well have sworn or quoted Sylvia Plath. All would have sounded the same. It was like the sound inside a shell, which, they'd told her in kindergarten, had nothing to do with the ocean. The same effect could be achieved by cupping a hand to the ear. Without the strength of association, it didn't sound particularly like waves crashing. It was all just trapped air.

Cass added to her cries the beating of her fists against the door. For a frenzied second, she thought she heard someone knocking back, then shaking the handle on the other side. It was an aggressive sound; she leaped back from the door. With a hand pressed to her chest, she felt and tried to soothe the ferocity of her heartbeat.

A sudden silence. The door was unmoving.

From a distance of a few steps, under the dull light of the torch, she imagined herself hurtling through it: splinters and blood. It would be embarrassing for Anika, if that was how she emerged on the other side. This thought energised her and, when she made contact with the wood, she cried out in pain. Tentatively, she touched her shoulder—bare, freshly freckled—where it hurt most. It wasn't wet enough to be certain, but she suspected she'd cut herself. She licked the pad of her forefinger. Dirt and salt.

She sat on the floor: damp rising through her legs, a creeping wordlessness rising up through her thoughts. It was from this new vantage that she saw on her left, high up where the wall joined the roof, a tiny speck of sunlight. She stood up, the expression 'blood rushing to your head' suddenly making sense. Standing at the base of the wall, she looked up and saw a gap, less than a centimetre. The roof was low. If she stood on her tiptoes, she could get her mouth a few inches beneath the gap.

She propped the torch on the ground, burying it by the handle so that the warm glass faced upwards. Then, with the dirt invasive beneath her fingernails, she grabbed at the wall for balance. Teetering there, with her chin tilted up towards the gap, she took a deep breath, preparing herself to unleash a loud *coo-ee*. Her father had taught her that this was how bushwalkers cried for help. It made her feel resourceful, rather than overwhelmed, to apply that Australian knowledge here.

As loud as she could, she cried out. A low, long *coo*, followed by the punctuating *ee*.

But, like all the sounds in this infernal hut, it echoed back to her, losing, in repetition, any of its structure, merging to become a single panicked shriek.

She tried to listen for any outside movement: someone running or calling out her name. The icehouse was silent. If anyone had heard her, they'd dismissed the sound.

Until this point, Cass had enjoyed a strange distance from her own entrapment. She had been more intellectually than emotionally engaged, as if she were reading about it in a book, intrigued to find out what the plucky heroine might think of next. Even as she dug her hands into that muddy wall, she'd thought about how she might relay it to Anika afterwards.

Now, the present gripped her. She began to think of herself not as the main character in a drama, but as a victim of inescapable circumstance. She was small and the icehouse was all the world.

It was not her mother who she thought of now, as her mind turned to the more practical matter of whether she might eventually run out of oxygen. She thought about her father.

Several times during this last week, she'd allowed herself to imagine that she was born of different parents. That Bruce, who knew what a langoustine was and how to cook it, who had an anecdote for every meal, was her father. And that Vanessa was her mother; her tenderness towards her favourite daughter only highlighted by how cool and remote she was with absolutely everybody else. Many times, she'd imagined Vanessa's jewellery chiming as she enveloped Cass in a soft, sophisticated hug.

But when survival was less about being polite and winning people over, and more about waiting for someone to notice she'd been gone for hours, she started to feel guilty. As if she'd betrayed her own real dad by failing to miss him more.

This time, when Cass opened her mouth to scream, she did not form words—not *help*, not even *coo-ee*. The sound that came out of her was punctuated only by the drumming of her hands against the wood, and the short pauses in which she drew increasingly ragged breaths.

CHAPTER 15

2024

WHEN CASS WALKED into the hotel bar at four in the afternoon, it was with nervous dread. She was still exhausted from the flight. Nauseous and faintly aching, she knew she wouldn't be comfortable until she was fully horizontal, until she closed her eyes and started a new day. A drink with Anika Kelly, at this juncture, seemed an impossible effort.

Cass was comforted, however, by her exit strategy. At five o'clock, there was a welcome drinks event for the wedding guests. This meant that, whatever it was Anika Kelly needed to confess, however awesome her outpouring, she would have to limit it to an hour.

Cass was not optimistic that much could be achieved by this impending conversation. Anika was going to try to diagnose her, she was sure of it. She would tell Cass that her seizures were the result of some trauma in her past. (From the tone of her message, it appeared she had a particular moment in mind.) Cass knew already that once this belief was formed there was nothing she could say to convince Anika otherwise. Any denials of alleged trauma would be attributed to shame about her illness, or a lifetime of repression.

This was why she preferred not to talk about her seizures. In fact, if it weren't for the wedding—the need to play happy families—and the fact that Anika's father had just died, Cass wouldn't have agreed to meet.

These fears were not allayed by the sight of Anika. She was sitting on a stool at the back of the bar, hunched over a bright orange drink. With a near constant, almost mechanised movement she took quick, furious sips.

Perched as she was on a stool, Cass could see Anika's whole outfit, from her singlet to her wide-leg pants, all the way to her red ballet flats. Anika had always been a trend dresser. At any given time, she looked like any other Hot Girl on the internet. Cass had always thought her interest in fashion seemed fearful. If clothes were a mode of self-expression, Anika's spoke only to her desire not to be left out.

'Hey!' Cass called as she walked over, trying to sound pleased to see her.

Anika didn't respond, not even when Cass greeted her again. It was not until Cass was standing right in front of her that Anika jumped, spilling some of the orange drink over her hands. She licked it off her index finger. 'Oh my god, sorry. I didn't see you.'

'You must have.' Cass took the stool next to hers. 'You were looking right at me.'

'Sorry, I've been jumpy since I got here. I don't think I'm a destination wedding girl. Like, if you drag everyone across the world and dictate how they spend their annual leave, you run the risk of amassing a big group of people who *used* to want the best for you but now kind of resent you.'

She spoke so quickly and concluded with such an abrupt bark of laughter that Cass suspected she'd planned this cold-opener while she was waiting.

'I'm joking,' she said, just as quickly. 'Of course I still want the best for her. I'm just tired. And I'm threatened by how chic this whole situation is.'

This time, Cass laughed with her. It was so like Anika: just when you suspected she had no self-awareness, she'd sum herself up with such sudden and painful acuity, you wondered where she'd been hiding her scalpel.

And, to be fair, the whole situation *was* painfully chic. The hotel bar was Instagrammable by any frame—from a wide shot, taking in the brass-accented bar and the monochrome armchairs, right down to a close-up of the tabletop: a clay bowl, filled with enormous green olives, a cocktail sweating at its side.

'Yeah,' Cass said, 'this hotel is fucked.'

'Right? It feels, like, not real life.'

'Actually, it reminds me of—'

Before Cass could finish her thought, Anika interjected: '—of France?' Then, absurdly, given that Cass hadn't actually said what it reminded her of, she added: 'Me too!'

While Cass ordered a drink, Anika pulled the paper napkin out from beneath hers and started drumming her fingers on it. 'That place was fucked-up beautiful, too.'

Cass ordered the same thing as Anika. When it arrived, they clinked their identical glasses.

Before Cass could steer the conversation to the wedding, Anika leaped in. 'Actually,' she said, 'that's what I wanted to apologise for.'

Already, little indents ran the length of Anika's napkin, like scratch marks. She went on: 'For what happened to you in the icehouse.'

'The icehouse?'

'When you were trapped in there.'

Cass knew exactly what she was talking about. She sipped her drink. Then, not knowing how to respond, she sipped it again. Of all the people who had said or implied that there was some trauma in her past, nobody had put it to her with such specificity. Nobody had mentioned the icehouse.

'I'm really not trying to pry. I just wanted to say how sorr—'

Cass tried to keep her voice steady. 'I don't know what you think happened, but I can tell you, it wasn't that dramatic.'

Anika finally stopped drumming on her napkin. The effect was as intense as sudden silence. In her stillness—taut and coiled—she seemed to demand an explanation.

'I was stuck in there for a few hours and then I got out.'

'I could've got you out faster. I'm so sorry. And I'm sorry I haven't raised it earlier. I think I always knew, or wondered . . .' As she trailed off, she looked down into her glass. 'But I comforted myself with the fact that you were obviously fine.' Now, she met Cass's eye. She almost whispered: 'I didn't know about the seizures.'

'It's got nothing to do with my seizures.' Cass had been sipping continuously throughout this short conversation. Now, she tilted her head back, emptied her glass, and placed it back on the marble bar with what she hoped was a resolute clunk.

'I'm sorry,' Anika said. 'I've upset you.'

It was true: she was upset. And Cass, who had been awake—or, at best, half-asleep—for over forty hours, didn't have the energy to pretend that she wasn't. She sighed and, with that brief exhalation, gave in to her emotions. The anger that had been aroused by her fight with Sam now poured out of her with all the inevitability of someone who, having fallen, must eventually hit the ground.

'Look, as fucked as it sounds, I wish you were right. I get the impulse. Honestly, it would be easier if I could just go to a therapist and talk about the one terrible thing I've never faced and then it could all be fixed. I'd love that! But my . . . what's happening to me . . . it's not as if we can say: *Oh, she's like X because of Y.*'

'I know.'

Because Anika's eyes were filling with tears, Cass attempted a less heated tone. 'I appreciate the apology. But believe me, it's not necessary. This isn't about you.'

She had meant that last part as a comfort, but she could see in Anika's face how it felt like an insult: an allegation of self-absorption. Immediately, Cass tried to take it back. 'Sorry, I didn't mean—'

'No, I know.' Anika was crying now, drops spotting the napkin, which she was tearing into pieces. She was breathing so heavily it was impossible for her to speak. When she'd calmed down enough to manage a few words, each one was an effort, as if strangled on the way out. 'I know. Because it happened to me too.'

'What?'

'That's how I knew. When we got you out, I knew straight away that someone had touched you.'

'Oh.'

There was not a moment, not even a fraction of a second, in which Cass doubted the truth of her friend's claim. She only wondered at her own stupidity for needing to be told something that was, she could now see, self-evidently true. Anyone sitting across the bar could see it: in Anika's thin, clawing fingers, the mascara-streaked tears, the uncontrollable shaking in her shoulders. But also in her intelligent eyes, the sharp angle of her jaw—tilted slightly upwards, as if in defiance. She wasn't her mother or her sister but in her own way she was beautiful. It was odd, for Cass, to see the girl she'd always known and, at the same time, to be confronted with an entirely new fact about her.

Cass had no idea—had never even suspected—that Anika had been assaulted in that icehouse.

'I'm so sorry.'

'It's okay. It's not a big deal, you know, in the scheme of things. Like, people get groped all the time. I think it really affected me because, you know, I was with my family and everything was meant to be safe. Not just safe—like, *idyllic*. Like, I should've been grateful to be there.'

Leaning forward, slumped with relief, Anika told Cass the whole story.

While she was talking—her hands quivering above her body, showing Cass where, exactly, she had been touched—Cass had the eerie sensation that this was a story she already knew.

Two girls standing in the dark; two anonymous bodies. And it was Anika who was touched. She thought, with a guilt that encouraged her to suppress the idea, not only *how horrible*, but also *of course*. Of course it was Anika. Such things . . . they happened to her.

After school, they had gone their separate ways, but stories made their way around. When they were not yet twenty, Anika became the first person Cass knew to have a restraining order against a boy.

Then, while she was doing her master's, she'd published a personal essay on one of those surprisingly literary websites that nobody had ever heard of. It told the story of the time Anika was backpacking through Israel and Turkey. She contracted a UTI and went to a local doctor who put his fingers beneath her underwear as a diagnostic tool.

Then another article a few months later about the emails she had received in response to the first one. Vile things—things Cass would never have conceived of, let alone typed out and sent to a stranger.

Then there were the occasional mentions of a stalker in her Instagram stories. She'd write: *The thing about having a stalker . . .*

Or, *This one's for the stalkers* . . . As if it were a relatable trope—a thing people just *had*. Like hayfever.

From afar, Cass had looked at these posts and seen a self-perpetuating cycle. It seemed that, by seeking love in all the wrong places, by going online and crying out for attention, Anika was inviting the very scrutiny she was so ill-equipped to cope with.

But now, sitting in that bar, it occurred to Cass that perhaps she hadn't always been like this. Maybe such things happened to her because of the icehouse. Maybe that was the inciting incident: the first random event after which a pattern emerged. Because her body was treated as a thing, it became an object: moving through the world ready to be picked up and used.

That whole holiday, Cass had been by Anika's side. A few inches to the left or the right in the dark, and it might have been *her* body that felt the foreign touch—felt it in her gut, knew it to be perverse, even though she could not yet comprehend it. A matter of centimetres. She was overwhelmed by the enormous smallness of this distinction.

She knew at some level that she was manufacturing a turning point, hinging all she understood of Anika and her accumulated struggles on this one crucial moment. But it was an inescapably chilling thought: that it might have been her, that it so easily, for such arbitrary reasons, almost was.

In a timid voice, Cass said, 'Do you know who it was?'

'I've always assumed it was Rupert. You know, that wri—'

'I remember Rupert.'

'Obviously, I didn't actually see him. It was so dark. And—not that it's much comfort—I imagine he was reaching for someone else.'

'Who?'

'For Skye, I assume. I think they were having some kind of fling and the icehouse was where they met. And I guess we got caught in the crossfire.'

Cass ignored the *we*. 'That makes sense.' And then, once more: 'I'm so sorry.'

Anika echoed her, without appearing to notice the repetition, as if she hadn't heard Cass at all. 'I'm so sorry. If I'd said something at the time, if I'd got you out sooner . . . I could've protected you.'

It felt nitpicky at this juncture to insist to Anika that what she'd surmised wasn't true; that Cass's assault by Rupert existed only in her head. What Anika didn't need to hear, in this moment of confession, was how *little* they had in common. How significant that gap of a few centimetres in an icehouse all those years ago. So, in an attempt to soothe her, Cass tried to connect on Anika's terms.

'But why would you blame yourself? You were a child. Surely, if you were going to blame anyone, it'd be Rupert.'

'I hate him. What he's done to you.'

'And to you.'

Cass knew she was misleading Anika, allowing her to think that she too had suffered. But, real or not, this story brought them together: Anika chained for years by guilt and regret, Cass realising only now how tightly they were bound. She couldn't assert that nothing had happened to her without renouncing this imagined bond. It was an instinct as uncontrollable as that feminine urge, upon hearing an intimate confession, to afford it the respect of reciprocation. As if to assure the other person that it's not their fault; that it can happen to anyone. To respond to the claim that someone else has suffered not by saying, *Poor you*, but, *I have suffered too*.

THERE WAS NEVER going to be an appropriate way to conclude such a conversation. Especially in a trendy hotel bar. The bounds of normality, of social graces, didn't allow for a proportionate response. Two young women sitting on bar stools, swapping stories of abuse. Between them, untouched olives as well as all that guilt: for not saving each other at the time, for not discussing it since. Anika allowed herself some tears (she tried to dab them with the shredded remnants of her napkin), and then Cass pointed out that it was time to go: the welcome drinks had well and truly started. They hugged on parting—a cursory embrace, no mutual clinging—and Cass whispered: 'Please, don't think any more about it. It's not your fault.'

To respond appropriately, to absorb the magnitude of that forgiveness—the relief, after all these years, that Cass didn't *blame* her for what happened—Anika had to retreat to the adjacent bathroom. There, she had a really big cry.

She was sitting on the toilet seat in one of the two small cubicles and unleashing such loud, refreshing sobs that she didn't hear someone come in.

There was a knock at the door. 'Anika?'

She recognised her sister's voice immediately. She wiped her eyes with toilet paper and tried to compose herself before opening the door.

'Have you been crying?'

'No,' she said. Then, because the evidence was overwhelming, she added: 'Don't worry. You should be at your drinks.'

'Oh, Anika.' Now it was Skye's turn to tear up. 'I wish he was here, too.'

'No, that's not it. I mean, obviously, I miss Dad. But that's not—don't worry about it.' At the sink, Anika splashed her face with water. She could see Skye in the mirror.

'Now I'm worried.'

'Just enjoy your night.'

'Well, I'm not going to enjoy it now.'

Their eyes met in the glass. 'It's literally nothing to do with the wedding or anything.'

With the dual authority of older sister and bride-to-be, Skye said: 'Can you just tell me?'

Anika turned to face her sister. The mirror had created an illusion of distance. In reality, Skye was just a few steps away. The bathroom was tiny. Blue tiles decorated the walls and gave it a swimming-pool feel.

Why had she rebutted Skye's first assumption? Couldn't she have just pretended to be crying about their father? Now Skye looked determined. Nothing but the truth would do.

Anika had to be careful: to dodge the sordid details. She had decided long ago that Skye was better off not knowing what happened in the icehouse. And she was determined not to expose the secret now, on the eve of such a significant occasion. Tomorrow should be one of the happiest days of Skye's life. It was already marked by their father's absence; it didn't need to be further blemished by guilt about an unchangeable, distant past. If Rupert hadn't reached for Skye in the first place, he would never have touched Anika or Cass, but that didn't make it Skye's *fault*, and she didn't want to suggest that it did. Unable to lie, she kept it vague and tried to distract her sister with other (true) irrelevancies.

'It wasn't anything to do with you—and, honestly, I'm probably delirious with jet lag; it's been such a big week—but yeah, Cass and I were just talking about that holiday in France and it made me weirdly emotional.'

'Oh.' Skye let her arms hang by her side. She seemed to sway a little. Were it not for the tiles, which made her voice rebound, Anika probably wouldn't have heard her whisper: 'You were talking about Rupert.'

Anika was so shocked by the swiftness with which Skye joined those dots, by the knowledge to which it attested, she could only nod.

Immediately, Skye stood up straighter and adopted a familiar, almost professional brusqueness. It was the same tone she had taken at their father's funeral: yelling at everyone, issuing instructions while Cass writhed on the floor.

'Right. I thought this might come up. But let's get through these drinks first and pretend to be, like, chill and drama-free. Then we should talk about it.'

'We don't have to do it toni—'

'No, I'd like to. I've put it off for so long. I didn't think there was any point telling you, because I knew it would only upset you and, like, make you judge everyone differently. But . . .' Skye had one hand on the door already. Over her shoulder, she looked at her little sister: closely, as if seeing her again after a long absence, trying to pinpoint the ways in which she'd changed. 'I guess you've known for a while.'

The door swung shut. Having just promised a drama-free evening, Anika didn't feel that she could call out after her. But the question felt urgent, the words pressing down on her tongue.

Known what?

CHAPTER 16

2008

'SKYE, WHAT'S WRONG?'

'Nothing.'

'If you say so.'

Anika was not fooled. It was obvious to her, from the moment she re-entered the kitchen, that her sister was upset. For one thing, she appeared to be cooking. Or, at least, she was being helpful in the kitchen, ripping the heads off the langoustines with real malice. Her expression, too, was revealing, with faraway eyes and her mouth no longer a lazy pout. Instead, it was pulled into a tense line, which made her look even more like her mother.

'Nothing's wrong, okay?' Skye raised a hand—part concealment, partly to swat her little sister away. Picking up the silver mixing bowl, she pushed past Anika. A severed head fell out, its brain juices oozing and yellow.

'Stock!'

Every member of the Kelly family stopped what they were doing. Vanessa's knife stalled halfway through a tomato. Skye froze, her arm outstretched towards the floor. Anika just stared at her father.

It seemed impossible that the shriek had come from him. It was too high-pitched. He sounded like a teenage girl. But there he was, mouth moving around the sound, his hands waving. 'Stock, Skye! Stock!'

He took the bowl from Skye's hands, intercepting its progress towards the bin.

'Oh,' Skye said. 'You want to *make* a stock.'

'The heads have all the flavour.'

Bruce retrieved the head, placed it in the bowl and left his hand in there, fondling its contemporaries.

Because everybody else seemed to have a job—Skye was wiping the table, Vanessa was chopping tomatoes, Bruce was leaning over a decrepit cookbook that came with the villa—Anika turned to her favourite occupation. She decided to goad her sister.

'What did Rupert want?'

Anika assumed they hadn't heard her.

'I saw him when we were driving back.'

Skye looked up from her damp cloth. 'Did you?'

'Yeah, it was so funny. He was literally sprinting from our place to his. He was trying to climb over the fence and he was, like, so awkward getting up. And then he just sat at the top for ages. Like, he was too chicken to jump down. Like this . . .' She stretched her hands out on either side, widened her eyes, and mimed someone who, at a dangerous height, realises they are about to lose control.

'I pointed it out to Dad, but he was "driving". And, you know, his eyesight . . .'

'There's nothing wrong with my eyesight! I can see perfectly.' Bruce looked up from his cookbook. 'It would help if I could speak French, though.' He removed his glasses and turned to face his wife. 'So is Rupert coming for lunch, now?'

Vanessa put her knife down. 'Not unless you invited him.'

'I haven't seen him!'

'Good.' Vanessa looked at her watch. 'Although, it'll be more like dinner by the time we sit down. Where has the day gone?'

'So what did he want?' Anika said.

'I don't know, darling. If he came over, it certainly wasn't to see us. Skye and I have been here the whole time.'

'Yeah,' Skye said, and then, as if Anika were being ungrateful, she added: 'cooking *your* lunch.'

Vanessa reached her hands out. They were glossy with juice. 'Are you sure you saw him, darling? It wasn't, I don't know, his housekeeper or something?'

Anika didn't move. 'It was definitely him. He was wearing his pink shirt.'

'It's very hot today. Maybe you should go for a swim.'

For a moment, Anika wondered whether her mother was about to burst into tears. Her eyes were shiny and Anika thought she recognised, in her pleading tone, a feeling she knew well: unutterable defeat. As if her mother—her perky, acerbic mother—was tired of living in her own skin.

She had no idea how they'd arrived at this point. It was meant to be funny: a grown man perched awkwardly on a fence. Maybe she'd told it badly. If her dad had told it, they all would've laughed.

Here it was again, that old entrapped feeling, like she was separated from the rest of the world—from her family, especially—by a dirty pane of glass.

In the car, Anika had been momentarily relieved of it. She had seen herself as not so different from those girls, like her sister, who were all over Tumblr doing wistful things like riding bikes through fields in denim shorts or going to a farmers' market in France. It had seemed obvious then that summer wasn't just about smelling of perspiration and adjusting your towel to cover your tummy.

Now, in the comparative darkness of the kitchen, with its bare stone walls and its cold-tiled floor, she felt herself slouching back into her usual shape. They were all busy. There was nothing she could do to help, not even make conversation. Nobody listened when she spoke, except to humour her, which didn't really count as listening.

'I'm going upstairs,' she announced, just to see if anyone would react. Nobody did.

IN THE POOL, a young girl's body floated on the surface with an eerie stillness. The hair bled out and conjured, in Harry's mind, the thought of Ophelia.

It was only a moment, broken when Anika pulled her head back—water droplets on Harry's bare feet—and gasped for air.

She treaded water. 'Oh. Hey, Harry.'

'Morning.'

'I'm looking for Cass.'

'Is she down there?'

'Ha.'

'Cassandra, Cassandra, Cassandra.' Harry lay back on a pool chair. He made a show of nestling in—hands placed across his chest, head back to the sky, a loud contented sigh. The splashing sounds suggested that Anika had recognised the opportunity to haul herself out of the pool unscrutinised.

When Harry looked back, her towel was wrapped beneath her armpits.

'Have I ever told you about the mythological origins of the name Cassandra?'

'Yeah, you have.'

Harry knew that he hadn't. He sighed. Poor Anika. She was forever tying herself in knots. Curious, but too shy to ask questions, she displayed that ultimate marker of intellectual insecurity. She preferred to remain ignorant than to *appear* ignorant.

Now, she lifted one corner of her towel to wipe her nose. 'So you haven't seen her?'

'No. Although I did get up quite late.' He touched his head. 'I like a sleep-in on a holiday.'

'What about Rupert?'

Harry didn't answer her. He had closed his eyes against the sun. Without opening them, he said: 'What do you think Rupert's characters are called? Do they all have posh names like Percy and Spencer?'

Anika smiled at that. 'Or Pamela and Patricia.'

Harry laughed to be kind, not because he found her funny. In fact, she'd misunderstood the category. He was going for *posh* not for *alliteration*. He amused himself with the thought that perhaps his performative pronunciation of the plosives had put her off. 'Or maybe he goes for more evocative names. Maybe he gets all metaphorical, like Inspector Forthright. Doctor Bloodstone.' Harry paused, thinking. 'Miss Treaclebum.'

There it was. Her laugh was still a child's. Then, with an adult's voice which made him sit up and look at her, she said, 'You hate him, don't you?'

'I don't *hate* him. I certainly dislike him. But that's only because everyone else likes him so much. I'm a contrarian, Anika. I'm suspicious of anyone *that* charming. It's not Rupert Tombe's fault. It's just a matter of principle.'

She was squinting past Harry up towards Rupert's villa. 'I hate him.'

She'd said it so softly it seemed almost private, like a prayer.

Then Anika turned, hitched up her towel—high enough to horrify Harry with the sight of her wet wedgie—and ran back up to the house.

He shook his head. Strange girl.

BACK IN THEIR shared room, Anika sat cross-legged atop her bed and picked at the soft skin on the soles of her feet. She tore chunks off and left a little pile on the bedside table. She'd have to remember to wipe it before Cass came back.

Cass had made her bed that morning, as she did every morning. She did it quietly, as soon as she got out of it, before going to the bathroom or changing her clothes. 'I just do it,' she'd said, when Anika pointed out that they weren't in the military or boarding school or a hospital. 'I do it without thinking.'

But she'd blushed—red cheeks and orange hair—when Vanessa called her a good girl and said: 'Your mother must have it so easy.'

Maybe Cass moved naturally through the world in a way that happened to delight authority figures and generate their praise. Maybe she was just a nice person.

Even now, Anika was sure that Cass was in the icehouse looking for her necklace. She wasn't in the villa or down by the pool, and Harry hadn't seen her. Anika was simultaneously certain that Cass would find it and dreading her return. She'd have to admit to her parents that she'd misplaced the necklace in the first place. And then, worse, be loudly grateful for her brilliant friend, who followed her around, picking up the pieces and finding the things that Anika had lost.

Just as her thoughts had turned to her necklace, her sister poked her head through the door. She looked no happier than she had in the kitchen.

'Here,' she said, something dangling from her hand. 'I found it yesterday.'

Anika was so shocked to see her necklace in Skye's possession and not, as she'd imagined, in Cass's triumphant fist that she looked at it coolly, without any sense of ownership. A delicate daisy pendant hanging from a very thin chain. One of the petals was bent out of shape.

'Where was it?'

When Anika didn't take it immediately, Skye threw it on the bed, as if impatient to be rid of it. 'You're welcome.'

'Skye? Where was it?'

She was already at the door. 'In the icehouse,' she said without turning around. 'Like you said.'

'Why were you—'

But Skye had already closed the door behind her.

All at once, several disparate concerns converged. What might have been a series of coincidences arranged themselves with such sudden elegance, the story came to her whole and entire, as if this were its only possible form.

It was a perfect plot: a silver chain, each event linking neatly to the next.

She recalled what Rupert had whispered in the icehouse. *Friday*, he had said. The memory of that word dripped down her spine. It was an invitation, never intended for Anika's ear. After all, it was Skye Rupert had reached for. He must have wanted Skye to return to that very spot and continue what they'd started. She must have wanted it, too. That's why Skye was always mooning around the icehouse. After all, 'Friday' had been whispered in the wrong ear. In another light, it might have been a comic miscommunication: Skye waiting in a dirt hut for a rendezvous, her dignity ebbing away, outrage turning into boredom, until, eventually, she picked at the dirt and unearthed a necklace.

That also explained her weird behaviour today. Anika felt a thrill of vindication. She *knew* that Skye had a secret! She knew it as soon as Skye had said in that shady way that she was too busy to go to the shops. And that explained, too, why Skye had been in such a foul mood just now in the kitchen. She'd been roped into cooking when she had hoped to meet Rupert. And she was never going to have a better opportunity: her father was out and her mother was occupied.

Anika recalled what her mother had said: *We've been here the whole time.* So Rupert, happily anticipating what he believed to be a firm plan, would have sauntered straight down, bypassing the villa entirely. He must have been coming from the icehouse, not the villa, when Anika saw him jumping over the fence. That's why neither Skye nor Vanessa had seen him.

What Anika couldn't understand, however, was why Rupert had been running so fast. It had looked like he was making an escape. But from what? He would've found the icehouse empty.

No, not empty.

Her thoughts moved quickly. Anika had pieced all this together in a matter of seconds. From the corridor, she could still hear Skye's retreating tread. Her hand, where she gripped the necklace, was starting to sweat.

Rupert wouldn't have found the icehouse empty.

Anika remembered only a few days ago how the hot breath had shushed her. The hands that were on her crotch and at her breasts and even at her neck—how one of them had covered her mouth, making it impossible to scream.

In fact, this situation—those hands on a young, confused body—was exactly what she had tried to avoid by refusing to re-enter the icehouse. To go down there was to be trapped in the dark and echoing quiet, stuck in a black mess of incomprehensible, overwhelming sensations.

She could not claim, not even in the privacy of her own conscience, that she had not considered this when she sent Cass down there. Wasn't that why she had been so reluctant to fetch the necklace herself? Because she knew, in the darkest, most instinctive part of her—in the part of the gut that can tell good people from bad—that dreadful things would happen down there.

She'd sent Cass in her place. And with such bitterness, after the horrible incident with the sanitary pad. An incident that now, only a day later, seemed sickeningly innocent. Cass hadn't really humiliated her. She'd laughed, of course, but not with malice. And for that? Anika had sacrificed her friend. Into the icehouse on the appointed day, to face whatever dangers lay in wait.

It was obvious that Anika had crossed a line. She could see it behind her, clear now that she was on the wrong side and there was no way back. To ask that of Cass, to send her into danger, was unforgivably naughty.

But *naughty* was an excuse of a word. Little children were naughty. Cheating at Monopoly was naughty. It let her off even as it claimed responsibility; as if she couldn't have known better, as if the line materialised only afterwards as a marker of her maturity, not as if it were there all along, wilfully crossed. What was the word, she wondered, for someone who puts their own friends in danger, who wants them to suffer? Someone who can exact revenge— can really want it—and only realise later the cruelty of their own intentions?

And yet, as the minutes accumulated, and passing birds flapped shadows on her walls, she couldn't move to undo what she had done.

She lay in bed, twisted herself in knots and made and broke successive promises. At three forty-five she would go down and rescue Cass. At four she would tell her parents and they could go down on her behalf.

She was scared, her fear mutating every minute.

First, she was scared to go down herself. Scared of what she might see.

She could stand back while an adult did the work. Her father might run in and emerge, carrying Cass. She might even be smiling. *Silly Anika*, they would say. *What did you think would happen?*

There were only two options. Either Cass would be unscathed and Anika would be called upon to justify her seemingly baseless panic. Then she could confess what had happened to her and see if they believed it, or she could say she'd just 'had a moment', and yes, she was mad, which they would find easy to believe. Then there was the other option—the stomach-gripping one, to which her mind feverishly jumped, like a reader skimming sentences, racing to the part where, at last, things can't get any worse. Cass was hurt in there: something worse than what had happened to Anika. And she would emerge changed, perhaps forever. And Anika's panic would prove entirely justified, her parents turning to her in horror, as if she were possessed of some supernatural power, and saying: *How did you know?* In this eventuality, too, she would have to tell them about the other night. It all came back to that. The story that she was just beginning to live with, that didn't need to be told, dragged up and out and foul-smelling into the light.

Scared to go to the icehouse herself, scared to alert anyone else to the threat, she did nothing. And finally, as unlikely as it now seemed, after almost an hour of paralysing deliberation, Anika lay and prayed in a fervid whisper to a god she didn't believe in and couldn't conceptualise that Cass might come back into the room, untouched and without a fuss, and that nobody would ever know what Anika had done. Not even her own mother.

Several times she tried to doze. She squeezed her eyes shut tightly and imagined her lids scrunched like paper into a ball, as if, with the force of will, she could turn the day into a dream. As if she could wake up and be someone other than herself: a person who wouldn't think to do such a thing; a person who cared for their friends naturally, easily, and not only after she'd already sent them to the wolves.

It was a tap at the window that finally got her to her feet. She leaped up, elated, expecting to see Cass tapping at the glass. It was absurd, but it was what she wanted to see. So intense was her desire, it bent the bounds of plausibility. As if it were possible that Cass would have sauntered out of the icehouse and—instead of walking through the villa, up the stairs, into their shared bedroom—scaled the peach-coloured walls to hover outside the window.

Through the glass, Anika saw several ravens at a distance, calling to each other across the stone fence that separated their villa from Rupert's. Leaning forward, so her nose almost touched the window, she saw a scratch on its surface. A raven must have sat on the sill and pecked at it.

Still, she was standing now, and after waiting so long, she no longer considered it a possibility that Cass might yet return with a simple explanation. *Sorry, I dropped the torch. It took me ages to find it.* She would go and tell her parents that—just that. Cass had been gone for hours. It defied explanation. Something must have happened to her. Perhaps they ought to check the icehouse. Her father would go with her, if she asked calmly enough. She took several deep breaths and tried to assure herself that she could pull it off: could convey urgency without panic, danger without hysteria.

On the stairs, she counted each step and tried to move at a measured pace. She took them two at a time in exaggerated—but not rapid—leaps.

VANESSA WAS TRYING to focus on what the boy was saying, when Anika entered the kitchen with a loud, 'Hey!'

She waved a shushing hand at her daughter.

'Hey!' Anika said again.

But she held her focus, and Bruce, Harry, and Skye held theirs. They were all looking at Sam. He was remarkably calm—that strangely expressionless face of his. But his voice trembled.

'So, yeah,' he was saying. 'I think she must have locked herself in there or something.'

'What's happening?'

Bruce was the first to acknowledge Anika. 'It's Cass,' he said. 'Have you seen her?'

Anika shook her head.

Vanessa drew her daughter to her. 'Sam was saying he saw her go into the icehouse hours ago, and he hasn't seen her since. He tried just now to see if she was in there but the door was closed.'

'I think it's stuck. And I knocked and I thought I could hear her moving but I couldn't open it. I'm worried she's—'

'We'll get her out. Don't worry, Anika.' Vanessa touched her daughter's face. It was sweet, really, how quick she was to cry for her friend. 'I'm sure she's fine. We'll just need to work on getting the door unstuck.'

'It's pretty badly jammed,' Sam said. 'I'll need help.'

He held up his hands. They were riven with splinters, the palms dotted pink. And across the fingers on his right hand, a bloody smear.

It was a detail Vanessa would remember for its gore—the way it set the tone and coloured the rest of that afternoon.

ANIKA WAS STARING with the sick focus that attends to catastrophe. It was not that she *couldn't* look away. She didn't want to. This, she thought, was the meat of life: the real muscle and sinew. It was high drama.

Sam was working on the door. They had tried first with screwdrivers in the latch—Harry and Bruce and Vanessa passing it between them, increasingly irritable with each other as they grew increasingly frustrated with themselves. Unhelpfully, Bruce tried several times to diagnose the problem. ('The wood has likely expanded in the heat.')

After asking about an axe, and being told that any heavy-duty equipment was probably *inside* the icehouse ('Bruce! That's not helpful!'), Vanessa had managed to procure from the kitchen an enormous meat cleaver. Sam was now using it to hack at the latch. Anika was frightened, watching him work. His arms were as hard and smooth as the handle of his knife, and his face—a mask of concentration—seemed to admit no human feeling.

'I think that's it.'

To the sound of sighs and whoops—applause, even, from Vanessa—Sam began kicking the door. Once, twice, and then, on the third time, it didn't swing open; it fell inward, thrust off its hinges.

From the angle at which it fell, it was clear there was something caught beneath it.

Anika and Skye stood back while Harry, Bruce, Vanessa, and Sam took one corner each. Anika cried out, then covered her mouth with her hand. It was a cry of relief. Only one body beneath it. Just Cass.

Although, as the door was placed to one side and the body remained unmoving, relief was overwhelmed by anger. Cass, covered in dust and splinters, her hands dirty and her clothes askew, did not look like someone who had been discovered. She looked discarded.

Skye placed a hand on Anika's shoulder, which made Anika notice that her legs had been shaking.

Rupert must have locked the door on his way out, to give him time to get away. Then he had sprinted straight back to his villa—that was when Anika saw him trying to jump the fence.

Anika looked over her shoulder. For once, Rupert was not watching them from his balcony. Of course, he had gone into hiding.

Cass was lying on her back, her knees up. Now, she dropped her legs so they were flat against the ground and raised her arms to shield her eyes from the sun.

Anika ran forward so quickly, her mother cried out for her to stop. Her arms around her friend, smelling the dirt that thickened her hair into clumps. 'I'm so sorry—I tried to get you,' she lied. 'I tried.'

Although Anika was scared of the answer, the question was too urgent. She needed confirmation in the same way that Cass, trapped and growing delirious, had needed fresh air.

'Did he touch you?'

CASS HAD, FOR several hours now, been fantasising about the moment of her rescue. Lying on the dirt floor, she had thought longingly of the fuss that would be made of her. That had been her only consolation, as the knowledge of her neglect—how easy she was to forget—festered: the idea that the Kellys and Harry and

Sam might all feel guilty about it; might, in the way that children do, *learn their lesson.*

But now Anika was dampening her shoulder with weepy apologies, it suddenly seemed an awful thing that anyone might feel bad for her sake.

'I'm fine,' she said, as many times as Anika said sorry. Then Anika asked whether she'd been touched.

Cass felt the question in her stomach, which tied itself into a knot.

Before Cass could answer, Vanessa inserted herself into their embrace. As she felt the soft crush of Vanessa's chest, Cass's stomach tightened further still. Fathers, she thought, don't hug like this.

Pulling back, Vanessa suggested that it was time for bed.

Although it was only early evening, the day an abomination of sunlight, this seemed a natural suggestion. It was because of the gentleness with which Vanessa had said it and because of the closeness of that phrase to the more childish *bedtime.* For teenagers who expended so much energy trying to be older and more independent, it was a relief, for once, to have an excuse to be a child.

Like little girls—like the girls they themselves had been only a few years ago—they followed Vanessa away from the icehouse and back to the safety of the villa, holding hands as they went.

Cass didn't answer Anika's question but she kept squeezing her friend's hand in what she hoped was a convincing gesture of reassurance. A reiteration of that same refrain.

I'm fine.

CHAPTER 17

2024

IN HER HOTEL room, Anika waited for her sister. The welcome drinks had wrapped up after about three hours. Most of the travellers were eager for an early night. Some wedding guests, like Cass and Sam, were too tired even to attend. As the crowd thinned, Skye gave her sister that universal look: eyes wide, head angled towards the door. The look that passes between partners in a crowded room, between children behind a teacher's back, between siblings across the dinner table. With her eyes, Skye said: *I have something to tell you.*

But Skye must have been held up talking to one of her guests—perhaps one of her fiancé's feral uncles—because Anika had been waiting for almost half an hour. She paced the room and tried to imagine what Skye might say. She was almost certain that Skye hadn't yet made the connection between Rupert and herself, or between Rupert and Cass. She'd looked shocked when they spoke about him in the bathroom but not concerned.

As Anika paced, her heart pounded. Her ears, which were still blocked from the flight, seemed to trap each beat. She found herself wishing—actually muttering, *please, please, please*—that Skye didn't have her own trauma to reveal.

She comforted herself with the thought that Skye was eighteen when they were at the villa. Only four years younger than their mother had been when she married their father. Rupert's attentions, however sinister, may have felt less like predation and more like flattery.

By the time Anika heard her sister's gentle knock, she was so agitated she jumped. She opened the door with one hand, clutching her chest with the other.

'You scared me.'

'Sorry. I was stuck with Angela. She literally can't *hear* the words "I have to go" until you've said them thirty thousand times. When you're on the phone with her, you have to factor in, like, an hour for goodbyes.'

'She's your mother-in-law.'

'Ugh.' Skye was tipsy. Her voice was too loud and she was picking up the hem of her dress, fanning herself with it. As she strode to the window on the far side of the room, she fanned so vigorously that Anika saw a blush of black underwear.

'It's so hot in here.' Skye opened the shutters. 'I'm going to smoke.'

Not tipsy, then. Drunk.

Anika threw her sister the packet from her open suitcase, first retrieving a cigarette for herself. Joining her by the window, she offered Skye a lighter.

Skye took a long drag and then coughed on the exhale. 'Is Mum next door?'

Anika shook her head. 'Her room's the other end of this floor.'

'Oh, thank god.' Skye leaned out over the railing into the hot night. Below them, they could see the pool. It was dusk and its surface was smooth and shiny. In the pale sky, whisps of cloud floated gently upwards, like smoke.

'You know,' Skye said, 'I'm actually really glad we're having this chat tonight. It's weirdly fitting.'

'Cass said a similar thing. She said this hotel reminded her of the villa.'

'A bit, I guess. But also, like, it's good to talk about it right before my wedding. Like, there's never going to be a better time to think about fidelity.'

Anika frowned. They were backlit by the room, so Skye's face was difficult to make out. 'Rupert wasn't married, was he?'

'No, but Mum was.'

Anika gripped the railing with both hands.

'I thought you might mention it after the funeral,' Skye was saying. 'But then, of course, you were in the hospital with Cass.' She tapped her cigarette. Anika's, meanwhile, burned closer to her hand. 'Mum made this weird comment in her speech about how she didn't deserve Dad. Or that was the gist of it. She said he was "more faithful" than her. I don't know if the others picked up on it. Maybe I was just hyper-alert to it.

'Anyway, I don't know whether Dad ever found out. I mean, *I* certainly never told him. And I really don't think it meant anything anyway. I always got the impression it was, like, a random moment of passion. Unless you told him?'

It took Anika a moment to realise that she had been asked a question. She was gripping the railing so tightly that her palms had started to ache. She uncurled her fingers slowly. 'No. No, I never told him.'

'So, how long have you known?'

Anika knew she had to be careful if she wanted to get the whole story out of Skye. Her family always kept things from her. She had been the last to hear of her father's diagnosis. Her mother had phoned her and asked her to come over, and when she arrived, she found Skye and Vanessa standing either side of him, looking so alike—two models of dignity and purpose: ready to support first, grieve later.

'I mean, Cass and I always suspected,' she lied. 'But I never said anything to Dad. Or to Mum either.'

'Wow.' Skye turned so her elbows were on the railing and she was facing into the room. 'I didn't suspect at all. I was so stupid. In my defence, I was young at the time and, like, having a slutty phase while I was travelling and everything. I thought Rupert was attracted to *me*. I was definitely into him. I just, like, couldn't think of anything sexier or more perverse than fucking this older guy on a family holiday.'

'Okay.'

'Sorry, but you know what I mean. Anyway, I'd built it up so much in my head, and I took all these little things, that are obviously all irrelevant in hindsight, as evidence that Rupert liked me back. It all culminated in—you probably don't even remember, but he took me to Saint-Tropez. On my own. It was just the two of us in his car and I was like: this makes perfect sense. I didn't even question it. It was the next logical step in this story I'd laid out. We were going to go to Saint-Tropez and he was going to invite me for a drink in some hotel and then one of us would suggest we get a room. You know how a teenager thinks trysts happen—in suites and whatever.' She used her cigarette as a pointer, motioning to Anika's hotel room.

Anika didn't react. She stayed still and silent, hoping that Skye, liquid-lipped with drink, would continue this flow of talk.

Skye's head rolled back down to face the ground and her voice took on a melancholy, almost grudge-bearing weight. 'But in the car on the way there, me all confident and putting my legs up on the dashboard and thinking I'm sexy and whatever, I saw your necklace.'

'What?'

'Remember, you had that silver necklace you were obsessed with, and you left it in the icehouse and you were so upset about it? Remember that weird old hut?'

'Yeah. Cass got trapped in there.'

'Oh, yeah.' Skye laughed. 'I'd forgotten about that. Anyway, Rupert—god, it's embarrassing how clearly I remember everything to do with *Rupert*'—(she said his name in a mock-British accent)—'he seemed to think that the necklace was Mum's. So then I was, like, why is Rupert hanging out in the icehouse and why is he lying about it?

'Anyway, so for the next few nights I waited until everyone was asleep and I went down to the icehouse.'

'Why?'

'I don't know! To snoop?' Skye laughed again. Now that she was on a roll, she seemed to be enjoying her tale. 'I was such a *teen*. Like, the speed with which I pivoted from vixen to, like, Nancy Drew . . . Anyway, I got more than I bargained for because one of the nights, Mum and Rupert were in there together.'

'Oh god.' Anika braced herself for one of Skye's abrupt punchlines.

'No, no. They weren't *doing* anything. Just having this excruciating, sexually charged conversation. Rupert kept being, like, "I can't stop thinking about last Friday," and Mum kept being, like, "It won't happen again." Eventually, she was like, "Bruce is going out tomorrow. Come over, we can talk about it then."'

And Anika had thought, all this time, that Rupert had been referring to the future: the Friday to come. That word, for her, had been prophetic: it readied her for the worst. But—Anika looked vacantly into her hotel room, an empty stare into a half-empty suitcase—the seduction had already passed.

She was right in one way, at least: it *was* Rupert who had touched her; who had whispered in her ear. But it was the mother, not the daughter, whom he was reaching for.

Anika wasn't sure she wanted to hear any more. She could imagine it all too clearly: the whispered voices, the dankness of the air around the hut, how lightly Skye would have had to tread so as not to snap a fallen pine needle. But it was Skye's story to tell: she would finish where she saw the natural end. Not, as Anika would have it, ending at the icehouse, looping back to where it all began.

'I totally dropped my bundle,' she was saying—an expression of their father's, which made Anika's throat tighten. 'I'm still mortified about it. I just—it sounds crazy, but you have to understand how much I'd built it up. I was heartbroken. It's all so embarrassing looking back, but I literally spent that entire holiday lying by the pool because Rupert could see it from his house. I was so bored! But in my head, it was like we were playing some kind of game. Like, I used to sunbathe topless when no one else was looking and . . . anyway, it felt like he'd betrayed me. And with my mother, of all people! So then I went into, like, revenge mode. I thought, if I caught them, I'd *show them*. So when Rupert came over the next day, I followed him.

'But I never really got my moment. I waited a while before following him, so it wouldn't be obvious. Then I looked in the bedrooms, obviously, and eventually found them in the kitchen. I stood there eavesdropping for a few minutes trying to work up the courage to burst in. Then someone outside screamed, which made me jump, and I, like, knocked something over. Then Rupert left. And that was it.'

'Who screamed?' Anika already knew the answer.

'Cass, I guess. Actually, that's right: I remember feeling really bad when we realised later. She must have been screaming from the icehouse.'

Skye threw the butt of her cigarette over the railing. For a moment, they watched its glowing descent.

So, Anika thought, the icehouse was the beginning and the end, after all.

She was exhausted by her sister's revelation. Most of all, she wanted to crawl into bed and think—about what this meant for her mother; about how it might change what Cass had shared with her today.

But she realised that Skye still needed her.

Anika knew enough about grief to know that it thinks like a writer: it wants to portray the random as inevitable, the inane as symbolic. It insists on conjuring, from the mess, a narrative. And the Kelly girls were grieving their father. So Anika reached again for the packet of cigarettes, knowing that she would have to stand out here with her soon-to-be-wed sister until they had decided what, exactly, this story *meant*. Together, they would identify a moral—a point more subtle than 'they loved each other, really' and 'people make mistakes' that they could use to put the past behind them.

It was dark now. The pool below had acquired an eerie night-time glow. In its indiscriminate surface, the lights from the hotel mingled with the moon.

WHAT SKYE DIDN'T tell her sister was that, in a way, she was granted her moment of confrontation. Rupert had already escaped the kitchen. So it was not the scene she'd imagined: the couple caught in the act. Instead, in that villa sixteen years ago, she faced her mother alone.

Skye was crouching by an armchair, only a few feet from the stone archway to the kitchen. A scream from outside caused her to jump. As she did, she knocked over a little ornament on the windowsill: a porcelain statue of a young lady, her skirt billowy enough to keep the whole delicate structure upright. Remarkably, it didn't smash. But it made a loud noise—loud enough to alert Vanessa and Rupert to her presence.

'You'd better go.' Her mother's voice had an unfamiliar note. Vanessa didn't issue this instruction from a position of authority; she was pleading.

Skye heard the door through to the laundry close—Rupert was leaving via the back way. Slowly, carefully, she placed the ornament back in its spot and crept out from her hiding place.

'Come here.'

There it was: the maternal authority was back. There was no doubt that Vanessa was addressing one of her daughters.

How she knew—how she had intuited that it wasn't Harry or Sam or Cass creeping by the archway—was a mystery which, in the moment, only seemed to enrich her mother's authority. On reflection, it made sense. It was what Vanessa was most dreading: being caught by one of her girls. Fearing something is sometimes a way of insisting on its truth—the instinct to face the worst thing, to survive it.

And because all people, even adults, are children around their parents, Skye came here when her mother said, 'Come here.'

She was still wearing her bikini. That was not a detail she'd spelled out to Anika, although it was probably implied. When would she have had time, in following Rupert from the pool to the villa, to put clothes on?

So her hair had dripped down her back and onto the tiles, and Skye had felt that it was unfair that *she* had to be near-naked, while her philandering mother was fully clothed.

From the laundry, she took a towel and wrapped it around her waist. In the kitchen, her mother sliced a stale baguette. It split with a crack.

She watched Vanessa move, familiar and new. There was the ever-protective glamour: her fingers thick with rings, her hair coiled and neatly clasped, showing off that long, elegant neck, bent now before a chopping board. But beneath it—children could always see beneath it—there was her mother as she'd always been. There, her knuckles, which bulged and made her rings impossible to remove, even for a child pulling with two hands. There, the white flush of her smallpox jab, whiter now because of her summer tan. A blotch that marked her as Older and having a Life Before Skye's. And there, on her feet (bare today, she never wore shoes around the house), the scar that ran from her big toe down to her sole, from her Life Before Before, of which they never spoke.

And then there was the knowledge, new to Skye, and freshly overwhelming, that she could see all this at once and still not really *know* her mother at all.

Vanessa asked her daughter why she'd screamed. Her tone was accusatory, as if this whole situation were Skye's fault. She tried to explain that it wasn't her—a bird, perhaps—but her mother didn't believe her; she kept saying, 'You didn't have to scream.'

This was what Skye had sought when she'd followed Rupert. Her mother was impotent, her annoyance about the scream a cheap, desperate attempt to find some higher ground. As a mask to cover her fragility, it was failed cosmetic surgery: advertising, in the obviousness of its attempts, the very frailty it set out to obscure.

A moment ago it had all been thrilling—when Skye's ear was flat against the wall. She could have writhed with the power: to have one *over* her mother. But now Vanessa was standing in front of her, in all her upsetting unknowability, and Skye realised that *having* the power was not the same as enjoying its exercise.

She told her mother tenderly—too tenderly to doubt—that it was none of her business.

Vanessa cried then, and Skye held her, the serrated edge of the bread knife pointing away from their embrace.

SKYE LEFT ANIKA'S hotel room just after eleven. She needed her beauty sleep, she said. Anika was tired, too: with jet lag, with emotion.

Alone once more, she sat on the edge of the bed. Skye was right: the room was very hot. They'd each had a gin and tonic from the minibar. The situation seemed to call for it. Anika felt dizzy as she knelt before the suitcase and reached into the chaos for her pyjamas.

Going slowly through the motions—getting changed, removing make-up, brushing teeth, applying creams—her thoughts turned again and again to Cass: to their conversation in the bar.

If you were going to blame anyone, it'd be Rupert. That's what Cass had said. And when Anika told her that she was sorry for what had happened to her, Cass had looked her right in the eye, nodded, and said: *And to you.* She had gripped Anika's arm while she said it, so hard she had left indents on Anika's skin. There was no mistaking her: they were bonded by what happened in the icehouse—what happened to *both* of them.

At the time, those words had made Anika sick with relief. But after Skye's revelation, they had lost their comfort. Cass's words were a spider's web which Anika had walked right through. Try as she might to brush off the tendrils, she could still feel their traces.

Anika had always assumed that Rupert had locked the icehouse door before making his escape, sealing off his crime. Now, she tried to remember what had actually happened. She spread out the sixteen-year-old story and searched its complicated pattern for the strands of fact. The icehouse door was open when Cass went in, that much was obvious. At some point, several hours before she was rescued, the door sealed and Cass was trapped. Anika had always assumed that Rupert was the one to seal it—she had, after all, seen him sprinting away from the villa as if from a crime. But now Skye said he was in the kitchen, not the icehouse, when Cass started to scream. So was it someone *else* who made Cass scream? Or did the icehouse trap her all by itself? It was decrepit, after all. Anika wondered, for the first time in years, whether she had embellished the story, adding human hands and nefarious intent to enliven a simple tale of bad luck and bad timing.

And yet Cass had said, *But why would you blame yourself?* Not: *It didn't happen.*

Clearly, Anika's suspicions were correct: Cass's seizures weren't just random eruptions; they were the ugly expression of what she had repressed.

Such was Anika's conviction that this became the foundation upon which she built her story. All other facts and recollections were bent to fit this reality: the one in which Cass was marked, too.

Anika climbed into bed and began to apply all of her imaginative effort to make sense of what Cass and Skye had told her today. Eyes wide and unseeing in the dark hotel room, she scrabbled in the dirt of her memories, plucking out the details, rearranging them to form new scenes.

She told herself that it was none of her business, that Cass would talk about it if and when she needed to. But no sooner did she make these sensible resolutions than her grip relaxed, she veered towards sleep, and fantasies encroached.

Jet lag caught her in a loop: her body was exhausted but her mind raced. She felt as if invisible hands dragged her down into the mattress and tightened strings inside her brain.

When at last she dozed, her thoughts returned to her father's funeral, to the sight of Cass writhing on the floor. She thought, too, of Sam, who hadn't attended the funeral that day, who hadn't come to drinks tonight either. She thought of what Skye had said on Monday night, when Anika finally found out about their relationship: *Too good to be true.*

With a jolt, it came to her, stunning in its simplicity. The threads, which, previously, she could only vaguely sense, now, with the light behind them, started to take shape.

Sam had been there the whole time. In the villa, in the icehouse—probably by her side only yesterday, when Cass read Anika's message and they arranged to meet for a drink.

What if Cass was so eager to blame Rupert not because it was true, but because it was *convenient*?

At last, all the pieces cohered. Rupert was a diversion: today, in the bar, Cass had let him take the place of someone else.

No wonder Cass had been obsessed with Sam in high school. She was thirteen on that holiday in France. It must have driven her mad, trying to understand what had happened to her: the significance of it. She must have been desperate to talk about it. Anika actually cried out—a low, pillow-muffled moan—to think how they might have helped each other; the conversations they might have had. But Sam had made it impossible! After finishing with her in the icehouse, he locked her in there, doubled back, waited several hours, then—and this was his masterstroke—raised the alarm. He entombed his crime: he sealed himself as her saviour.

It made sense now why Cass was so secretive about Sam. She hadn't even told Anika about their relationship until that phone call in the hospital forced the point. Even then, she'd been reluctant to talk about it.

This version of events explained too—or could explain—why Cass's seizures had become so difficult to manage. Hadn't Anika, just the other day, read about a woman who'd been abused as a child, whose seizures started when she encountered her abuser decades later?

Looking at the ceiling now—the shadow of the low-hanging lamp like a spider crawling across it—Anika wondered when, exactly, Cass's seizures had become unmanageable. At the beginning, they were several months apart, that's what Cass had said at the hospital on Monday. Anika regretted now that she had been so distracted by the handsome doctor. She couldn't recall the exact dates. But hadn't Cass gone on to say that it was only after she came back to Australia—*after she reunited with Sam*—that the frequency of her attacks increased?

As awful as it was, Anika was exhilarated by the horror of it. There was a sense of triumph, an oddly satisfying kind of resolution, in the totalising depiction of someone else's pain. No more secrets, no more mystery. At last, Anika felt *sane*. At the bar today, she had sensed that Cass was withholding something. Now she knew what.

But her exhilaration did not last long; it morphed quickly into fear.

Sam and Cass were both coming to the wedding. What would she say when she saw them together for the first time? How could she look at them without giving the impression of really *seeing*—of shattering their mirage?

She was in such a frenzy of clarity that decisions presented themselves to her without the mediation of her will. It was obvious: she needed to let Sam know that she was on to him.

In fact, it seemed the *only* thing to do. Almost feverish with focus, she thought it through.

She couldn't message Sam on social media: she wasn't friends with him, so it would go straight to his 'Other' inbox, and he might not check it. Of course, she couldn't tell him in person—Cass would be by his side all day.

Still in her pyjamas, she opened the door and ran three flights down to the hotel's reception. There, she asked what room Cass and Sam were staying in. 'I have a message for them,' she said, speaking too loudly and slowly, before it became apparent that the receptionist's English was perfect.

He offered to call their room 'at a more regular hour' (it was two in the morning) and deliver the message on Anika's behalf. Anika insisted that the message needed to be in writing.

'It's a very important message. I don't want to risk calling in case they miss it. Like, in case they're out or something.' Really, she didn't want to risk Cass picking up the phone.

Nodding, he handed her a sheet of the hotel's stationery. Anika wrote out a short note.

'Have you got an envelope?'

That, too, was embossed with the name of the hotel. She licked it closed and wrote Sam's name on the front.

'I'll have it sent up straight away.'

Anika held the envelope flat against her chest. 'No worries. I can do it.'

Over the top of his computer, the receptionist eyed her carefully.

'Please. I just want to make sure they get it. It's important. I . . .' She gestured maniacally, 'Wedding stuff!'

At the invocation of a wedding, the receptionist bounced into action. He leaned forward, peering at the screen. In a matter of clicks, he gave Anika the room number.

She ran all the way up to the top floor, then walked on tiptoes, her heart pounding from the climb, pounding even more when she arrived at Cass and Sam's door. She slipped the letter under it.

Back in her own room, Anika took a sleeping pill. In her dreams, she saw a pool at night. Sometimes she was looking down on it. And sometimes she was submerged, a hand strong at her head. She kicked and writhed, she opened her mouth, she screamed. Again and again, the water absorbed the sound.

CHAPTER 18

2008

IN HER ROOM on Friday night, Vanessa Kelly was grappling with a maddening distinction: the difference between believing something and wanting it to be true.

When she'd stood back and watched Sam hack at the icehouse door, Vanessa had begun to imagine what would happen if they found Cass unmoving inside. The phone call to her father. The body bag in the hull of the plane. The difficulty of explaining it all to the French police. Would Rupert translate for them?

Once Sam had broken the door down, revealing the girl stirring on the ground, there had barely been a moment of relief before Anika had whispered the next-worst thing.

Did he touch you?

Vanessa had taken them straight upstairs after that. It was only six in the evening: an absurd time to send them both to bed. Through the shutters, the late afternoon sun laughed at her. But fetching towels and snacks and water, folding clothes, straightening the sheets, tucking the girls in, these were the little things that Vanessa could do to prevent her hands from shaking.

She'd asked Anika, while Cass was in the shower, what she'd meant by her question.

'What question?'

It was Skye in the kitchen all over again, telling her that the scream—the human woman's scream—was a bird, or maybe no sound at all.

But she *had* heard it. She'd heard her daughter say: *Did he touch you?* Just as she'd heard Cass's scream and mistaken it for Skye's. It had cut through the kitchen, slicing the thin curtain that separated Vanessa and Rupert from the real world.

Now, Vanessa trembled at the thought of what she might have prevented had she understood that scream at the time instead of yoking it to her own petty drama. She'd been distracted then: flirting, worrying about getting caught, rather enjoying it all.

Outside her window, she could hear Harry, Sam, Bruce and Skye eating dinner on the terrace. Beneath the clink of cutlery and the murmur of voices, the crickets picked up where the cicadas left off. And beneath their thrumming, Anika's whispered question: *Did he touch you?*

Although she knew it was precisely this self-absorption that had led her to dismiss Cass's screams in the first place, she couldn't help but think that this drama—the child half-buried, perhaps violated too—was all because of her. The two events seemed connected: one the transgression, the other its awful consequence; her flirtation with Rupert, Cass's ordeal. It made sense. By her selfishness, by her indiscretion, she had reached into the dark and set this disaster in motion.

IT HAPPENED ON their second night at the villa.

They'd spent the day at Saint-Tropez. Anika was jet-lagged and grumpy. Cass was characteristically even-tempered. Skye was still recovering from the shock of being reunited with her parents (and, therefore, being once again a child). And Bruce was irritable: stressed about the stock market, cloaking his stress in self-importance. He kept complaining about the internet and, when Vanessa asked what was going on or whether he needed to go home, snapping that she didn't understand.

Like most men of his generation, Bruce was only capable of conceiving of his talents as his alone—never the culmination of circumstance. Later in his life, he would learn to say things like, 'I've been so lucky,' and, 'It's so much harder for young people now,' when it became fashionable to do so. But luck, in his mind, only ever set the scene—prepared the stage—for Bruce Kelly's entrance. He was lucky, for example, to be born in the country, in the time, to the parents that he was. Luck provided the opportunities of which he made so much. It did not fashion his character, put the thoughts in his head; it did not make him *him*. It was difficult, then, for Bruce to acknowledge a distinction between ignorance and incapacity. When he said to Vanessa, *You don't understand,* he meant, *You can't.* Not, *You haven't had the opportunity.*

In pursuit of a distraction from her holiday, from her family, that evening Vanessa knocked on the door of the chateau on the hill and invited Rupert around for dinner.

The girls were all shy and went to bed early, while Bruce was the most glittering version of himself: slapping Rupert's back and speaking self-deprecatingly awful French and talking about the books he had not so much read as studied for just this sort of occasion. Non-events from their flight and their daytrip were recounted with a verve that was on the funny side of convincing. Such was the force of his charm: Vanessa's memories, even of her own marriage, were all sorted over time into the library of Bruce's anecdotes. She remained quiet but for the odd cutting remark. Like a heckler at a comedy show, she was a better audience if she gave Bruce someone to spar with.

Rupert irritated her to the point of fascination. He seemed an obvious type, faintly ridiculous for being recognisable from films and books rather than from real life. His posh voice sounded put-on. His appearance, too, was cinematic: over six foot with neat stubble. His smile was so consistent, it very quickly started to look like an effort of will. All night, he did not seem to laugh with them so much as humour them.

Bruce had drunk several glasses of red. When he began to shout, Vanessa suggested that he might go straight to bed. 'I can do the washing-up.'

It was a marker of how drunk he was, and how well he had disguised it up until that point, that he went at once.

The two of them—Rupert and Vanessa—sat at the table, scrutinising each other in the freshly raked soil of the silence that Bruce's absence had created. (He really had talked a lot.)

Vanessa looked at her watch. It was only ten o'clock.

'He's still jet-lagged,' she said. 'It's a long flight.'

'Of course. He's a lot older than you.'

'Not that much.'

Rupert pinched the stem of his wineglass between thumb and forefinger. 'What's the age difference?'

'Twelve years.'

'My father was older—'

'I bet he was.'

'—than all his wives.'

Vanessa laughed. Rupert's pause had been deliberate, and she'd walked right into it.

She stood and started to stack the plates. Behind her, she could hear Rupert following her inside. The glasses he was carrying tinkled as they rubbed together.

'Dinner was delicious, thank you.'

She put the plates by the sink. The tap let out a single, languorous drip.

'Oh,' she said, watching the next drip take shape, 'Bruce did most of the cooking.'

Rupert reached around her to put the glasses down. She turned, knowing that he was standing right behind her and would not step back.

She hadn't wanted to acknowledge it at the time, but all night, while he smiled and laughed at Bruce, Rupert's eyes had been returning to hers.

So it was not a surprise—in fact, she stood deliberately still—when his mouth rushed forward. She could feel his beard. Sharp against her cheek and then blurred beneath her hand. How wet, a stranger's mouth, how urgent, the tugging upon her hair.

She had known that this would happen. Her walk, when she'd taken him into the kitchen, had moved to suit his gaze. She'd known it from the moment she surprised herself by lying about the age gap. *Twelve years*, she'd said. Not, *Twenty*. What surprised her most was that she had said it for her own sake, not for Bruce's. A rush of vanity.

Vanessa had never thought of herself as a pliant person. Indeed, her whole sense of humour—her brashness, her dryness—was an attempt to resist such descriptions. It seemed a special indignity to affirm people's expectations for a white man's much younger Asian wife. Lately, however, she had worried that she *was* affirming them.

Her days were dull and dutiful, like she had no personality to assert on the world. Back in Australia, she seemed to end up in their local Westfield shopping centre several times a week. The car park—the fumes, the depth of it, the way the exits were deliberately hard to find—always made her feel trapped. Bruce never came with her or the girls, never even dropped them off. He didn't approve of 'malls'. How was it that she had deviated so far from where she wanted to be while Bruce, seemingly, never strayed at all?

Married at twenty-two, faithful for eighteen years. Like all ages, twenty-two only seemed young in hindsight, and younger all the time. Vanessa was hardly a woman of great sexual experience. It was possible that she did not know the difference between what she liked and what she had grown accustomed to. And backed right up against the sink—the porcelain chill on her upper thighs—she liked kissing Rupert.

Rupert may have leaned in for the kiss, but she was the one who whispered, 'Not here,' and led him by the hand, a finger at her own lips, to the icehouse.

There, she took the torch from its spot by the door and propped it up in the corner. With their bodies, they formed inhuman shadows on the cave walls. The dirt held their secret, cocooning them in sighs and whispers and, eventually, in moans.

It was over quickly. They were scared of being caught, hardened in their resolve by the fear that it was only a matter of time until they were. They did it standing, Vanessa's leg raised, her heel digging into a bulge in the dirt. Now, she held on to his back as she slid down, placing both feet on the ground. Through his shirt, she could feel the rise and fall of his gradually steadying breaths.

Without speaking, they rearranged themselves. Rupert opened the wooden door—Vanessa flinched at its creak—and, with a parting smile, walked out, unashamed, into the night.

Vanessa crept back to the kitchen alone. There, by the sink, she took off her dress—a summer shift—and rinsed the dirt from the hem where she had lifted it up past her bum, where she had rubbed it against the icehouse wall.

Fortunately, the dress was brown linen, the stains unlikely to show. But she threw it in the washing machine anyway. For a few minutes, she watched the evidence rotate.

In just her bra and underwear, she crept up the stairs to bed. Bruce, who was already snoring (as he always did after drinking), did not see her come in.

If she hadn't wanted it so much—hadn't, in some way, invited it—Vanessa might have flagellated herself more. But for the next few days, she didn't dare think about it, lest chastising turned to fantasising. It remained apart from her life: an out-of-character act in an exotic location, with all the consequences, the moral weight, of a dream.

'DO YOU THINK Cass will be alright?'

At last, Vanessa was alone with her husband. She was sitting upright against an old mahogany bedhead, while he, standing, tightened his dressing-gown. Her nightie had ribbon about the throat. She coiled it around her index finger.

'She'll be fine.'

'When she got out,' Vanessa said, 'Anika asked her whether anybody had touched her.'

'Touched her?!'

'That's what she said.'

'But the door was jammed. Nobody could get in.'

Vanessa pulled on the ribbon until the pad of her finger went red. 'Maybe someone was already in there. Or followed her in? They could've jammed it on their way out.'

'Who?'

Vanessa looked at him, hoping he'd get there on his own. But his face was so baffled, she quickly realised: he didn't have all the pieces.

If someone had touched Cass—if that was what had prompted that hellish scream—it couldn't have been Rupert: he was with Vanessa in the kitchen. And it wasn't Bruce, either, who had been out with Anika. Nor was it Harry, whose desires were a mystery, except for the fact that they didn't pertain to women.

All evening, Vanessa had been circling the obvious conclusion, looking for a better way. But it made perverse sense. His recent trauma, his lack of family support. The boy was, in a way, damaged.

But whatever sense it made was only theoretical. She found it impossible to imagine that polite, shy boy, the one who had said 'please' all week, behaving so monstrously. She didn't need to imagine it, however, to accept that, rationally, it was the only possibility.

She whispered it, as if afraid that saying it any louder might make it more real.

'Sam.'

For a moment, Bruce was speechless. 'Vanessa'—he shook his head, already denying what he couldn't yet comprehend—'this is nonsense.'

She marvelled at Bruce's certainty. She had always envied this ability Bruce had: to adopt a position first, then begin substantiating it. And then—most enviable of all—to call it *rationality*. It was why she brought all her concerns to him: so he might dismiss them, so she might borrow from his seemingly endless store of confidence.

On this holiday alone, they had already adopted these roles several times over: Vanessa full of worry and regret, Bruce a font of reassurance. On Tuesday morning, Vanessa had gone straight back to bed and recounted the scene in the kitchen—specifically, her comment about Anika's cereal, how accidentally hurtful it had been. And Bruce had insisted that the cereal wasn't a big deal, that Anika must have been worried about something else instead. And on Wednesday night, before they went to sleep, Vanessa had wondered aloud whether she should have let Skye go to Saint-Tropez with Rupert; she had seemed uncharacteristically snarky when she returned. Bruce thought she seemed absolutely fine.

And it wasn't just worries about the girls. Whenever someone seemed excessively interested in how she and Bruce first met, or how Vanessa came to live in Australia, or the story of 'her biological parents', she could rely on Bruce to smooth and to soothe. Nothing was personal; everybody had their reasons; she wasn't a bad mother. And although sometimes Vanessa suspected that her husband just *missed* things, she allowed herself to be persuaded.

Tonight, however, his confidence was aggravating. He was speaking loudly and standing over her. A defence of her character, her sanity, depended on justifying this accusation against Sam.

'She passed out, Bruce. People don't just pass out from sitting in the same room for several hours.'

'The icehouse is not especially well-ventilated.'

'You honestly believe she suffocated?' The tip of Vanessa's finger was white now, the flesh bulging about the ribbon.

'She probably got herself all worked up. You know, let her imagination get carried away.'

Vanessa suspected that he wasn't really talking about Cass. Bruce only resorted to clichés when he was trying to impart a moral—in this case that maybe *she*, Vanessa, was letting her imagination get carried away.

'Anika seemed really worried,' she said.

'Anika's addicted to drama.'

Again, she wondered whether this accusation was really aimed at Anika. 'She's hardly *that* macabre, to wish that on a friend.'

'Just because the boy isn't your usual sort—'

'Oh, for fuck's sake.'

'—doesn't mean he's a criminal.'

Vanessa always knew he was winning an argument when Bruce accused her of classism. Even though Bruce's family had been comfortable—his father was a banker—they had not been so illustrious or respected as Vanessa's adopted parents. Because it was levelled in response to her biography, not to her behaviour, it was an irrefutable accusation. Vanessa, on the other hand, never stooped so far. She would tell Bruce if he was rude or patronising or inconsiderate, but never *racist*.

In her rage, however, she found another way to stoop. 'I know it's horrible to think about,' she said, 'but we can't ignore the possibility just because it's unsavoury.'

Bruce sat on the edge of the bed, his back to Vanessa. He took loud breaths through his nose. 'Did you ask Cass what happened?'

'She said she was fine.'

'And you don't believe her?'

Vanessa almost shouted, 'That's what we all say!'

'Then why don't we put it to her outright?'

'That's a horrible thing to put in her head.'

'We could just say: *Was anyone in the icehouse with you?*'

'Why don't we ask Harry?'

'What?' Bruce turned now to face his wife. His dressing-gown opened, revealing, beneath his boxers, a pair of stubborn legs. She reached out across the duvet and took his hand.

'We'll just ask him where Sam was this afternoon. You could do it casually. Just in passing.'

She wouldn't let his hand go. She squeezed it and kept squeezing, even when he started to pull back.

There was no way she could explain why this meant so much to her: the superstition that one had caused the other, that if she'd been a better, more faithful wife, Cass would never have been trapped in that icehouse.

'Okay,' Bruce said. 'I'll ask.'

BRUCE DID NOT go straight to Harry's room. Instead, he went down to the pool. He passed the terrace on the way—Sam and Harry both gone, the tabletop freshly wiped. The girls were all in bed. On the hill, two sparse windows glowed in Rupert's villa. No sign of the man himself. Rupert had been conspicuously absent from his balcony earlier today, when they were trying to get Cass out. At the time, Bruce kept looking over his shoulder, waiting for Rupert to emerge, as if he might be able to tell them what to do.

Now the night was still. Bruce pulled a lighter from one pocket of his dressing-gown and a cigar from the other. He lit it and admired the starkness of the little flame. To his left, the wreckage of the icehouse door formed a vague mound. If he didn't know what it was—hadn't seen Sam hack at it in such a frenzy, hadn't winced at the thought of the email he would have to send to the owner describing the damage—he would have found the shape impossible to interpret. A bonfire, perhaps, or a hunched and sleeping beast.

He smoked slowly, each puff its own pleasure. He was procrastinating.

The question was impossible to pose—what was Vanessa's word?—*casually*. Harry and Bruce had known each other too long for that. And Harry was too clever, he would know that Bruce wasn't just *casually* curious about the boy's whereabouts. It would be obvious at once what Bruce was really asking: did Sam have an alibi?

It seemed unjust even to hold the accusation in his mind. Sam was a nice boy who'd been through a lot. Harry, it seemed, was starting to love him. Bruce was loath to unsettle them both. And such a question would be unsettling. Either Harry would take Vanessa's suspicion as his own and doubt the boy, or, thinking it ridiculous, he'd doubt his oldest friend for entertaining the idea.

It seemed that saying it out loud, putting words to it, could only enliven the possibility that Sam was, in some way, *evil*. It was a thought better buried.

He exhaled slowly: a cloud of frustration.

This wasn't really about the boy or about what he may or may not have done to Cass in the icehouse. It was, in some obscure way, about Anika. His fights with his wife always were.

For years, Vanessa had been afraid that Anika might hurt herself. Hence her wheedling, and constant acquiescence, her refusal to ever say 'no'. Bruce had always thought this a kind of selfishness: wanting your children to *like* you. Being optimistic about them, demanding more from them—this was his way of wanting the best for them.

But then Anika had taken a razor to her upper thigh. She could never know—not until she had children of her own—the damage she did with those few small incisions. The fissure she carved in her father's sanity.

Suddenly, Vanessa's parental paranoia looked like prescience: warnings that Bruce ought to have heeded. If they weren't kinder, more forgiving, if they didn't try harder to make Anika happy, then she really might do something drastic.

Bruce had always had the gift of confidence. At home, at work, he was the person who assured others that everything would be okay.

What's the worst that can happen? was one of his favourite clichés. Occasionally, his daughters would attribute his confidence to 'masculinity', as if he were exercising a privilege in being decisive, rational, in accepting that there was no point worrying about what was outside his control. As the only man in a house of women, as the boss of a team of forty, all with families of their own, other people relied on his mettle. If his girls were right, if it was a privilege, then he also felt it as a responsibility.

But in recent weeks, ever since the incident with Anika, he'd been shaky.

Like a hand-wringing housewife, he fretted. Even now, instead of asking Harry, instead of dismissing Vanessa's fear as ridiculous, he smoked by the pool and let the question fester.

He found himself raking over previously resolved questions. Just yesterday, by the pool with Harry, he'd thought about the time when Harry made a pass at him in the sauna. He cringed at his own sentimentality. Imagine sitting in this French idyll and wondering whether, forty years ago, he could've been a better friend.

It was as if Anika had climbed into his mind and was now weaving away: sitting at the loom of his conscience, braiding together old mistakes, ever-tightening, ever-lengthening this shroud of regrets.

A few days before they left for France, he had found in his desk a document that, for years, he had managed not to think about. How many times had his hands passed over that manilla folder when he was reaching for something else? It was only lately, in this strange mood, that he had settled on it.

Just after Skye was born, Bruce had written to Vanessa's orphanage in China. She'd become fixated on finding the identity of her biological parents. Initially, Bruce attributed the changes—the crying, the unwillingness to leave the house or shower or change her clothes—to postnatal depression. Despite her curiosity, she didn't want to reach out to the orphanage. It would only be a disappointment, she said. He offered to do it for her. *What's the worst that could happen?*

The orphanage had responded within a fortnight. Their reply was written by hand. The use of capitals was presumably for neatness and legibility, but Bruce read it as a shout. This, plus the missive's brevity, made reinterpretation impossible. The message was unambiguous.

WE HAVE MADE CONTACT WITH VANESSA'S MOTHER AND FATHER, WHO ARE ALIVE AND WELL.

THEY HAVE REQUESTED TO REMAIN ANONYMOUS AND HAVE ASKED THAT WE DO NOT CONTACT THEM AGAIN.

IN SUCH CASES, IT IS OUR POLICY TO RESPECT THE PARENTS' WISHES. WE HOPE YOU CAN UNDERSTAND.

Having unearthed it, after all these years, the letter now posed a dilemma. Why hadn't he told Vanessa? Perhaps she'd been too fragile at the time. Now, it felt like a deception, which only deepened the longer it went on. But he dithered. He left it face-up on his desk, hoping she would find it. It was there now, the single white sheet stark and unblinking, while the whole Kelly family was here: in a villa in Provence.

Bruce bent down and stubbed out his cigar in the grass. Perhaps he should bury the letter again: retrieve it only in moments such as this. Whenever he felt the urge to dismiss Vanessa's fears as paranoia, her warnings as improbable, he would pull it out: a paper-white rebuke, the sheer, physical fact of it a reminder of the limits of his own imagination.

Of course, he never did. Over the years that followed, the letter just shuffled shamefully between the four drawers below, until it finally came to rest second from the top, in a pile of papers that contained, among other things, Bruce Kelly's final wishes.

BRUCE STOOD AT the door to Harry's bedroom, unsure how to interpret the scene before him. A body was kneeling on the floor, the head bent out of sight, as if decapitated.

The smallest room on the top floor was lit by a lamp, which was perched on top of an old chair. With its wicker seat, it called to mind a painting by Van Gogh. This and the light, yellow on a low ceiling, set an old-fashioned scene. You could imagine the servants bending beneath a sloping roof. It was this sense that people had lived so very differently in these exact spaces, the sense of a history that survived and whispered, that allowed Bruce to contextualise what he was looking at.

Harry was praying.

Right up to the threshold, Bruce had been unsure. But now, he took this as a sign. It was, perhaps, the most intimate they had ever been. Like watching someone sleep: unrecognisable for being so unmasked.

He decided to leave his old friend in peace.

As Harry's right hand rose to his forehead and he began to make the sign of the cross, Bruce crept back from the door.

'DID YOU ASK him?'

The lights were off and Vanessa was lying on her back, wide awake. In the dark, Bruce began to climb into bed.

'Bruce?'

'The boy was with Harry all day.'

'Oh. Oh, good.'

Her relief was obvious: her body went slack and she rolled over into a trusting sleep. How easy, Bruce thought, to drop a topic that disgusts us.

It was only after her breathing grew deep and steady that Bruce thought of a question to ask her. *Why did it have to be Sam? Why not Rupert?* Suspecting he knew the answer, Bruce had no sooner formulated the question in his mind than he'd resolved never to ask it.

They had been married for almost twenty years. Doubt was a habit they'd long outgrown. Instead, like his wife, he rolled over and closed his eyes—to the whispers, the cracked shards, the shiny, silvery clues.

SATURDAY

CHAPTER 19

2024

FOR ANIKA, ONE of the great joys of weddings was the inevitable imperfections. She was sincere—sentimental, even—about love and commitment and the witnessing of these things by a crowd. But she still saw in weddings, as in all pursuits of order, the glorious clash between a determination to perfect and to predict, and the universe's refusal to let it happen.

As a legal event—the exchanging of vows and the formation of contracts—weddings made sense to her. But as a figurative representation of the smooth union of two families, they were doomed to fail. There would be a crying baby or confusing dietaries or a drunk uncle who made everybody uncomfortable.

And there was nothing Anika loved more, no surer way to wet her eyes, than seeing such disturbances navigated with grace: the unique humility of a bride who can say, *This is important and it means the world to me, but it's out of my hands.* That, to Anika, was romance.

So when Anika had set out for Italy with her mother, she was, in a way, eager for chaos. Waking on the morning of Skye's wedding, however, anticipation had turned to fear, and Anika had an eye out for a different, more sinister disruption.

As soon as she was awake, she pulled on her joggers and headed into town. It was the first time since her arrival in Italy that she'd left the hotel. The old monastery was situated on a hill at the edge of a small town—it only took her ten minutes walking down an empty, one-way road to reach the church and main square. There, market stalls were selling fresh produce. Anika was grateful for the solitude afforded by a crowd.

She had woken late; the sleeping pill held her until past ten. Now, she needed to think, before the wedding frenzy began in earnest. She already regretted slipping that letter under Sam and Cass's door. Her conviction that Sam deserved some kind of comeuppance—a calling out—persisted, but the method she'd chosen was rash. He was clearly a dangerous person, who, for a long time, had been allowed to get away with his crime. The fact that Anika knew what he'd done all those years ago would make him feel exposed. He might lash out at her, try to silence her. Or, worse, he might take it out on Cass.

The heat was already reflecting off the stones; she could feel it through her trainers. And, standing at the edge of the market, the fish were growing pungent. Anika walked away a few paces so she didn't look like she was browsing. She contemplated running back to the hotel and asking reception to let her into Cass and Sam's room. It was possible that they hadn't opened the letter yet. She might be able to say that it was some kind of wedding-related invitation which, owing to a change of plans, she now needed to retract. It was ridiculous, but at least it was trivial enough not to inspire much curiosity.

Just as she turned on her heel, resolving to give it a try, she saw two people moving through the crowd towards her. The man's hand hovered behind the woman. He didn't touch her but he floated, ever-protective, as if ready to catch her should she fall. While she was focused on her phone—the unbroken, slow-stepped attention of looking at a map—he was looking straight at Anika, as if he recognised her. The woman wore her orange hair clipped up. Now, the man placed a hand on her exposed neck, summoning her attention.

'Anika? Hey!'

Cass rushed forward, Sam trailing a few paces behind her. She gave Anika a hug.

For the sake of peace and order, of good manners, she hugged Sam next, even turned her cheek to accept a kiss. It was amazing, Anika thought, this iron grip of politeness—how easily it was confused with sanity. She was incapable of doing anything else. Civility bound her with the intractability of instinct. The effect of its codes, so consistently applied over so many generations, was to assert a natural order. Anika had *evolved* to never cause a fuss. And what a fuss it would be, to claw at a man's face, to scratch his eyes out, when chancing upon him in a foreign street.

And civility rendered her a puppet right throughout their conversation: her mouth pulled into an obliging smile, her head nodding along. 'You're real, then,' she said.

'Apparently.'

'I thought Cass might've made you up.'

'Not at all. No, it's a great gig. I had to beat out a lot of other actors.' When Anika didn't say anything, Sam prompted: 'For the part of Cass's fake boyfriend. You know: take her out in public, bump into people.'

'Oh! Ha.' Her laugh sounded false. Throughout this little interaction, she'd been too busy studying Sam to realise that he'd attempted a joke. He was giving her the smallest smile that could still be considered polite. His arm was around Cass. Every now and then, he yanked her closer to him. In another couple, it might have been a sweet display of affection. But Anika eyed it with suspicion: she identified in it something possessive.

Cass, meanwhile, was wearing a wide holiday smile. She motioned with her head to the market. 'Did you miss breakfast, too?'

'Yeah. Slept through.'

'We just bought some fruit and cured meats and whatever, if you want to join us? We were just going to eat it in our room. There's a nice balcony.'

At Anika's hesitation, Cass's smile fell.

'Oh, wait, you've probably got wedding duties and stuff.'

'No, actually. I'm not getting my make-up done till three.'

'Fab! Let's go.'

In the moment, it had seemed like a good opportunity to access their room. But the short walk back to the hotel provided sufficient time for Anika to doubt this decision. If she was too late, if Sam had read the letter, he was more likely to lash out at her in private than in front of the crowds at the wedding.

Cass, meanwhile, skipped ahead, peppering Anika with questions about the Big Day. Anika had never seen her in such a mood before. Where she was normally composed, her humour stretching as far as irony, now she was playful, almost childlike in her excitement.

Anika wondered whether Cass was nervous. Perhaps they had read the letter together. Sam's secret was Cass's too, after all: it bound them together.

There was no lift so they had to take the stairs. They went single-file and grew quiet as they climbed. With every step, it seemed more likely that Anika was walking into a confrontation.

There was some fumbling for the key card. Sam thought it was in Cass's bag; Cass insisted that he'd taken it (she was correct: it was in the pocket of his shorts).

As soon as they heard the electronic *beep*—before they had even crossed the threshold—Cass grabbed Anika's arm.

'Do you want a drink?'

'What?'

Sam mistook Anika's panic for a more innocent confusion. He put a restraining hand on Cass's shoulder. 'Isn't it a bit early?'

'It's past twelve. And we might as well start. We'll be drinking all day. What do you reckon, Anika?'

She heard herself say: 'Sure.' But she was distracted. On one of the bedside tables, she'd spotted her letter. The envelope was name-side up—she couldn't see whether the seal on the back had been broken.

While Sam and Anika fussed at the minifridge, she backed towards the letter. It was to her left now, almost within reach, when Cass turned around, a bottle in hand.

'Prosecco?'

'Why not.'

Cass frowned. 'We don't have glasses.'

'They were in the bathroom in my room. Randomly.'

Sam and Cass gave her a quizzical look, but it did the trick. They both poked their heads into the ensuite, which gave Anika just enough time to flip the letter over.

She almost giggled with relief. It was unopened.

Luckily, there were, in fact, glasses in the bathroom—two water glasses, which Sam now emerged with. He passed one to Anika. Cass, meanwhile, had found a mug inside the wardrobe, next to the kettle.

Anika didn't dare reach for the letter again while they were watching her. She didn't want to draw attention to it. She would have one drink with them then leave, saying she'd forgotten about some minor but essential wedding duty. She had to pick up the flowers, or something. Fortunately, the bedside table was close to the door. If she timed it right, she might snatch the letter unnoticed on her way out.

Even though she had confirmed that Sam did not yet know what the letter contained, his presence still made her nervous. She hesitated before stepping out onto the balcony. They were on the top floor. If she lost her balance—if someone pushed her—she wouldn't survive the fall.

'You first,' she said to Cass.

BEFORE CASS LEFT for Italy, she had imagined the very scene she was now living: a round, glass-topped table, an ashtray sitting very European at its centre. On it, a plastic tub of olives, a white plate with several strips of cured meat, a bunch of grapes, two peaches and, by their side, a knife.

While Anika faced inwards, looking through the French windows to where Sam stood in the hotel room, Cass sat on the wooden bench with her legs curled under her. This gave her a few precarious extra inches from which to lean out over the sloping roof tiles and look at the view. Green fields lined with poplar trees. The dots of houses that made up the town. Although the palette was different, more yellow than purple, there was something about the neatness of the landscape that really did remind Cass of the south of France. Sam had made a similar comment that morning.

He was holding her while she lay on her side, looking out the window. They had reached for each other instinctively before they were really awake, so that their bodies warmed as they slowly rose to consciousness.

'Beautiful day.'

'Mmm,' Sam said. 'It reminds me of that villa.'

'Are you getting sentimental?'

His laugh was a soft breath in her ear.

'I thought we didn't talk about that holiday,' she said.

'I don't go on about it, like you. With your "crush".'

She kicked him. 'I never mention it.'

After a long, cosy pause, in which she almost fell asleep again, he whispered, 'I had a crush, too. Not a crush-crush but, like, I knew, even then, that you were a special person.'

They might have left it there. Going back to sleep, or with a kiss that led elsewhere. But their conversation that morning had a freshness to it. Perhaps it was because they had woken somewhere they had never been before. Perhaps it was because they both knew that sex would soon follow, and were lying in lazy anticipation, savouring an intimacy that was both physical and personal. For whatever reason, Sam wanted to talk in a roaming, exploratory way. It was as if they were back at the beginning of their relationship, back when being loved was still a novelty, when her desire to understand him was gentle and coaxing and he seemed to surprise himself with what he was capable of revealing.

'I was thinking about it yesterday,' he said, 'after what you said about my mum.'

'I'm sorry.' She was still lying on her side, his face at her shoulder. She squeezed his arm to show that she meant it.

'I was actually thinking how true it was. I didn't want to bring it up when we started dating, because I didn't want to make it weird or be, like, I don't know, pervy, but I did think about that holiday a lot. About how you got stuck in that icehouse.' He held her more tightly, as if to better protect her. 'And how I got you out. I think it really affected my, like, self-esteem. To know that I wasn't useless. It was just . . .'

He paused but she didn't prompt him.

'I think,' he went on, his voice thick, 'when you lose someone, like when Mum died, there's this feeling that you matter less. Like, because there's one less person in the world who really needs you, it almost feels like your life really *is* less important. And that holiday, with everything that happened, I just felt like I meant something again. Like I didn't need to just skim over the top of life. I could, like, commit to things and my choices could mean something. I was so lost after she died. And then I came back from France and I knew what I wanted to do and, in a way, I've been on that path ever since.'

Cass was silent for several seconds. She thought about the girl she was all those years ago—more alone than she realised. Her eyes started to sting, thinking how happy that girl would be to know where she ended up. Her contentment, in that moment, was so total that it was everywhere: in the sunlight; in Sam's eyelashes, each its own perfect parabola; even in the fading curves of a stain at the foot of their hotel bed, which the sun illuminated. The sense that everything was ordered and perfect, and exactly as it ought to be. It was naff to say that their love felt right; but that was what Cass thought, lying there: that the world had been made right.

There was only one way to convey this feeling—the enormous, almost physical fact of it. She rolled over so she was facing him. Her smile was a prelude.

'Frankly,' she said, 'that does all sound a bit pervy.'

NOW, UP ON the balcony, Anika was jittery. She and Cass were sitting side by side on the wooden bench, their backs to the view.

Their knees touched, so Cass could feel it when Anika continually bounced her leg. And Anika kept glancing from Cass to Sam, while never looking *at* them. Cass wondered whether there was a residual awkwardness after the intensity of their drink yesterday. Or maybe the whole wedding thing was upsetting for her, as a single woman in her early thirties. She probably didn't relish the opportunity to third-wheel Cass and Sam; she was likely sick of the whole performance of marriage—heightened, in this case, by how far everyone had travelled, and how many photos they would need to post to justify the effort. The recently married or soon-to-be-married could be self-serving at these events, in how much they proclaimed to 'love (romantic, heteronormative) love'. As if to be surrounded by other couples made any two people more of a couple.

Even as Cass tried to account for Anika's discomfort, she was, at the same time, happily unfazed by it. How very Anika, to be so wound up amid such serenity. Cass felt an expansive love for her old friend, for her predictability. Maybe, she thought, that was what love was: knowing people so well that they made sense—not by objective standards, but by behaving in the ways you have come to expect.

Looking inside, she saw Sam standing by the wardrobe, holding his glass up to the light. He looked unsatisfied with its cleanliness.

She had an urge to stand up and go to him. She wanted to touch him—just on the shoulder would do—so he'd know that she was thinking of him, even while she sat and made small talk with Anika. So he would understand that what she wanted most of all, always, was to be alone with him, and that she, too, considered this drink with Anika an interruption.

She was still that girl of thirteen, watching Harry and Sam drive away from the villa. That urge to cry out and run after him, to have one more conversation, to extract, even if only for a moment, more time.

CASS'S ORDEAL IN the icehouse ended not when they knocked the door down and dragged her out into the sun, but when she heard Sam's voice.

When screaming into the tiny gap of light did nothing except echo and mock her, she started to really panic. Once, in class, she had seen a girl have what was later identified as 'a panic attack'. At the time, Cass had found it suspicious. They were about to sit a test and the girl in question wasn't particularly academic.

Now, as each breath brought no relief and her chest started to burn, she thought back to that girl, to her tears, and the wet stretch of her open, voiceless mouth. How could Cass have thought she was faking it?

She registered dizziness with relief. Lying down, the floor seemed to tip and sway. She was breathing so heavily now that, with her face pressed to the ground, she sucked in grains of dirt. They didn't taste like anything, but she could feel them scratching her tongue.

For several minutes she stayed like that: in the foetal position, heaving in the dirt. Eventually, as she started to exhaust herself, reason crept back in. They would find her. Even if she had to wait until they all sat down for lunch. They wouldn't pass a whole day without realising she was gone. And they would look everywhere, including in the icehouse. Her screams were obviously inaudible, so she just had to make sure she stayed awake so she could hear them when they knocked.

The biggest challenge, as she sat with her back against the wooden door, was managing the panic. Every now and then, she felt its hands tighten around her throat. She tried to distract herself:

playing memory games; trying to recall the exact events of each of her birthdays; the order of scenes in her favourite childhood films. When her concentration lapsed, her breathing would grow shallow. Then she'd stand and stretch and start again. At no point did she lose consciousness. In fact, the ordeal was made worse by her remaining very much awake.

Her salvation came, as she thought it would, in the form of a knock at the door. Except the voice was not Anika's.

'Cass?'

She banged the door until her fists bled.

'Cass? I'll come back and get you out. Just wait there. I'll get you.'

It was then that she fainted. The relief was so complete she actually swooned with it. Because there was something about Sam's voice—low and confident—that convinced her she could rely on his promise. As if words and action were the same. It would happen, because he had said so.

She was roused by the sound of some instrument hitting the door. It withstood the assault longer than she'd expected: the bashing was louder, the splinters more painful in her legs. But at no point did the panic return. Between each stroke, Sam would pause to say, just so she could hear, 'I'll get you out.'

And at the fulfilment of his promise, when the door finally collapsed and he lifted it off her, he knelt down and put his arms around her. She wished intensely that he would keep holding her like that, right next to his chest, for a while longer.

It was funny, thinking of it now, after a gap of so many years. All this time, ever since her first seizure two years ago, Cass had resisted the suggestion that her life might turn on a single traumatic moment: that her fate could be so determined.

But, in a different way, her fate *had* been determined by that incident in the icehouse. Sam had changed her life. Not all at once, perhaps—not in a single, decisive act. But she loved him from that moment. There it was, the crux of the X: the cleaving of Before and After. Her story was not Before and After she got sick. It all started after she heard him through that door: the promise of safety.

He'd been there in her teenage years, too. Not just when she looked him up on social media, but when she started going on dates with boys her own age and was secure in her belief that they were too young, too immature, that she could wait and find someone better. And he was there—subtly, almost imperceptibly—in the adulthood that followed. In her boldness; her determination to leave home and seek out a new one; her quiet confidence that, no matter where in the world she went, she could find people who would look out for her. And it now seemed obvious and not at all like a coincidence that their paths crossed as soon as she'd retreated to Australia. When she was at her most helpless, he found her again.

All because, all those years ago, he had noticed that she was missing. He had cared, when nobody else did. There was an alchemy in that. When he finally held her, splintered and blinking against the light, they were both already changed. He had whispered through the door that he would get her out, and—before he'd even saved her, when it was only a promise—she had believed him.

His hands had been outstretched ever since. Sam was there—had always been there—to catch her should she fall.

THIS MEMORY, WHICH had come to Cass emotionally whole, now departed just as quickly. She was back on the balcony, but with the distinct sensation that she was looking down at herself as if from a great distance.

Seeing those two women perched on a bench at the edge of a tiny balcony, Sam in the comparative darkness inside, Cass's mind was flooded with a dazzling light. All the seizures and the fights and the misunderstandings made perfect sense, insofar as they were the necessary steps leading to this balcony, under this bright, benevolent sun.

This time, for the first time, Cass did not smell burning. It was only Anika's face—terrified, as if a predator were advancing—that alerted her to what was about to happen.

THE DISORIENTATION OF an abrupt, unflattering angle. The sky a bald and mocking blue. Hands—the wrong hands—touching her.

Cass sat up. No longer on the wooden bench, she was sitting on the tiles. With her head in her hands, she moved first her right leg, then her left, checking that they didn't hurt. She first clenched one fist and then the other. Nothing appeared to be broken, although her right foot was throbbing.

Opening her eyes, she saw Anika. She was crouching down, both hands on Cass's shoulders. She was crying—too much, it didn't make sense. A sound was coming out of her that Cass had never heard before. It was animal. Anika seemed to be yowling.

Cass looked at her body again, looking for something terribly, terrifyingly wrong. Beneath the black straps of her sandals, her feet had blood on them, although she couldn't identify where from.

Anika's fingernails were now digging into Cass's forearm.

'It's Sam. I'm sorry. He came running.'

'Did I . . .?'

'It was my fault.' Five half-moon scratches, dragging along Cass's skin. 'I'm sorry. I'm sorry. It's all my fault.'

Slowly, Cass stood up. First, on her hands and knees, which was when she noticed, beneath her palms, shards of glass. Anika's hands were bloody too. In one of them, she clutched the broken neck of the prosecco bottle.

Walking to the edge of the balcony, Cass made a crunching sound. Her feet were wet. Everywhere, falling from her summer dress, smashing against the floor, shards of dark green glass.

She placed both hands on the tiles, where the balcony met the sharp slope of the roof. The pool was far below them. Before looking down, she allowed herself the thought that he might have landed there, in its forgiving waters. But she was without real hope.

In her dread, Cass was a prophetess, knowing already, because it was the worst thing imaginable, exactly what she would see.

EPILOGUE

LIKE BRUCE KELLY, Sam was mourned at a private burial (family only, which is to say, just me and Harry), followed by a more public funeral service.

For the funeral, Harry organised a service at his local church. To my knowledge, Sam never went to church, but I didn't have an alternative to suggest—I'd left all the arrangements to Harry.

In the days after Sam's death, while I was still in Tuscany, I had been remarkably proficient with what Sam and I would've called 'life admin'. If he were alive, one of us would have joked that it was really 'death admin'. There was a whole holiday to cancel and flights to rearrange. There was an embassy to contact, a morgue to visit, a body to place in the hull of a plane. All problems of a heightened world, a different genre of experience, where people travelled internationally, where dramatic beauty was disrupted, equally dramatically, by a body falling from the sky.

When I arrived home, however, back to the life I'd built with him, his absence was inescapable. For days, I didn't change my clothes or leave the apartment. My phone died and I didn't charge it.

I left bed only to go to the bathroom. Looking at my own face in the mirror, I was shocked to find it familiar. I'd expected to see a ghoul.

Harry dropped by every day under the pretext of bringing me dinner. He can't cook, apparently, so it was usually takeaway: sushi, a roast chicken with packet coleslaw, a plastic container filled with tuna pasta. Walking to the front door each evening was as far as I ventured from bed. There, I'd lean against the frame while he babbled—usually telling me logistical things like, *The funeral is tomorrow*, or, *I'll pick you up at nine*. Eventually, he'd lower his plastic bag onto the threshold and back away from it, trying to smile at me.

Not once did I invite him in. What was I going to do? Try to smile back, my mouth twisted like his, my eyes dead above it?

Harry was my reflection. And it was too soon, too painful, to share a meal with my grief.

HARRY'S CHURCH, AS it transpired, was offensively quaint. The grass that surrounded it was velvety and the morning sun caramelised its sandstone walls.

Inside, at least, the sunshine took on a sickly, anaemic tint. The windows were thin and made of dull-yellow stained glass. At the back door, there was a square of unmitigated white light. I stood at the front near the altar and watched as the mourners arrived: stepping first into the blinding, anonymising square, then clarifying as they proceeded into shadow.

I had only been at my post for a few minutes when I saw the people I had been waiting for. Two thin figures, their hair an unyielding black, even where they stood in that first patch of abrupt sun. Pausing there, where their faces were difficult to make out, they might have been sisters. I recognised Vanessa's dress from Bruce's funeral.

They made their way down the aisle towards me. Skye reached me first. She held me so long and hard, I had to pat her arms to suggest that she might let go. Vanessa's greeting was much more painful. Not because she held me even tighter, but because she stood about a foot away and looked at me, really looked at me, until her lower lip—that subtle instrument, usually deployed in an upward drift of derision—started to wobble.

'Oh, darling.'

She held out a hand and cupped my cheek. I felt like a child. More so than if she had crushed my head to her breast.

'Is Anika with you?' I asked.

Now Vanessa hugged me. She whispered in my ear, 'He was such a special person.'

Behind her mother's back, Skye met my eye. 'She's . . .' she paused to swallow, then shook her head. 'No, she's not.'

There was a note of regret in her answer, which told me Anika wasn't just *not* with them. She wasn't coming at all.

THE LAST TIME I saw Anika Kelly—the only time I have seen her since Sam's fall—I did not yet regard her with suspicion. If anything, I felt sorry for her.

It was the Saturday afternoon of her sister's wedding. I bumped into her as I made my way from the coroner's office back up to the hotel. The orange-plastered buildings were five storeys on either side and so close together that the whole street was in shadow. The path inclined upwards on uneven stones. Anika was making her way down. When she stopped a few paces away, she towered over me.

She was still wearing her exercise gear. Looking at my watch, I felt a bizarre intrusion of panic. But she said she had a make-up appointment at three!

She reached out and gripped my arm. It was probably years of under-eating, but her head, in that moment, acquired skull-like proportions: her jaw huge, her teeth exposed in the semblance of a smile.

'Cass,' she said. 'You're free.'

I assumed she was talking about the interview I'd just had with the coroner—the one she was about to have herself. 'Don't worry, he's really nice.'

'No, I mean'—she widened her eyes, filling them with an insinuation I was yet to grasp—'you're free.'

I thought to myself: Truly, this woman has gone mad.

As we parted ways, I worried about her, wondering whether Anika, with her infinite sensitivity, was capable of processing a shock of this magnitude.

IF I HAD seen Anika only a few hours later—if, for example, I had attended Skye's wedding that evening instead of haunting my hotel room—we might have had a very different conversation.

To Skye's credit, she offered to cancel the wedding. I insisted she go through with it but said I doubted I'd be able to attend. I assumed that everybody understood. In fact, I thought they might welcome my absence. Tragedy can mark you: suffering renders you a pariah. Not knowing what to say, understanding that there's nothing to be said, people prefer to avoid you.

So I was in the cramped room that Sam and I had shared, the wedding raging outside, when I found Anika's letter.

In an attempt to stop myself from thinking about the balcony, I had closed the shutters. Nonetheless, the revelry was audible. I was reaching for the top drawer of Sam's bedside table, looking for the sleeping pills he'd brought with him for the flight. There, blinking innocently on top was a white envelope. Flipping it over, I saw that it had no address, just Sam's name scrawled across the front.

Inside, I found a single sheet of hotel-branded stationery. The handwriting was immediately damning. It crawled along the page at an angle, each slash snarky. It wasn't signed, only initialled. But I would have known who wrote it even without the identifying AK.

Dear Sam,

I know what you did to Cass in France.

(Here, Anika had crossed out in France and written: *when she was thirteen*. For moral clarity, I suppose.)

You disgust me and I want nothing to do with you. But I do need you to know that I know.

She will stay sick as long as you're both trapped in denial. If you care about her, if you have any regret about what you did, if it pains you at all to see the damage it's still causing her, you'll help her to face it.

Let her go.

AK

THE CORONER'S REPORT, when it finally arrived six days after Sam's death, was clarifying, if only by way of contradiction. Hunches I'd had about what happened on the balcony—what Anika did while I was unconscious—became convictions, as I read it and thought: *No, that doesn't sound right.*

I typed the whole thing into Google Translate: first in chunks; then in discrete phrases; then one word at a time, mining for nuances. I read it so many times, I can still reproduce whole sentences in the original Italian. *Trauma cranico. Infortunio.* Foreign words, now tainted with intimate meaning.

According to the coroner, this is what happened on that balcony: when my attack started, I fell sideways off the bench where I'd been sitting. Because our room was on the top floor and the balcony was cut into the roof, when I slipped, my torso hung out over the sloping tiles. Sam came running and attempted to lift me down. He couldn't reach me—my legs were thrashing too much—so he squatted on the bench and tried to get his arms around me from above. That was when I jerked violently, and knocked him off balance. He rolled out onto the tiles. The roof sloped at an acute angle, the tiles descended without the interruption of a gutter, so he slipped straight down, unable to find a handhold that might stop his fall.

Sam hit his head and was dead on impact. There were small abrasions on his body from the glass. These were easily explained given that, up on the balcony, a bottle of prosecco had been smashed.

If it weren't for Anika's letter, the coroner's report may have seemed exhaustive. But its omissions struck me as glaring. Where was Anika? What did she do, while Sam wrapped his legs around me, straddling me, forcing me to lie still with his own crushing weight? I could only imagine how the scene would have looked in the eyes of a woman, who believed that it was Sam, not Rupert, who had preyed on a child in an icehouse all those years ago.

In my frustration, I recalled the shards I had walked over on the balcony. And the thin neck of a bottle, smooth and unbroken, protruding from Anika Kelly's closed fist. As if it had been held—held like a weapon—before it was smashed upon its target.

Sam's head was the first part of him to hit the ground. There was no way of identifying, on the wreckage of his skull, whether it had in fact been damaged twice: once by the fall and, before that, by a blunt object.

I recalled, too, what Anika had said. Up on the balcony, she told me: *It's all my fault.* And then, in that alley on the way back to the hotel, she'd gripped me and her eyes had widened, perhaps with pride, as she emphasised that final word: *free.*

SO THAT WAS why I arrived at Sam's funeral desperate to see Anika Kelly. I wanted to look her in the eye and, by my presence, pose that still unanswered question. *Did he fall? Or did you hit him?*

I retained remarkable composure during the ceremony. It was the rage that did it. I felt galvanised, probably to the point of seeming callous. Not like the burial, which had taken place a few days before. There, my legs had shaken so violently that I sat down at the graveside. I had pulled up fistfuls of grass and, where I wiped my eyes, drawn smudges on my face. Now, however, I was calm. The funeral passed in a series of impatient glances over my shoulder. I kept looking at that square of light, expecting to see Anika Kelly standing there, vague as a ghost. Even on the way out, I scanned every face, pew by pew. With each face that was not hers, the screw of my fury rotated a few degrees.

I felt cheated. As if I were entitled to the confrontation I'd been fantasising about for days. I had already imagined what I might say; whether I would point at her and cry out my accusation, or whether I would slink up to her and whisper, like conscience, in her ear: *You hit him, didn't you?* And then, by watching her reaction—seeing in her eyes a blink of confusion or a flicker of guilt, quick as a snake's tongue—I would know whether I was right.

And more than the promise of closure, there was the idea that confronting Anika might be a way to punish her. It felt good to picture her shame, her guilt. If she could only look at me, haggard and stripped by grief, she might see how wrong she was. She'd realise that the villain she'd slain was a figment. And that the man she killed was innocent—not in the sense of being untouched, in that more remarkable way of being kind and gentle and all the purer for the darkness he had overcome. A man whose goodness was endlessly regenerative, who lost his family and made a new one—with Harry, with me.

But Skye was right: Anika hadn't come. Harry and I were walking out first, the whole congregation watching us go. I walked slowly and saw every single face, even those who stood at the back, right by the door, their heads bowed.

I squinted as I passed through the open door. I had a brief, mad hope that Anika might be waiting outside. Perhaps she changed her mind at the last minute.

I blinked against the sun. Down the stone steps, on the grass, were several suited figures. None of them looked like Anika Kelly. One of them—a man wearing sunglasses—snapped his head towards me, as if in alarm.

I KNEW AT once that I had not had a seizure. Not only had I remained conscious the whole time, my fall was totally without warning.

One moment, I was squinting at an attendant from the funeral parlour, the next, I was on the ground at the base of the church steps, inelegantly easing myself into a crouch.

I heard her perfectly. From her urgency, her professional authority, I gathered that she was addressing a crowd.

'Stop, don't touch her. I'm a doctor.'

I brushed the dirt from my black knitted dress. The same dress that I had worn to Bruce's funeral. By the time she reached my side, I was back on my feet.

'Skye, it's fine.'

'Are you alright?'

'I just tripped.'

'Oh.' She looked at me for a moment in disbelief. And then, as if suddenly realising that I was standing and cogent, she let out a loud laugh. 'You're fine!'

'I'm fine.'

I turned so the crowd exiting the church might see that I really *was* fine. Around me, several people smiled with relief. But then, amid all those well-wishing eyes, I felt a subtler pressure. Harry's hand at my shoulder.

'Cass,' he whispered, 'you don't have to—'

I placed my hand on his, squeezing it, so that he might feel my desperation, even though I managed an emotionless whisper.

'Take me home.'

I HAVEN'T HAD a seizure since that balcony in Tuscany. That's hardly notable: in the past I have gone for several months without an attack. What *is* unusual is that, between reading Anika's letter, and tripping at Sam's funeral today, I hadn't thought about my condition at all.

In a way, Anika's letter spared me.

I'd locked myself in that hotel room on the night Sam died, intending to make a cage of my guilt. Before I closed the shutters on the unbearable scene of *my* mistake, I'd taken one final look at the balcony. It was evidently precarious: a low wall and a high drop.

I admonished myself for ever having ventured out there at all. Knowing I might have a seizure, I should have managed the risks better. Worse, I should have never had a seizure in the first place.

It all seemed to hinge on whether my condition was psychological. I longed for the clarity that Sam had attributed to me the day before he died. I wished that I'd decided to leave my pills at home, in the full confidence that I had been misdiagnosed, that only therapy—not anticonvulsant drugs—could help me. But I'd told Sam the truth, feeble as it was. I hadn't left the pills at home on purpose: I just forgot. And to my mind, there was still a possibility that my diagnosis was correct, that the pills *did* help. In which case, my omission in forgetting those pills, had been fatal.

I had my suspicions, of course, about what was wrong with me. For a long time, I had wondered whether the seizures had something to do with my head, if for no other reason than because they started when I was twenty-eight: the same age my mother was when her mental health fell off a cliff.

But suspicions weren't enough. I craved the absolution of a formal diagnosis. I wanted someone with authority, like a doctor or a judge, to point to me and say: *Those drugs have no effect. Even if you hadn't forgotten them, even if you'd taken one that very morning, you would still have had a seizure. There was nothing you could have done.*

In the dirt outside Harry's church, the blame came back to me. My search for Anika suddenly seemed childish and attention-seeking. If it were closure I really wanted, or even just the truth, I might have contacted Anika at any point in the last few weeks. No, what I really wanted was a scene.

When I searched the crowd and didn't find her, my fury was nourishing. In her absence, Anika strengthened my convictions. Because to look at her—to see a woman I have known since we were both children, to feel, under her gaze, like the girl I once was—would be to witness an endlessly complicated human mess. *Not* seeing her, however, I am afforded the space to hate her.

Anika, of all people, would understand why I might prefer to avoid her, or, failing that, to only engage with her in the most dramatic terms. After all, wasn't that what she did to Sam?

She was the one who sent me into that icehouse, all those years ago. And it was easier, having identified herself as the cause of all my suffering, to add another link to the chain. Of her own regrets, she can say: *Yes, I sent Cass into that icehouse alone. But it was Sam, with more sinister intentions, who caused the deeper trauma.* It would have been the easiest thing in the world to smash a glass bottle over that man's head. It might have even felt good. In her mind, Sam was the predator, and I was—had always been—his prey.

And so it is for me. Of Sam's death, I can say that yes, it was my seizure that erupted our idyll, I was the one who caused him to rush out to the ledge. But it was Anika Kelly who delivered the fatal blow.

HARRY HAS GONE. He stayed with me for several hours. Mercifully, he didn't talk about my fall, or ask about my seizures. Instead, we sat and chatted over the TV. He got up at regular intervals, usually to make tea. Once, he was up for twenty minutes, with so much plate-clanking and cupboard-closing that I assumed he was making a whole meal, and wondered where he'd found the groceries. When he invited me into the kitchen for 'lunch' I saw that he had laid out and opened every condiment I owned—mustards, jams, butter, jar after jaunty jar. On a plate beside them was a modest tower of toast.

After lunch, which we ate around five, he left. At the door, I said, 'See you tomorrow?'

His surprise converted so quickly into elation, I had to shut the door.

Now, I am alone. Outside, the sky is several different colours. Navy darkening the horizon; up higher, the clouds a resilient pink. I turn the TV off and sit in the thickening silence.

I am still unsure whether to tell Harry my theory: that Anika lashed out; that she was the reason Sam died. I worry it would only compound his suffering. It makes Sam's passing all the more painful: to think that he was, in some sense, pursued.

Of course, there is the possibility that Harry wouldn't believe me. But I tend to think that, if I told him, my theory would quickly become his, too. He'd probably want to press charges. I can see it already: the whole harrowing, expensive process. Most likely, we'd fail. I'm the only witness and I was unconscious at the crucial moment.

Whether I tell Harry one day or not, whether justice is pursued, does not really matter. It seems to me that the important work is done. It started with Anika Kelly's letter; that first link in the chain, which led me to that sun-illuminated square at Sam's funeral, wherein I found, at last, an answer to the coroner's question.

Now I know what really happened on that balcony. Without qualm or complication, I can say: Anika Kelly is to blame.

I have decided, as we all do, every day, which version of the story is the one that I can live with.

AUTHOR'S NOTE

SIGNS OF DAMAGE opens with the epigraph: 'Unexpressed emotions will never die. They are buried alive and will come forth later in uglier ways.'

When I chose it, I believed the quote to be by Sigmund Freud. That seemed a fitting epigraph for a novel which is about, among other things, the omnipresence of psychoanalytic concepts—not just in art, but in the stories we tell about our own lives.

Months later, my ever-rigorous copyeditor, Ali Lavau, went looking for a citation. Within easy reach were hundreds of websites and blogs and graphics attributing the quote to Freud. We were unable, however, to find a precise source.

As embarrassing as it was, I was also delighted by this synchronicity of art and fiction. By lazily misquoting the father of psychoanalysis, I had fallen into the same trap as my characters. We all defer to familiar narratives: we see someone's present suffering and immediately wonder what buried trauma is being expressed, we encounter a quote that appears to legitimise this way of understanding other people and don't pause to question its authenticity.

So I decided to keep the original epigraph, although its meaning had changed. Where originally it was intended as a droll comment on the pervasiveness of trauma narratives, now it's a testament to subjectivity—to that inescapable human tendency to bend the facts to suit our story.

ACKNOWLEDGEMENTS

MY THANKS:

For the research: to Dr Tobias Winton-Brown, for providing me with essential resources on functional neurological disorders, and to Dr Richard Kanaan, for being so generous with your time and professional insight. For further information about epilepsy, functional neurological disorders, and hysteria, I am grateful to FND Australia and Epilepsy Action Australia for their many resources, as well as to several authors for their work, especially: Colin Grant (*A Smell of Burning*), Suzanne O'Sullivan (*It's All in Your Head*), and Fiona Wright ('This Woman is Hysterical'). I am especially indebted to two essays which proved formative in conceiving of this novel: 'The Case Against the Trauma Plot' by Parul Sehgal, published in *The New Yorker*, and 'The Art of Pain' by Beejay Silcox, published in the *Australian Book Review*.

For the words: to my dear friend, Tom Davidson McLeod, who was—yet again—the perfect first reader; to my publisher, Robert Watkins, for saving this novel via an early and very necessary structural intervention; to my agents, Felicity Blunt and Duvall Onsteen, for their passion and rigour, which infinitely improved the final text; and to my copyeditor, Ali Lavau, and proofreader, Rebecca Hamilton, for their unflagging insight and enthusiasm—I feel so privileged to have worked with you both for the third time now.

For the publication: to the whole team at Ultimo Press, in particular Alisa Ahmed, Andrea Johnson, and Zoë Victoria.

And a special thanks to Amanda Wildsmith—I couldn't ask for a bigger champion.

And for the author: to Lauren Gale for very welcome company in many libraries. Most importantly, to Patrick Still and to my family, Karen Reid, Peter Reid and Maureen Ryan.

Diana Reid is the Australian author of the bestselling novels *Love & Virtue* and *Seeing Other People*. Her debut, *Love & Virtue*, won the ABIA Book of the Year Award, the ABIA Literary Fiction Book of the Year Award, the ABA Booksellers' Choice Fiction Book of the Year Award, and the MUD Literary Prize. She was also named a *Sydney Morning Herald* Best Young Australian Novelist in 2022. Born in Sydney, she is currently based in London. *Signs of Damage* is her third novel.